The Water Diviner and Other Stories

The Iowa Short Fiction Award

The Water Diviner and Other Stories

Ruvanee Pietersz Vilhauer

University of Iowa Press · Iowa City

University of Iowa Press, Iowa City 52242
Copyright © 2018 by the University of Iowa Press
www.uipress.uiowa.edu
Printed in the United States of America
Interior design by Sara T. Sauers

The University of Iowa Press is a member of Green Press
Initiative and is committed to preserving natural resources.
Printed on acid-free paper

ISBN 978-1-60938-598-9 (pbk)
ISBN 978-1-60938-599-6 (ebk)

Cataloging-in-Publication data is on file with the
Library of Congress.

For my parents, Chandra and Vernon Pietersz

Contents

The Water Diviner and Other Stories

Beauty Queen

WHEN I SAW Suja waiting for me at the airport, I had reason to hope that Dr. Aronson had been right. We were different people. Suja was the beauty now. She was wearing a milky blouse with an elaborately embroidered neckline, and her hair was like a black silk veil against it, falling almost to her waist. I remembered her fingering my hair. How much time had she spent brushing with her head upside down, trying to make her hair wavy like mine? Now there was no need for that.

Two girls in their early teens were gawking at her and whispering. When Suja turned around, they waved, giggling. She waved back, looking amused. I had forgotten she was a celebrity.

When she embraced me, I noticed that she also smelled different. When we were kids, she had always smelled of Pond's talcum powder.

She used to cover her face and arms with it. She thought it made her skin look fairer. I had never wanted to tell her that it only made her look ashy. Now she smelled of a musky perfume. This was progress, I thought.

We fell easily into conversation, as if we had not changed, as if seven years had not passed, as if the banner-carrying incident had never happened.

Sri Lanka had changed too, I thought. My plane landed after midnight, so I could not see much of the countryside on the way to Colombo. But even in the dark, I noticed that the roadside shops were different. The familiar thatch- and tin-roofed shacks filled with biscuit tins, powdered milk, and soap had given way to glass-fronted two-story structures selling ladies' garments and ceramic tiles. I remembered that the shacks had been set back from the road, their ramshackle doors open in a way that was welcoming but not pushy. These modern-looking shops were pressed up against the road as if they were too eager for business. There were few stretches of road with no shops; I saw hardly any open fields and wild lantana bushes. The airport road was better, though. It was wider, and the ruts were no longer deep enough to throw us up against the car roof.

"Remember what a hoot it was, going to the airport? How we used to shriek," Suja said. "All those holes in the road, and the lorries thudding over them. Your father muttering at the pedestrians. Remember how irritated he used to get?"

"Donkey! Goat! Bloody cattle!" I said, laughing, mimicking my father's growl. "He still does that. Even in Berkeley, he mutters at the SUVs that cut him off."

"And your mother still gets that martyred look?" Suja said. Her laugh was still the indelicate snort I remembered.

"Plus she gives him the cold shoulder until he apologizes. Then she goes on about how she doesn't want to put up with road rage." Suja understood my parents almost as well as I did. Until the banner incident, there had not been a day when she had not spent time at my house. "Nothing's changed with them," I said. Unlike with us, I thought, hoping that Dr. Aronson had been right. "But around here, things look different."

We talked companionably about the traffic on the road and the shops full of export surplus clothes until we passed a billboard showing a beige-skinned young man entering a Land Rover. His dark suit, which was unsuitable for the heat, looked crisp. He was wearing a felt hat, oblivious to being in a country of bare-headed, umbrella-carrying people. "Look at that man," I said. "Some things don't change. Remember that crayon color we used to call 'flesh color'? That pinkish-beige? Wasn't it weird that we colored all the people we drew with that? Didn't we realize we were brown?"

I thought I saw her flinch and realized I had let my guilt steer me to a topic that was too close to trouble. But she started talking about Miss Matilda, our grade five teacher, who had always wanted us, inexplicably, to draw feet and shoes in art class. It was only then that I realized how tense I had been. The banner incident was so far in the past, I reminded myself. From an adult's point of view, it should have seemed trivial. But the guilt I had held for seven years was still there. Although it had got smaller, it had enough weight to influence my interactions with people. Dr. Aronson said childhood experiences could leave a long trail. But he had pointed out that Suja and I were grown-ups now. I believed him when he said we could leave our childhoods behind. That was why I had come to Sri Lanka: to forge a new adult relationship with Suja.

We went to St. Catherine's the next afternoon to look around. It was the August holidays, so school was not in session. The metal gate looked smaller than I remembered. When we banged on it, the gatekeeper who peered out was Jamis. His face had shrunk, and he had a bald spot, but otherwise, he looked the same as when I had last seen him, when I had been in grade six.

New multistory buildings stood in the school compound, and a concrete walkway circled its perimeter. I felt as if I were in a dream, the kind where you are in a strange place that seems oddly familiar. The sun was merciless, and I was groggy, maybe from jet lag or maybe because my memories were weighing me down. I looked past the recently tarred basketball courts to the playing field. It had not changed. Around it was the hard-beaten dirt of the track where we had held the march-past.

In grade six, Suja's dream had been to carry the Aloysius House banner for the march-past at the school's annual sports meet. She wanted to start practicing early, months before the meet. She insisted that it was the only way to ensure success. We were both in Aloysius House, but she knew I had no interest in being the banner carrier. She persuaded me to practice with her so that she could learn to synchronize perfectly. We marched around each other's gardens after school, our backs straight as broom handles, our arms swinging stiffly, yelling, "Laaayft, right. Left right left!" Suja carried a broom with its business end in the air, raining dust on our heads, to simulate the banner. During these sessions, I giggled and horsed around, kicking my legs in random directions, or pretended to be other people: Saddam Hussein, Charlie Chaplin, the army guards outside the prime minister's residence. But Suja was deadly serious. Sometimes I saw her practicing marching on the spot before the full-length mirror in the dining room of her house, her face set in fierce concentration. By the time we began doing synchronized marching in our physical training classes, she had perfected it.

Five days before the sports meet, the three prefects in charge of picking the banner carriers had all of us girls march past them. Suja and I, with our hours of practice, were the finalists for Aloysius House. I misstepped on purpose and lifted my knees lackadaisically when the prefects shouted, "Maa-ark time!" At least, that was how I seemed to remember the scene, although much later I began to doubt myself and wonder whether I misremembered what I had really done. The prefects had us stand at ease while they debated our merits. They were in grade twelve. They must have been a foot taller than us, and they had plucked eyebrows and fashionably cut hair. They were whispering, but we heard them clearly.

"Not that one. The other one can practice and then she'll be fine," one prefect said. I remembered how she kept pinching a raised black beauty mark on her cheek.

"Like milk and molasses," another said, snickering.

"No question," the third said.

"Beauty and the beast," the snickering one said, pulling at a dangling earring that had somehow escaped Sister Bernadine's censuring eyes.

That was how I ended up carrying the banner for Aloysius House. Suja said hardly anything to me the rest of the school day. She was silent during our drive home together too. I could not recall what I said to her. Maybe I did not say anything at all. I was only twelve.

Because we were next-door neighbors in addition to being first cousins, we usually had our after-school eats together, either at her house or mine. But that day, I had my snack alone; I remembered trying to eat a roti with fish curry and having no appetite. Suja refused to play afterward. I sat on my garden swing and read the same page of my Tintin book, *The Prisoners of the Sun*, over and over again.

The next day, Suja stayed at home with a stomach pain. Over the years, there must have been other days when she had been sick and missed school, but that was the first time I could remember it happening. When I got back home, I found out that she had been hospitalized for appendicitis. For years afterward, I believed I had been the cause of it. Children do not think in terms of coincidences.

Suja did not come to the sports meet. She needed to recover from the operation, my aunt said. Neither my aunt nor my mother knew that I had been chosen over Suja. I never said anything to them, and apparently, neither did Suja.

I remembered a few things about the sports meet. It was one of those cloudy days, not too hot to enjoy. The place was teeming with all of us in our starched white divided skirts. It was noisy. You had to shout to be heard. The Aloysius House tent was decorated in yellow, our house color, with nylon ribbons, crepe-paper streamers, and masses of araliya flowers. Some of the flowers had fallen onto the grassy ground and got crushed. Their thick smell was in the air. I sat with a group of other girls on the grass inside the floorless tent, watching the track-and-field events. Clouds of dust fogged the track every time girls ran a race. The cheering inside the tent sometimes turned into screaming. Whether the girls came back to the tent triumphant or dejected, they streamed sweat, their uniforms dusty and plastered to their backs.

By the time of the march-past, I had finished the Necto in my drink bottle and eaten two of the small boxes of powdery glucose that girls were passing around for energy. That might have accounted for the excitement I felt. The Aloysius House girls selected for the marching squad lined up behind me. Someone handed me the banner, a yellow satin flag embroidered with the house crest and mounted on a wooden pole that had been planed smooth. Because Aloysius House came first in the alphabet, we were the first squad to step onto the track. Silence descended, and then the marching band began playing. I followed the band, feeling the ground vibrating with the stamping of our feet and the thudding of the big drum in front of me. For the four minutes it took to march around the field and past the guests of honor, I forgot everything else. I was lost in the experience: the dust and the sticky air, the rumbling music and the rhythmic pounding of our feet, the landscape of watching faces, the taste of left-over sugar on my lips, and my hands clutching the banner pole. I loved it.

Later, when I got home, I found out that an infection had ambushed Suja. My mother and my aunt had rushed her back to the hospital. Then I remembered how Suja had cried silently when the prefects had picked me. She had stepped to the side, the tennis shoes that she had painstakingly whitened the day before soiled with dust from the track, her face wet with tears that smeared messily across her face as she rubbed her cheeks. I thought about what I could have done differently. I could have refused the honor for which I had been chosen. Even if I had not done that, at least I could have not enjoyed the march-past.

After she recovered, Suja and I stopped hanging around together in and out of school. I could not remember whether and how much I tried to talk to her about other things. I knew I did not bring up the sports meet. There was no big confrontation. Our time together just petered out. After school, I sat for endless, friendless hours on my swing, reading or staring at the squirrels chasing each other on the cocoplum tree.

"Ready to go?" Suja said, turning back toward the basketball courts. I must have started, because she said, "Were you dreaming? You must be sleepy still from the flight."

That was when I realized she had put the incident behind her. Maybe she did not even remember it. That seemed strange when the incident and its aftermath had affected me in so many ways. At the end of grade six, my parents and I had emigrated to the US. In school, I did well in my classes but poorly at any big exam. The only prize I ever won was for an essay I had written in my tenth grade history class, not knowing that it was going to be entered into a contest. I scored low on the SAT although the tutor my parents had hired predicted an excellent performance. My teachers had said I was Stanford material, but I ended up at a modestly ranked state university. In university, I joined the debate club to get over my fear of public speaking. I was always afraid I would talk too much. At a debate on stem cell research, I froze up at the podium and let my team down. I abandoned the debate club after that. I joined the drama club and got a star role in the season's play. But I lost my voice on the day of the show; my understudy, who was one of my good friends, got her chance in the limelight. That was when I had first gone to see Dr. Marcus Aronson. In the course of months of talking to him, he had pointed out the many other incidents involving Suja that had affected me, but the only one that I could not get out of my mind was the march-past.

It seemed unfair that Suja had been unaffected, although, of course, I was happy for her. All she talked about on the way to tea was her hope that she would get picked to model for the new Neemia Shampoo advertising campaign.

. . .

The days flew by. The term paper I had to email to my Asian studies professor was overdue, but Suja liked to shop, so we went to the Liberty Plaza and Majestic City shopping arcades instead. I craved the pastries from Sena & Sons, the bakery near St. Catherine's that we had haunted during our school days. Modern chrome furniture had replaced the old wooden chairs and tables, and ceramic tiles now covered the cement floor. The glass cases looked new, but there were still a few flies flitting around inside, as if for old times' sake. The pastries had not changed: Cornish pasties, steak and kidney pies, bacon and egg rolls, mince pies, and the sugar-topped cakes I especially liked. Suja insisted on paying, but she did not eat much; she had to keep her figure, she said.

Once, when we were lounging over a table littered with pastry crumbs, a round-faced lady stopped near us, clutching the end of her sari to her chest.

"Rupa, no? Still so lovely!" she said in a voice that could have carried to the road.

It was only when Suja said, "Hello, Beryl Aunty," that I remembered her. She had lived down the lane when Suja and I had been neighbors. Climbing her jambu tree had been one of our pastimes. She had appeared so suddenly from her kitchen once, bellowing at us, that Suja had fallen off a branch and sprained her wrist.

"Beryl Aunty, how are you?" I said, rising.

Beryl Aunty patted my cheek with her plump fingers. "Good, good, but how are you, Rupa? I ran into your aunty and she said you are visiting for only two weeks."

"I have to get back home to California," I said, wiping flakes of pastry off my hands. "My fall semester classes start soon."

"Already in university! My, can't even believe," Beryl Aunty said, as if she had expected me to be twelve still. "Growing up to be a beauty. Even fairer now that you are living in the States." She laughed. "Not so much sun there to make you black, no?"

I thought I saw Suja's back stiffen against her chair.

"Only because I've been inside the library studying," I said. "But this is the beauty queen." I nudged Suja's chair forward.

"Of course, of course," Beryl Aunty said. "We were all so proud when she won."

Suja smiled, but her back still looked stiff.

There were times when people we did not know recognized Suja. They would stare until Suja smiled at them. Sometimes she pretended not to notice, but I could tell how much the recognition pleased her.

I was ten days into my stay when I found the Lanka Chitchat website. Suja and I had been lolling on the sitting-room sofa. It was overcast outside. The sitting room was dim although it was midafternoon, so we had turned on the glass-shaded lamp that sat on the side table. We were Googling ourselves on my laptop computer. The only hit I had was about the essay prize I had won in high school. Suja, on the other hand, had dozens of hits, all having to do with her Miss Green Sri Lanka status and her participation in the Miss Planet Earth pageant. There were pictures of her with other semifinalists in newspapers from India, Brazil, Canada, Germany, Sweden, Indonesia, the UK, and the US. One picture had her in a modest one-piece swimsuit going down a waterslide with some of the other contestants. There were also pictures taken during the pageant's swimsuit and evening gown competitions. The *Los Angeles Post* had interviewed several of the semifinalists on the day of the pageant. The newspaper quoted Suja saying, "I've always dreamed of this." Clearly, being a national beauty queen was much better than being the Aloysius House banner carrier. I thought of saying that out loud, to confirm my absolution. But I did not.

I had watched the pageant on TV in my off-campus San Diego apartment with three of my friends. We had eaten samosas from the Patel Brothers store and cheered during the question-and-answer segment, when Suja talked about wanting to get people to stop polluting the Indian Ocean.

"Look, you're famous," I said, clicking on one link after another.

When I clicked on the Lanka Chitchat website, I was probably slower to read the comments than Suja. The comments were transliterated from Sinhala into English, and it had been a while since I had spoken Sinhala. Later, I wondered if I could have read faster and shut my laptop as soon as I realized what we were seeing.

The first comment was, *Did you see that Suja Tissera?*

The second said, *The one they sent to Miss Planet Earth?*

The next comment was, *A she-devil.*

I laughed, pointing at the screen. "What do they mean by that? You're so hot you're a devil?"

After that, someone had written, *I wanted to vomit.* It confused me, and then I thought the commentators had gone on to another topic. But I saw that Suja was craning forward, gripping a sofa cushion, so I kept reading silently.

No wonder we didn't win. Which idiot sent her?

Must have given a bribe to get in.

"This is stupid. Let's just close it," I said, although later, I had to admit I had been curious. Suja pushed my hand away and kept scrolling down to read the rest.

If they told me, I would have found them a good-looking girl.

They don't want a good-looking girl. All they want is one who will show herself.

The showing ones are the ugly ones.

If they don't show, how will they get noticed?

Should have put coal on her face. Then she would have been fairer.

Did they pick the blackest girl on the island?

Black like a devil.

Maybe she'll see these comments and drink poison.

Then there'll be one less ugly one.

There were no more comments. I snapped the laptop shut and shoved it onto the coffee table. "Can you believe how ignorant people are?"

Suja did not say anything. She was slumped against the sofa back.

Her face looked as if it had fallen in. My mouth was dry. I could not think of anything to say.

Finally I said, "They don't even see they're still under the British this many years after independence." I tried to laugh, but I sounded as if I were choking.

Suja did not even try to laugh. She leaned over and fumbled with the lamp switch. After she had turned it off, she curled herself into the corner of the sofa. "Look at what everyone is thinking," she mumbled.

"Don't be crazy," I said. "You should have heard my friends when we were watching you on TV. You know you're gorgeous."

"I don't care what people say over there," Suja said. "But here? I can't believe everyone here is saying this kind of thing." Strands of her hair were straggling over her eyes, but she did not try to wipe them away.

"This is not everyone," I said. "This is a bunch of people who are still caught up in the old ideas. They sound like they know each other. All people working at the same company probably."

She went on as if I hadn't spoken, squeezing a cushion as if she were trying to burst it. "I didn't show anything. That swimsuit was the most modest of the ones I had to choose from. My evening gown was so covered up."

"Don't worry about it, Suja," I said. "You can't let yourself be affected by every little thing." I wanted to say more, to ask her why she cared so much about the way she looked to other people. But I did not want to jeopardize our relationship further. I tried to put my arm around her shoulder, but she brushed me off. She slipped into her bedroom and shut the door.

The next day, a Saturday, was busy.

Ratna Aunty, who knew nothing about what had happened the previous day, was rushing around, cooking the kind of dinner you might expect at a wedding. Upul, the suitor I had heard so much about, had returned from a trip to the hill country, and he and his family were coming to dinner. Suja and I helped in the kitchen, stuffing chilies, scraping coconut, rolling cutlets, and frying strips of brinjal. The rain that had been threatening to come down since the day before had not yet arrived, and it was muggier than usual in the kitchen. Ratna Aunty did not want the fan on when the oil was hot, so we were sweating as we did our tasks. I was grateful for the heat and the work because they seemed to be keeping Suja's mind occupied.

When I went into Suja's bedroom before dinner, she was standing in front of the mirror wearing a blouse with ruffles at the neckline, the ends of her hair still damp from her bath.

"Is this too transparent?" she asked, considering her reflection.

"It's fine," I said, adjusting the narrow straps of my own dress.

"Upul is conservative. And even more, his parents. Old-style." Suja brushed out her hair. She stretched her lips wide to apply lipstick. "But still his mother thinks we'll be a good match, he says. Mummy also thinks so but she won't admit."

"So you're really thinking of marrying him?" I said. "I thought you had been joking about that."

She turned around to look at the back of her pants in the mirror. She was at least five inches taller than me in her high heels. "Why would I be joking? He's a good catch, I told you."

"Yeah, but," I said, "you're so young. Don't you want to have a career? Get a job you like first?"

There was scorn in the look she gave me. "What for? Of course I'll do advertisements. The Neemia job . . ." She paused and looked at herself in the mirror. I could tell she was thinking about the Lanka Chitchat website from the way her expression turned somber.

"You are going to make a great Neemia model," I said.

She turned her head this way and that, grimacing. Then she turned to look at me. "But not without getting married. What would be the point?"

She had always been more into boys than me. After I went to the US, we hardly communicated at first. The first two years, we only exchanged Christmas cards. Then she started writing occasionally, about boys she had met. When I was in the eleventh and twelfth grades at Berkeley High, she wrote me some real letters, not emails. They were on old-fashioned notepaper with leaf borders. I used to read them after school when I was in the public library doing my homework and trying to study enough to not go blank during exams. Those were the first two of the three years Suja lived in Manchester, after her father, Neil Uncle, had been posted in the UK. She seemed most interested in the boys who showed no interest in her, although there were few of those. She had become popular when she moved to Manchester; boys offered to carry her books and begged to take her out. It was those few years in Manchester that gave her the confidence to try out for her first pageant.

Upul held an umbrella over his parents' heads although the walk from their Volkswagen to the front door was a few feet and it was only sprinkling when they arrived.

"See how well he treats his parents," Suja whispered to me. "I told you he was a good catch."

Upul was several years older than us. He was a few inches shorter than Suja, which surprised me. Suja liked tall men. But he did have the kind of wolfish face and runner's build that attracted her. From the beginning of the evening, he went out of his way to engage me in conversation. It did not seem to bother Suja; I was not sure whether she was making such an effort to make a good impression on his parents that she did not notice at first or whether she wanted him to get to know me.

While Upul's parents were telling Suja about a car accident they had seen on the road from the hill country, Upul was leaning over the arm of his chair, stroking his thin mustache and asking me about my university studies.

"Ah yes, I was also a big reader before I started working," he said when I told him I was majoring in comparative literature. "All the good books. Dickens, Robert Louis Stevenson, Sherlock Holmes. And when I was small, the usual Tintins. And also Enid Blyton, Biggles, Billy Bunter.

You can't get those books so easily nowadays, but my parents had them from when they were small."

"My parents also had those," I said, trying not to feel flustered at the way he was watching me. "I loved those books, but can you imagine what they must have done to all of us? Remember the Nabob of Bhanipur in the Billy Bunter books? He was the only brown kid in the whole school. Everyone calling him Inky this and Inky that wasn't so bad, I suppose, but remember the way he talked? 'The awfulness of the esteemed class is terrific'? A complete laughingstock."

"Yes, yes, I remember. He was very funny," Upul said, taking a fish patty from the plate Ratna Aunty had set on the coffee table.

I wondered if I had been too incoherent in my self-consciousness; he seemed to have missed what I had said. "Too bad we didn't have any books in English around with Sri Lankan characters," I said. "Actually, when I was small, I don't remember reading any books with characters from the subcontinent. Indian, Pakistani even. Real characters, not ones that were there for laughs."

He dismissed the idea with a wave of his hand. His fingers were surprisingly slender. I wondered if he played a musical instrument. "Sinhala books, of course there were," he said. "But no good compared to all the English stories. You know our Sinhalese fellows can't come up with those kinds of things."

"But don't you see?" I said. When I smelled his aftershave, I realized that I was leaning too close in my enthusiasm to get my point across. I settled back in my chair. "Why we think that? Everything from when we're small stays with us."

He did not say anything to that. He smiled and fingered his mustache. He did not agree, I thought. He sipped his whiskey, still smiling, and it dawned on me that maybe he had not even been listening. Then he said, "Maybe you can write some stories yourself. With your American education, you could come up with some good stories."

"I'm no writer," I said. I crossed my legs and tugged the red linen of my skirt over my calves. "I want to teach. But that I can only do after graduate school." I had a little of the sherry Neil Uncle had poured for me. The wind had picked up, and the branches of the neem tree outside were scraping the windows. Rain started to patter on the roof. I heard thunder rumbling in the distance.

Upul swirled his whiskey and looked at me over his glass in a way that made the hair stand up on my forearms. "Very lucky your students will be," he said as if he had known me for much longer than thirty minutes.

Before I could say anything else, Suja turned to ask if he wanted another drink. He waved a no with barely a glance in her direction.

His mother twisted her sari *pota* over her shoulder. "So you're at university in the States, I hear," she said.

If I had been quicker to answer, maybe Upul would not have jumped in. "Not only so lovely and fair," he said, raising his voice over the sound of rain on the roof. "But so accomplished. You should hear her talk."

"I wish," I said, a familiar panicky feeling in my chest. "I can't hold a candle to Suja." It was no use though. Her face had crumpled, although maybe only I noticed because Upul, his parents, Ratna Aunty, and Neil Uncle continued talking as if nothing had happened.

Upul came to the house every day during the few days I had left in Colombo. I tried to stay out of the way. I said my hellos and excused myself on some pretext or other as soon as possible, although it was flattering to have his eyes following me. I knew Suja noticed because of the way her attitude toward me cooled. By the time I left the country, we could have been acquaintances.

Shortly after I returned to California, Upul friended me on Facebook. After I had accepted, I wished I had not. I worried that it would upset Suja, so I suspended my account. Because of that, I no longer had any contact with her. I did not email her. Maybe it was because she did not write to me.

I tried to put my trip to Colombo out of my mind. When the leaves began to fall from the oaks outside my apartment, I began going to drama club meetings. Auditions for the spring play began, and I managed to land a leading role. I was thrilled for a day, and then terrified that I would lose my voice on stage. I told myself I would see Dr. Aronson before practice sessions began in January, after the holidays. I had not seen him after returning from Sri Lanka.

I went home to my parents' house in Berkeley for the holidays, where I spent long hours reading while my parents were at work. It was late December, the suicide season of urban myth, when my mother called me from her office downtown. She told me, crying, that Suja had overdosed on a mixture of alcohol and sleeping pills.

It took me twenty-five minutes to get through to Ratna Aunty's mobile phone. I dialed and redialed. My fingers were shaking. The guilt was like a rock in my gut.

Ratna Aunty was at the hospital, watching Suja sleep after having her stomach pumped.

"She is okay now," she said, her voice wobbling. "But how can I leave her alone?"

I tried to think of something to say, but all that came out was, "I'm so sorry, Aunty," over and over again.

"After Upul lost interest, she got depressed," Ratna Aunty said.

I couldn't speak. I had not known that Upul was not in the picture.

Ratna Aunty blew her nose and continued talking. "I don't know if that was why she didn't get the Neemia job. She lost her confidence. And without confidence, how can she model?"

That told me everything. The day before I found the Lanka Chitchat website, two days before I talked to Upul for too long, Suja and I had gone to see a *Harry Potter* film at the Regal Cinema. The film had not yet begun, so the lights were still on in the theater. When we walked down the aisle, stepping over bits of discarded peanut shells, a few people began whispering. I heard someone say Suja's name. I could tell how pleased she was to be recognized. After we sat down, a young girl in high heels tottered over to us and asked for Suja's autograph on the back of a crumpled envelope. Suja was thrilled. She had been confident then.

Dr. Aronson insisted that I was ignoring the societal causes of Suja's depression. He said I was blaming myself too much and forgetting that Suja's dreams had repeatedly been squashed simply because her skin was a few shades darker than mine. He reminded me of anecdotes I had related to him: how my old-fashioned Ida Aunty had asked a matchmaker to find a fair wife for her dark-skinned son, even if that meant someone uneducated, and how my mother's friend Lakshmi had expressed disappointment at the birth of her first granddaughter, a beautiful but dark cherub. He pointed out that I had not written the comments on the Lanka Chitchat website or talked the prefects into choosing me for an honor at the sports meet. I tried to keep Dr. Aronson's words in my thoughts as I biked down endless park trails and cleaned out my parents' garage to keep myself occupied. But the sounds of marching feet and band music plagued my dreams. Rows of rapt faces watched me step across a dusty track as I slept. When I woke up in the mornings, sometimes I'd taste glucose on my lips. All I could think of then was how much I had enjoyed carrying the banner for Aloysius House.

The Water Diviner

WHEN PRIYA came home, Kusuma was chewing a bite of fried brinjal, ignoring its insipidity. "Home at this time? Something is wrong?" Kusuma said.

"No, no. Just forgot I had a dentist's appointment," Priya said. She was wearing the scarf Kusuma had crocheted for her the previous year. She jerked her head at the television. "You watch him even during the day?"

Kusuma wished she had had time to switch the thing off. She did not want to have the same old conversation again. "Occasionally at lunchtime," she said, lowering the preacher's voice with the remote. "There's plenty of buriyani left and I thawed that frozen brinjal." She added, "Shall I fry you a papadum?" although the thought of heating the oil was exhausting.

"No, Amma, I ate already." Priya made her way to the stairs, a thread from the scarf trailing behind her. The scarf had taken five months of careful bullion stitches with a tapered needle Kusuma had ordered from a knitting store in Seattle. The unraveling thread snagged on the switch of a floor lamp. The scarf was getting ruined, but Kusuma could not bother with it.

A caller was arguing with the preacher. Priya turned to watch, so Kusuma had an excuse to turn her attention back to the television.

"Look, Mr. Hatter," the caller's voice said, louder than was necessary. "My sister used to be a real Christian. But she been listenin' to this horse manure and now there's no reasonin' with her. What I want you to do is tell her this is nothin' but a joke. Then I won't have a reason to come down there and squeeze it out of you. Sir."

The preacher did not flinch. He looked gravely into the camera. His ears stuck out from his face, huge. Somehow they fit his unflappable manner. "No one can be forced to believe the truth," he said. His mouth drooped at the edges, but the rest of his face barely moved. "What I am saying is in the Bible, plain for anyone to see. The world will come to its end in eight days. On the twenty-fifth of October." He laid his hands over the wooden arms of his chair. His bony fingers curved along them. "Prehensile" was the word that came to Kusuma every time she saw them. Those fingers, oddly long, were the reason she had started to watch the preacher more than three months ago. Their strangeness had caught her eye. And now she could not stop watching.

"Amma," Priya said. Her eyes skimmed over Kusuma's face, as if she were afraid of what she might see there. "Why don't you come with me to the dentist?"

The preacher said, "Thank you for sharing. Time for the next caller, please." His fingers twitched briefly on the chair arm.

"No, Priya, you go. I want to lie down a little before I make dinner." Kusuma swallowed her last bite of rice and curry, trying to keep her eyes on her daughter's face. In her side vision, the preacher was smiling. "Maybe I will make a chicken stew I saw on the Food Network," Kusuma said, because Priya would be happy to hear that she was watching other television shows. There was no need to tell Priya that the stew recipe was one she had seen months ago or that she would probably end up heating a can of stew rather than using the recipe.

On the television, another caller, a woman, was speaking in a timorous voice. "I can't thank you enough, Mr. Hatter, for trying to warn everyone." She tripped over the words in her eagerness to get them out. "I haven't had the best life, you could say. But now I'm trying to do God's will. I am waiting for the end."

The preacher's smile crept toward his enormous ears. He tapped a long finger on the chair arm and waited for the caller to go on.

"You can't keep watching this craziness, Amma," Priya said. "Come with me. We can go to Lofty Lou's for some yarn afterward."

Kusuma started to shake her head, to remind her daughter that she had not crocheted in months, but then Priya said, "You have to get out, Amma," in a voice that sounded almost frightened.

Quite an irony that Priya was so keen to spend time with her now, Kusuma thought, as she trudged to the sink with her plate. Their small argument had happened less than four months ago. It had started because Kusuma had said, "How nice to finally see you," when Priya came home from work almost two hours later than usual. There had been nothing to see through the front window except the withered white flowers that had fallen from the trees lining the street. The neighbors' children had finished their pirates game by then and disappeared indoors. The rush-hour noise on French Hill Road had petered out. Kusuma could not even hear the boy down the street who banged on his drums in the evenings. When Priya clicked open the front door, the suffocating silence had broken. That was why Kusuma had said those words. "How nice to finally see you."

But Priya had crimped her lips as she kicked off her pumps. "It's Friday, Amma. I went for a drink with Sully and the rest. And it's only seven-thirty." She had looked at the black bangle watch Kusuma had given her for her birthday five years previously. That had been the year

Kusuma had come from Colombo to live with her daughter, the year Kusuma's husband had died.

"Yes, never mind," Kusuma had said. Of course, it was good to relax with coworkers. "Are you ready for dinner?" Three yellow Easy Going floribunda roses were in a vase she had placed on the table. She had chosen them over the Bronze Stars because the Easy Goings' fruity fragrance went better with the special *pittu* and chicken curry dinner she had made. She had set out plates and goblets only for two. Ranjith, her son-in-law, almost always had client dinners on Fridays.

"I already ate, Amma," Priya said. Her lips were still tight. "Some snacks at the café."

Kusuma only said, "Fine then. We can just sit and have a chat. Everything was good at work?"

She poured some iced water and brought Priya a glass.

"Work was good?" she said again, settling down next to Priya with her own glass.

Priya played with the stem of her goblet. All she said was, "Hm."

Kusuma had plumped the sofa cushions and waited for Priya to get comfortable. But then Priya had said, "Amma, I have a bunch of work to finish still. I don't have time to be chatting."

Kusuma had said, "What is the world coming to when a daughter does not have time to talk to her mother?"

Priya had stood up at that. "Look, Amma," she had said. "I know Sara not being around, on top of Evelyn leaving, has been hard on you. But you have to find things to do. Go out more, walk around. I try to come home early so that you don't have to be alone. But I do have to work, you know."

It was the tone of her voice that had upset Kusuma more than anything. "Are you telling me that I am a burden?" she had said. She did not remind Priya that she would have preferred to remain in Colombo, that she had only left everything familiar behind and come to the States five years ago because of Priya and Sara's pleading.

And now, after three months of watching the preacher, Kusuma needed nothing from anyone.

. . .

The next day, in the hour between heating a frozen lunch and the start of the preacher's afternoon program, Kusuma found three email messages in her inbox. One was from Sheila Abeykoon, a friend from her school days in Sri Lanka. Sheila still lived in Colombo with her husband. Her two married children and the three youngest of her grandchildren lived down the lane from the Abeykoon house, so Sheila's emails usually had an account of some triumph or small calamity. Sheila's oldest married grandson had got a new job at a software firm, and he was now driving a Benz, Sheila wrote. Her daughter had got into a shouting match with a neighbor over an oleander bush he had had no business pruning.

The second email was from Kusuma's friend Evelyn Brooks. Kusuma had been close to Evelyn and still missed their daily walks around the lake, past the rowboats and the neatly trimmed hydrangea bushes that stood by the half-mile markers. Pleasant Lake was what Priya called a yuppie community. After Evelyn had moved away five months ago to be closer to her son in Texas, Kusuma had started to feel like the only senior citizen in the neighborhood. She had thought about trying to find some others. But then she had got her mind set on October 25. She had started counting days. Now she did not see the point of getting to know other people. It had been a long time since she had even replied to emails.

The third email was from Mr. Pillai. This was the sixth time she had heard from him.

My dear Mrs. Homagama,

I have been wondering how you are keeping. Staying in good health is what I am hoping. I understand from my old friend Bertie Silva that this time of year is cold in the States. Bertie's daughter is in New Jersey, so he goes once in a while. Very clean and nice, he says the place is. Maybe California also is the same.

Just today, I got back from the hill country. Three wells in Kandy and on the way back, one in Ratnapura. Truly, this is my calling.

Last night was when I was to have got back, but I had to stay the night in a guesthouse because the Kandy road was blocked. Big lorry accident. Bananas all over the road. Luckily the driver was not hurt. And a very good thing for the monkeys, all jumping around and having a good feast.

Tomorrow I will have a small get-together for a few friends. The food from New Majestic Hotel is not as tasty as the buriyani my late wife used to make but still quite good. That is what I will get. Please drop me a line and tell me how you are faring.

Yours,
James Pillai

Kusuma closed the email and leaned back in her chair. Her right shoulder was stiff. She moved it up and down to loosen it. She twisted her hair into a bun. It showed more than an inch of gray at the roots from three months without dye. In the small mirror next to the computer, her cheeks looked sunken, making her skin appear more wrinkled than she remembered. Tony Perez, the elderly checkout clerk at the Safeway, had often remarked on the liveliness of her eyes. But now they were dull. She did not know what Tony Perez would say if he saw her. She had not gone to the Safeway for months.

Mr. Pillai's first email, received two months ago, was in her Saved Messages box. She clicked on it to remind herself of what he had written.

My dear Madam,

This is in response to your advertisement in the Sunday Observer dated August 5. Your interest in roses is what caught my attention. My garden has several rose bushes, although now not as many without my late wife here to look after them. You know certainly that roses need tending here in Colombo.

First and foremost, I am a water diviner. For thirty-nine years I was a Mathematics lecturer at the University of Colombo. Now I am retired. Who thought there could be a higher truth than Maths? But I have found now sixty-two wells all over the island. It is giving me great satisfaction. There is nothing like having the dowsing stick jump up when I cross an underground stream. For free, I find these wells, although occasionally I will accept a small gift. For finding a well on the grounds of the Coral Sand Hotel in Galle, I got a present of a stay recently.

My children are grown and living in Kandy. My grandchildren are all past university age. Please be so good as to correspond with me. I must say, but, that I am very happy in our Lanka and not so keen to be resident in the States.

Yours truly,
James Pillai

Kusuma had only consented to an advertisement in the online "Matrimonials" section of Sri Lanka's *Sunday Observer* after Priya and Ranjith had pestered her for two weeks about it.

"You must stop isolating yourself, Amma," Priya had said. "Let us put in this ad."

"For five years, your father has been dead," Kusuma had said. "Do you think I can't take care of myself?"

"There is nothing wrong with having a companion," Priya had said.

Kusuma had reluctantly looked at the advertisement they had prepared and asked that the word "Sinhalese" before the word "gentleman" be removed and that one last line be added.

The revised advertisement read, "Sri Lankan–born widow, 69 years, retired teacher, crocheter, rose grower, Scrabble player, USA citizen, seeks educated gentleman for correspondence, companionship, possibly marriage. Caste, race, religion immaterial."

Twenty-three gentlemen had responded to Kusuma. Priya had studied their surnames and pointed out that fourteen were Sinhalese, five were Tamils, and three were Burghers. One might have been a Muslim. Sinhalese or not was irrelevant, Kusuma had reminded her daughter. Her late husband, Priya's father, had turned too nationalist during the worst of Sri Lanka's civil war, Kusuma remembered. He had written to Priya regularly to convey his thoughts about the war. That was why Priya made such distinctions despite living in the States for over two decades, since her college days.

Twenty-two of the gentlemen had, Kusuma thought, been more interested in becoming USA citizens than in becoming companions. One, who claimed to be a Scrabble champion, had been, shockingly, thirty-eight years old.

"That one is a freak, Grandma," her granddaughter, Sara, had said. She had still been at home then, collecting printed cardboard storage boxes and posters of flamboyantly dressed celebrities Kusuma did not recognize, for the start of her freshman year at the university. "Some of these others sound good though. You have to write to them."

But Kusuma only wrote to inform them that she was no longer interested in seeking companionship. The only one to whom she had sent a different email was James Pillai.

Priya had tried to dissuade her. At first, she had said, "He's a Tamil, you know," as if this were not obvious to Kusuma. Kusuma had only given her a look.

Then Priya had said, "What's the point if he's never going to want to live here? And a dowser? Does he also sell snake oil?"

Priya was truly her father's daughter. Kusuma's late husband had been an accountant, and also the overly logical sort, much better suited to the States than to Sri Lanka. He would have adjusted well to living here, Kusuma thought. He would have laughed at the idea of water divining. In fact, he had laughed when their old friend Kenneth De Souza had once invited a water diviner to find a well on his property in Negombo.

But now here was a mathematician water divining. That was why she had written to Mr. Pillai. She had written only once, but Mr. Pillai had written back five times. In her single email, she had told him that most of her rose bushes had died over the past few months, since her granddaughter had graduated from high school and begun planning her move to the university. That was when Kusuma had started counting days, although she did not tell Mr. Pillai that. She also did not tell Mr. Pillai that the roses went untended because she was spending most of her time watching the preacher.

Lately Priya had changed her tune. "Why not write to him?" she had said recently. "No harm getting to know him. And maybe he will change his mind about coming here."

Sometimes Kusuma thought about writing to Mr. Pillai when she sat at the computer, but the preacher's program always interfered.

Kusuma looked out at the wrecked rose bushes in the backyard. There were no blooms on any of them. The climber she had planted on a trellis over the brick garden path looked drab without the swirled yellow and pink flowers it usually produced so copiously. The Bronze Star surrounding the bird bath and the stately Glowing Peace in the far corner had died of thirst; only twigs remained. The leaves on Kusuma's prized hybrid tea-rose bush had lost their gloss. Weeds had taken over the miniature roses bordering the path. The floribundas she had planted beside the wrought iron bench, for their fragrance and bright colors, had withered.

She knew the bushes needed tending and water. But she could not force herself outside. The garden would be too silent. No songs would blast from the window of Sara's room. The afternoon would drag on without Evelyn coming by to request a Scrabble game. There would be no need to keep track of time; Sara did not need to be urged toward her homework, and no one would ask for special dinner dishes to be made.

Out of the nine rose varieties she had planted, only one looked robust: the Wild Blue Yonder, a grandiflora variety. Two six-foot high bushes of it were still thriving, thanks to being situated near the sprinklers. But weeds were thick at their bases, so they too would soon be suffocated. Not before the end of the world though, Kusuma thought. She thought of Mr. Pillai, oblivious to what could happen, and wondered if she should write to him.

But the preacher's program had already started, so she went to turn on the television, to fill the living room with the comforting familiarity of his voice.

The preacher was relaxed in his chair, listening to a caller ranting. His fingers were lying over the pages of the Bible in his lap. Prehensile.

"You're making a lot of money with this program, Mr. Hatter," the caller said, his voice shrill. "The world is ending and still you ask for donations! What is the money for if the world is going to end in four days?"

The preacher laid his fingers carefully on the chair arm. His finger nails were square and faintly yellow in the light from his reading lamp. "Excuse me," he said calmly, but the caller continued his accusation.

"This is all about the money!"

The preacher interrupted, his voice barely rising, although his fingers looked more tense than usual. "Excuse me." Then louder and louder, until he was speaking over the ranter's voice, "Now excuse me. This is not a money-making operation. We don't ask for money. We tell people where to send money if they want to get God's word out."

The caller broke in, but the preacher raised his voice further. "Thank you for sharing. Time for the next caller, please." He smiled. His teeth were very white for an old man, Kusuma thought.

The next caller wanted to know what would happen if the great earthquake did not happen on October 25.

The preacher's fingers moved as if he were writing with a phantom pen. He gazed calmly into the camera. "Now everyone is getting too worried about that because the day is near at hand," he said soothingly. "There is no reason to speculate. I know the world is going to end in four days. The global earthquake will begin at dawn in the United States and then the rain will come. But you don't have to take my word. You can see it for yourself in the Bible." He flicked the thumbed edges of the book's pages with one long finger.

It was too absurd to believe, Kusuma thought, for the umpteenth time. But she could see no sign of doubt on his face. Could it happen? There would be no need for regret then, for the roses she could have resurrected, for the time she could have had with Priya, for Sara's promised Christmas visit, for letters she could have written to Mr. Pillai.

She heard a Skype call on the computer, so she went to answer, hoping to hear from Sara. But the call was from Mr. Pillai. Kusuma stared at the screen, unsure what to do.

Then she heard the preacher's voice, reassuring another caller, offering the peace of finality. "There is no room for doubt here. The end will come and it will come on October 25."

She left Mr. Pillai's call unanswered and went back to watch the program.

On the day before the end of the world, Mr. Pillai sent Kusuma a video clip. It was attached to a short email.

Dear Mrs. Homagama,

I trust that you are well and that I will hear from you one of these days. I am sending a video my grandson took in Kandy when I was looking for a well on my son's estate.

I tried to phone you on the Skype. Next time I am sure I will get through.

Yours,
James Pillai

He was a persistent man, Kusuma thought. Or perhaps optimistic. She remembered the accident he had mentioned seeing on the Kandy Road. He had looked on the positive side then too, leaving her with an image of full-stomached monkeys instead of a chaos of smashed bananas. He was the kind of person for whom everything might seem a godsend. That had not been the way with her husband, who had not wanted her to play the lottery because he worried about the taxes a winning ticket might incur. But then, that had been years ago. If he had been alive now, he might have been less cautious than he had been in middle age.

The video opened with a close-up of Mr. Pillai. Kusuma froze it to study his face. He was not as she had imagined him. His gray hair was thick and pushed haphazardly back from his forehead. His short beard was rather carelessly cut, suggesting a lack of vanity. One of his eyes was a little droopier than the other, giving him an asymmetry that Kusuma found strangely pleasing. His eyes were bright-looking; there was hope in them, Kusuma thought.

She clicked on the Play icon, and the camera zoomed out. Mr. Pillai walked across a patch of scraggly grass, both hands palm up, holding a forked stick parallel to the ground. His gait was almost bouncy, and his eyes were intent on the stick in his hands. His shoe struck a stone, sending a flurry of smaller pebbles skittering, but Mr. Pillai did not slow down until, at last, he came to a worn-looking fence. Then he turned around and walked away in a different direction. Perhaps twenty steps later, he paused in midstride and came to a full stop. The camera zoomed in. Mr. Pillai was smiling triumphantly, and the stick was pointing to the sky. His hands were gripping the ends of the stick with such force that the veins in his wrists stood out. Evidently, he had found water, although the patch of ground at his feet looked parched, with only a few blades of dusty grass in view.

Kusuma played the video again and again, mesmerized by the way the scene changed. Mr. Pillai walking, then stopping. The stick horizontal, then upright. Mr. Pillai's fingers loose around the stick, then tight. One minute, Mr. Pillai was searching, and the next he had found water.

She wondered what it would be like to live in Sri Lanka again. Sheila would be good company, and there would be no shortage of relatives who would visit. Her first cousin, Loretta, would come to gossip when her husband was busy selling cisterns and sinks in their hardware store. Even her third cousins from Ragama would be sure to come, their arms loaded with gold bangles and their mouths stuffed with stories about their neighbors' jealousies. And Kusuma's brothers-in-law and their wives were fond of gatherings; they would talk into the night if the whiskey and sherry were flowing. If she wanted to do a little gardening, her husband's nephew, with his rusty van, could be counted on to bring tools and fertilizer.

And what about Mr. Pillai? What would it be like to travel with him around the island, finding wells for other people? There had been a time in middle age when she had wanted to do a little traveling, to see again the remote places she had visited as a child: the crumbling ruins in Anuradhapura she barely remembered, the old temples with streaks of moss on their whitewash, square after square of paddy fields in the interior, the dirt roads through the dense scrub jungle in the east where elephants could suddenly appear. But her husband had not been a traveler, even when he was not busy with his work. Anuradhapura was too hot and arid for a comfortable trip, he had reminded her; the sun would burn up any pleasure she might derive from the ruins. The best temples were in the middle of nowhere with snakes and bad roads to spoil the day. And the elephants in the east were not just clumsy spectacles. They were so dangerous that even experienced lorry drivers were frightened of passing through their territory.

But here was this mathematician, this water diviner, gallivanting around the country. Kusuma played the video again. She watched the way Mr. Pillai's hands tightened around the stick, and the smile that grew on his face, and felt excitement stirring.

The wall clock beeped, signaling one o'clock. Kusuma clicked the video shut. She rose, pushing back her regret, and went to turn on the television. There might be no time left, after all, she thought, as the preacher's serene face appeared.

The evening passed quickly. Kusuma shut the door to her bedroom and listened to the preacher's last broadcast on the small television before her bed. He took no questions from callers. He laid his head against the plain velvet back of his chair. His hands lay limply on the book open on his lap. His voice was calm, admonishing his followers to wait without fear for the end.

After the program ended, Kusuma cooked Priya's favorite dinner of southwestern chili and garlic toast.

Priya said, "This is so good, Amma. Isn't it, Ranjith?" with an anxious look at her husband. The air was faintly smoky from the jalapenos Kusuma had roasted over an open flame.

Kusuma understood that Priya hoped her mother would return to her former self: the recipe tryer, the crocheter, the rose grower, the Scrabble player. She did not want to tell Priya about the end of the world. And besides, Kusuma was not sure what to believe.

She sat for a while at the table after dinner, the smell of the garlic she had crushed still on her fingers. It had been a long time since she had made a good meal. She watched Priya scrubbing the saucepans, and remembered the recipes she had yet to make, scribbled in the canvas-bound journal on her bedside shelf. The journal must have grown dusty. She had not touched it in months. Also on the shelf was a book with fifty-two crochet patterns, a present from Sara. The book had remained unused. Now Kusuma thought of things she could have made: a new throw for the love seat, table mats to send to Sheila, hats for Sara's college winter, maybe a light scarf Evelyn could wear in Texas.

She wrote long-overdue emails to Sheila, Evelyn, and Sara. They could be the last messages she sent them. She wrote that she missed them, but she said nothing about the possibility of the end of the world.

She lay down in her bed and thought about what her days might have been like with Mr. Pillai, until finally, she fell asleep.

The twenty-fifth of October, a Saturday, was cloudy. Kusuma woke later than usual, but a light mist was still lying over the dying rose bushes in the backyard. On the Wild Blue Yonder bush by the fence, a ruffled purple flower had appeared, its lavender eye visible even from a distance. Kusuma wondered how long it had been tucked under the leaves, unnoticed. Then she saw the time: eight o'clock. Of course, there had been no earthquake. She switched on the television for news. A space shuttle launch. A serial killer convicted. A protest about an anti-immigrant proposal. A hurricane watch in Florida. A few local tragedies but nothing about an earthquake or any global disaster. She thought about the preacher's followers waiting, and wondered what had happened to him. On the preacher's channel, soothing music played, and Bible verses floated over a still shot of his empty velvet-covered chair. The preacher did not appear.

After breakfast, Kusuma ventured out to the backyard to pull weeds away from the bases of the few surviving rose bushes. The weeds were tangled, clinging steadfastly to the ground. She bent low to tug them loose. She hefted the shears and pruned the overgrown rose branches. She wetted the soil and uprooted dead bushes, piling them in a corner to be hauled away.

Priya called to her from the kitchen doorway. "Amma, the Skype's ringing on your computer." She did not say anything about her mother's morning gardening, although Kusuma could see that she was pleased.

The Skype call was from Mr. Pillai. Kusuma was not surprised. She cleaned the damp soil off her hands and wiped the sweat from her face before answering the call.

"Hello, Mr. Pillai. How are you?" she said, sitting down at the computer.

The Fellowship

IN EARLY SEPTEMBER, Dean Emory summoned me to her office and told me that my teaching fellowship would be discontinued at the end of the fall semester.

My fellowship covered tuition and included a small stipend for rent, utilities, and a limited supply of food.

"I am so sorry," the dean said, fiddling with a paper clip she had twisted apart. "The division's new budget will only support one-third the number of fellowships. I know you can't get a job with your visa, but maybe your family can help."

Although my bank balance often fell to a single digit before my paycheck arrived, I had never told my mother I needed money. The previous week, my sister Manel had cut herself by being careless with my family's broken bread knife; they had not wanted to spend money on a new knife after the handle came off.

The dean must have noticed my expression change. She leafed through a notebook and wrote down a number on a piece of paper. "This is contact information for an alumnus who might be able to help," she said. "He made a generous donation to the library recently. Perhaps he would help a fellow countryman. His name is Edward Piyaratna." She stressed the syllables oddly, but I sensed their familiarity.

"He's Sri Lankan?"

"He's been here for some forty years," the dean said.

Mr. Piyaratna's house was in a neighborhood of brick pathways and ivy-covered walls. The oaks around his property had trunks that looked too thick for my arms to circle.

The door, which was made of heavy blackish wood, reached high above my head. "Yes, yes," Mr. Piyaratna said when he opened it, as if I had been in the middle of a conversation with him. Three cats slipped around his legs and ran into the front yard.

What struck me immediately was the smell of Old Spice. I hadn't smelled it on anyone for eight years, since first coming to the States. It had been my father's aftershave. Every morning when he was not outstation doing one of his factory inspections, he had stood in front of his bedroom mirror in a sarong and no shirt, and slapped aftershave on his cheeks. As a child, I had often wanted to stand next to him and do the same morning ritual. I never asked him if I could. Sometimes I had seen him stare at his reflection for long periods and rub his haggard eyes before I slipped away.

"Come in," Mr. Piyaratna said. He was several inches taller than me, although his back was slightly bowed. His eyes, under untidy black brows, were thoughtful, and his crew-cut gray hair was thick. He was wearing a faded denim jacket that had threadbare cuffs and rips in the collar and breast pocket. When he turned to lead me into the house, I saw that one elbow was patched with a piece of rough gray fabric.

Two more cats joined us as we went down a marble-tiled hallway past a spacious sitting room full of furniture whose simple lines spoke of their costliness. Every available surface was covered with bric-a-brac that looked as if it had been purchased at garage sales. The walls were crowded with what appeared to be original drawings and paintings tacked up without frames. The dining room was no different. Several side tables with graceful legs stood by the wall, loaded with knickknacks. Mr. Piyaratna waved me directly to the dining table, which was laid with green glass goblets and white crockery, the plates a little chipped. An array of takeout containers stood on the middle of the table's glowing surface. They were from Chez Michel, a restaurant on Dorchester Avenue that I could not imagine affording.

"I don't want it to get cold," Mr. Piyaratna said. "Come and sit."

The food he had ordered seemed out of place among the clutter in his house. I had never had such dishes: snails in butter, maple-glazed duck breast.

"So you're the division's emissary," Mr. Piyaratna said, pouring wine. "Kind of them to send you, but I don't need thanking." That was when I realized Mr. Piyaratna had no idea I was there to ask for money. I wondered if his ratty jacket pointed to stinginess. But then, surely he would not have made a donation to the library or ordered food from Chez Michel.

The idea of getting to know him with an ulterior motive made me uncomfortable, but what could I do when I had no other way to complete my studies?

I asked him where he was from in Sri Lanka.

"It's a long way off," Mr. Piyaratna said. He sipped his wine and examined his glass.

"I am from Colombo," I said. "Same with you?"

"Matale," he said.

"Your family's still there?"

"No," Mr. Piyaratna said, and in the same breath, "Dean Emory tells me you are doing a PhD in Philosophy?"

That was when I noticed the scars on his throat and the lower half of his face. There were dozens of them, small like almond slivers, faintly silvery, smoother and a paler brown than the rest of his wrinkled skin. There were some on his hands as well. I wondered if he had been in a car accident.

"I am hoping to finish next year," I said, cutting into a piece of duck. "If my dissertation goes okay."

His eyes closed briefly as he tasted his wine. "And your topic is . . . ?"

"Desert," I said. "You know, what one deserves. Punishment or reward, that kind of thing."

"Aha, I see. Merit, karma," Mr. Piyaratna said. "I am Buddhist myself."

"I don't come across many Buddhists here. Let alone Sri Lankans," I said.

He started to fiddle with his fork.

"When did you leave Sri Lanka?"

"Long time ago," he said. He placed his glass squarely on the table. "For a long time I have been here. I had a business here, an insurance company." He started talking about the way he had run his company. Every summer, he had picked two of his sixty employees and sent them to Paris for an all-expenses-paid vacation. Apparently he had done this not only to reward his employees for faithful service, but because he wanted them to experience luxuries they could not otherwise afford. His generosity was promising, I thought. Maybe it would not be too demeaning to ask him for financial support.

While Mr. Piyaratna talked about the clients he had insured, I looked at the junk arrayed on his shelves and side tables: wood and metal sculptures, candle holders, drawings in standing frames, smooth rocks in bowls, statuettes. He seemed to care about these things, because they did not look dusty. There must have been seven or eight very small vases, and they all had fresh wildflowers in them. On a corner shelf, an ornate pipe sat on a burnished wooden plate. The pipe was a deep reddish color, its bowl similar in shape to one my father had smoked.

When I had lived in Sri Lanka, my practice after dinner had been to follow my father to the verandah of our Colombo house, where moths killed themselves by flying at a hanging light. I usually sat in a cane bucket chair next to my father's rattan recliner, and we both read while the sweet smell of his tobacco floated around us. He probably did not know I was there. Sometimes, out of the corner of my eye, I saw him put down his pipe and hold his head in his hands. There were times when I wondered if he was crying, but I never said anything. After a while, he always went back to reading.

I did not say much at Mr. Piyaratna's house that day, other than to describe my work and my university-owned studio apartment, which I reached by means of an ancient manually operated elevator that stopped between floors unless I paid careful attention to when I pushed the Stop button. I could not think of a way to broach the topic of a donation when I had just met Mr. Piyaratna; the idea of asking a stranger for money seemed inconceivable.

When I next Skyped with my mother, I told her about meeting Mr. Piyaratna. I said nothing about the loss of my university funding. I called my mother each week because I knew she worried about me. I tried to have some innocuous topic to discuss whenever I called because I did not want to know about how my family was doing, whether the apartment manager had fixed their leaking roof, and whether the shower head that had come off had been replaced. I was thankful my mother had no webcam. I did not want to see her looking older, frailer, and more fatigued.

"Piyaratna is a fairly common name," my mother said.

"He has scars on his face and hands," I said. "Do you know a Piyaratna in Matale who was in a car accident?"

"There was that Piyaratna family with the tea estate in Matale. The worker riot," my grandfather said in the background. I wondered if he was having his beer. He had cut it down to once a month because of the expense.

"That terrible incident?" my mother said. "That was back when I was small. We talked about it in school, I remember."

"Bloody estate workers got fed up of the living conditions and started a riot," my grandfather said. "Attacked the owner's house with machetes. Big news item at the time. They all got hacked. The old couple and the grown children. They were managers on the estate. The youngest fellow must have been about twenty-five or six. He was the only one who survived, but he also got badly hacked."

"What was his name, the Piyaratna who survived?" I said.

"James? John? Could be William?" my grandfather said. "Some English name. That was the problem, you see. The government took the estates from the English, but the workers' conditions were no better than before. Worse even. The Sinhalese owners were still high and mighty like the English fellows, treating the workers as if they were dirt. Especially the old man, I heard, and apparently he was not much better to his own sons."

"So what happened to the son who survived? And to the estate?" I said.

"The estate got sold-off eventually, I think," my grandfather said. "The fellow, I don't know. Maybe he's your friend."

Mr. Piyaratna invited me back for dinner a second time. "I don't get much opportunity to talk to young people, especially students," he said on the phone message he left me.

He was wearing the same threadbare jacket. I sat at his dining table and ate Penang lobster curry and fried noodles while his cats took shifts rubbing themselves against my ankles.

I answered his questions about the Kant class I was assistant-teaching and the progress of my dissertation, wondering when I would have the courage to ask for money. Perhaps if I told him about the money problems graduate students had, he would suggest supporting me himself, I thought. Maybe I could have found a more interesting or pathetic graduate student experience to describe, but what came to mind was the coffee hour I had organized as chair of the Social Relations Committee in the philosophy department. I described how I had gone to the

Eloise to get wine and cheese and crackers, and sat in my double-parked Honda, ignoring the vacant metered parking spaces and the honks and curses from other drivers, until a free curbside spot opened up.

"The best part about going there is getting to taste cheese that I can't dream of buying," I said. "There are some good smoky ones. Also the wine."

Mr. Piyaratna listened to every word I said, nodding and hemming encouragingly.

"This fellow was in there buying a four-hundred-and-eighty-dollar wine," I said. "And he was young. I don't know what kind of job he had."

"Not a philosopher, I suppose," Mr. Piyaratna said.

After dinner, I went over to look at the pipe on the corner shelf. The bowl's rim had a carved border of leaves. Underneath was an elaborate carving of a man with a flowing beard that wound its way around the bowl, forming an intricate design.

"I bought that ten years ago at an estate sale," Mr. Piyaratna said, coming up next to me.

"It reminds me of the pipes my father used to smoke," I said, sniffing its faintly sour odor.

"That pipe has a history," Mr. Piyaratna said. "The English fellow who smoked that attended the Independence Day ceremonies in Colombo in 1948. When I heard that was when I initially got interested in the pipe. I have a photograph of the fellow, seated in the audience with the pipe in his hand, listening to the Duke of Gloucester—Prince Henry— talking on a stage with the governor general and his wife, and also Prime Minister D. S. Senanayake and his wife. This fellow—his name was John Chapin—must have been waiting to get outside and have his smoke. Apparently John Chapin was posted in Colombo for a time. The chap who sold the pipe claimed Chapin was a relation of Harry Chapin. Maybe you have heard 'Cat's in the Cradle.' I listened to that song too many times when I was younger. Whether or not John Chapin was really a relation I am not sure. The seller had no authentication."

Mr. Piyaratna laughed, and I thought that might have been the first time I had heard him do that. "But never mind," he continued. "It's not only because of the spit in there that the pipe is valuable. This is a very rare pipe, you see. I found out only after I bought it. Meerschaum, more than two hundred years old. Hand-carved, one of a kind. Apparently it was passed down through Chapin's family. This craftsman, here, is a famous pipemaker." He turned the pipe over and showed me the name carved on the bottom.

"You are interested in antiques?" I said, putting the pipe carefully back on the shelf.

Mr. Piyaratna shrugged. "The past matters," he said.

I was about to ask what he meant by that when Mr. Piyaratna said, "Your father doesn't smoke now?"

I told him how my father had died four years ago, on the day I had gone back to Colombo with my undergraduate degree in engineering from the US. I had not thought my father would take the day off just because his only son had come back after a four-year absence. But I did think my completed degree might have drawn him to the airport. Engineering had been his idea, although finding a scholarship to study in the States had been my mother's. I had the degree certificate in my hand, rolled up in a glossy cardboard tube, because it was too precious to be placed in the luggage hold. But only my mother and grandfather came to pick me up. My father had been doing a health inspection at a jam factory in Negombo. On the bumpy drive along the Katunayake Road, from the airport back to our house, I talked about my years in the States and how glad I was to be back. After we got home, everything changed. A message was waiting from the Negombo hospital; my father had collapsed at the factory from a heart attack. By the time he reached the hospital, he was dead.

"I am very sorry to hear," Mr. Piyaratna said. He did not ask me why I was back in the US studying philosophy. He looked as though he might cry, which I thought was odd for an elderly man.

It was the first time I had related to anyone the story of my father's death. Mr. Piyaratna seemed to understand exactly how I felt.

"Come back next week and have dinner," he said.

The taste of Mr. Piyaratna's red-bean-and-sesame dessert was still on my tongue as I drove back home. I thought about how I had sat on the verandah of our Colombo house when I was eleven and twelve, watching my father read *The Russia House* or *The Day of the Jackal* or whatever book he was reading at the time. Every evening, I imagined telling him about the things that had happened in school: how Suresh Ponnamperuma got awarded the English essay prize even though he had written about banning homework, how Karunatilaka Sir went flying across the room during social studies class after tripping over Mahinda Aluwela's foot, how Cyril De Silva had to stand in a wastebasket for half a period because he shot a paper ball at Father Damien. I never told my father about any of those happenings.

I started visiting Mr. Piyaratna regularly, usually on Friday evenings. I looked forward to these meetings.

Over grilled Chilean sea bass, he asked me how my family was faring in Colombo. I told him that they lived on my mother's widow's pension and Manel's salary.

"Manel is working as a teller at Hatton National Bank. An okay job, but she has to go to the Bambalapitiya branch by bus. She takes the number 198. I don't like to think about her hanging on the footboard, jammed in with all those sweating men who take the bus."

"Yes, difficult to think of bad things happening to family members," he said, and again he looked as if he might cry.

"They manage all right," I said. "Of course, if my father had not gambled everything, they would have been more than all right."

At my father's funeral, and the reception afterward in the high-ceilinged hall of St. Mary's church, my mother, my grandfather, and Manel had sat quietly next to me. We didn't say much to each other or to the guests. The light from the modest glass chandelier seemed too bright for a funeral, and the sympathetic whispers of our relatives and friends standing around in clusters sounded to me as loud as the rush-hour traffic on Galle Road.

"The worst part about the gambling problem was that I only found out after he died," I told Mr. Piyaratna. "In the end he left my mother with nothing except his pension and his son—me—to look after everyone."

In the weeks after my father's death, I had sat for hour upon hour on the verandah of our Colombo house, gripping the feather weight of the pipe he had left lying on the arm of his recliner, examining the dusty carvings on it that I had not noticed before. The bougainvilleas had grown over the edge of the verandah steps. It was my job now to prune them, but I could not bear the thought of handling the thorny branches. I watched black ants meandering along a row of cracked bricks in the garden path, and geckos sliding around the loosened knob on the front door. There were many tasks that had to be done. Instead of doing them, I applied for entry into the graduate philosophy program at my alma mater.

"I see," Mr. Piyartana said. "Being the man of the house is a lot of responsibility for a young fellow."

It was not the response I expected. I had thought he would ask me why I was in the States instead of helping my family.

"We had to sell everything," I said. "Our Mazda. Also the piano and an old teak settee—the only pieces of heirloom furniture my mother had—and all her good jewelry. And of course our house—it was a little shabby, but fairly big."

He only said, "How sad that must have been for you."

I couldn't help comparing him to my father. I remembered a night on the verandah when I had put my Marvel comic down and told my father that I had approached Leitan Sir, the sports master, and tried out for the cricket team. My father was reading *The Eagle Has Landed* that night, the smoke billowing around his face. He didn't hear me, so I said my news again. He had been a cricketer himself in his school days.

"What?" he said, as if I had appeared out of thin air.

"I asked Leitan Sir if I could try out for the cricket team, but I didn't get in," I said, for the third time.

I remembered the look of annoyance that crossed his face. "When you get into the team, tell me," was what he said.

I started telling Mr. Piyaratna about what had happened each week.

"Have you ever been to the thrift shops on Milwaukee Avenue?" I asked him, over octopus in soy sauce and ginger. "I told him that I had gone to look for a frying pan," I said. The Teflon had peeled off the second-hand one I had had for four years.

"Did you find one?"

"In the second shop," I said. "One dollar. And I found a good pair of trousers. Two-fifty."

"I always like a good deal," he said.

When Sarah Harris had a party at her apartment, I told Mr. Piyaratna about her rented glass-sided apartment by the lake, with room after room of glossy hardwood floors and stark white walls hung with real paintings, not prints. I and all the other starving students she had invited had swarmed around the table spread with endless French bread and gnocchi, pate and Brie, sushi rolls and cocktail sausages, baklava and tiramisu.

"This is the one student I know who is not going to be worrying about the job market when she graduates," I said, tucking into quail with truffle mousse. "A philosopher queen."

"This is a girlfriend, maybe?" Mr. Piyaratna said.

"No, no, I don't want to think about all that until I finish my degree," I said. "And even then, I am not sure I would ever want to marry."

One Friday, I had to walk to Mr. Piyaratna's house because my Honda's brakes, which I had needed to replace for a couple of months, finally gave out completely. My trunk had groceries when it happened: bread and produce, generic brand condiments and cereal, which were too heavy to lug home. I had to drive home slowly with the emergency flashers on, using the parking brake at traffic lights.

"I am going to have to walk until my paycheck comes in. On Tuesday," I said to Mr. Piyaratna, over pan-fried foie gras and scalloped potatoes. In the back of my mind was the idea that he might offer me a small loan for the repair.

"Good exercise," he said, stroking the head of a cat that had climbed onto his lap. "That is why I gave up having a car years ago. I only take a taxi if it is too far."

In November, during the second to last pay period of my fellowship, and a month before I needed to pay the tuition for my next semester, my bank balance fell to zero four days before payday, something that had only happened three times before. I had to scour my apartment for loose change, plunging my hands under the sofa cushions, rooting in the desk drawers and feeling under the floor mats in the Honda. All I came up with was two dollars and twenty cents. I used it for milk and discounted bread, and made do by eating unusual combinations of foods from the back of the kitchen cupboards.

"On Sunday, I had chickpeas. I mixed up a sauce with ketchup and mustard," I told Mr. Piyaratna, as I ate the butterflied filet mignon with horseradish sauce and the creamed spinach he served that Friday. "On Monday, I put some condensed milk on bread for lunch. Luckily there was a tin of sardines for dinner. With a little brinjal pickle I had in the fridge."

"Doesn't sound too bad," was all he said, filling my wine glass. I had thought briefly of asking for Mr. Piyaratna's help when my money ran out, but I had decided against it. Now I thought he should have expressed regret that I had not come to him.

The week before the end of my fellowship, I got food poisoning from eating a slice of lemon meringue pie someone had left for general consumption in the philosophy department lounge. When I went to the local emergency room, the nurse took one look at my threadbare shirt and the scuffs on my shoes and thought she knew everything about me. She mistook me for a fellow from the housing projects on the south side of campus. There had been stories in the news about how the hospital treated people from the projects. I vomited several times while waiting for a doctor. It took nearly three hours for me to be seen, and then only because I insisted that I might be getting dehydrated.

"That nurse thought I was ignorant because I look poor," I said to

Mr. Piyaratna that Friday, spooning tandoori chicken onto my buriyani. "That is why I've got into the habit of talking about my being in a doctoral program. That's the only weapon I have. Otherwise I get dismissed as a no-good bum."

"Good to remember that poverty is a relative matter," Mr. Piyaratna said. "I am sure that once you finish your PhD and get a job, have responsibilities, you will have a different understanding about what poor is." He opened a newspaper that had been lying on the sideboard and showed me an article about hunger in sub-Saharan Africa, with a photo of children with flies on their lips and their stomachs bloated to the size of pumpkins.

I did not say much after he showed me the newspaper. I did not look at him standing there in his tattered jacket as if he knew everything about poverty. I left without waiting for the grand dessert he had ordered, whatever it was, and walked away from the lofty house he had chosen to fill with junkyard knickknacks. I thought about my family's apartment: the green walls that must have grown duller over the years, the narrow windows that made the cramped space seem prison-like, and the books, old letters, brass vases, and pantry items that they had no choice but to cram onto open shelves in the small sitting room.

I could imagine my father saying the same words Mr. Piyaratna had said to me, expecting me to be responsible while he was gambling away everything that we owned without any regard for my family's future.

I had decided not to go to Mr. Piyaratna's the next Friday, but that day, Dean Emory called me into her office and asked me what I planned to do about my next semester.

"Maybe there is nothing you can do but withdraw," she said gently.

I knew it was the last day I had to ask Mr. Piyaratna for the donation, so I went to his house. I did not have a plan for bringing up the topic. I had an unpleasant feeling in my stomach when I thought about the fact that however generous he might have been to his employees, and however good the food he served me had been, he did not seem particularly interested in parting with his money. It occurred to me that I did not really know him despite having told him about my life for so many weeks.

Mr. Piyaratna asked me about my week as usual as his cats wound around my feet. He pushed takeout containers of Mongolian lamb and asparagus tempura toward me and did not seem to notice that I was not saying much. But after the meal was finished, he led me to the corner of the room. It was too late in the year for wildflowers, I supposed; he had placed sprigs of pine in the small vases.

"I want to give you something that will help you to complete your studies," he said, and handed me John Chapin's pipe. "You can sell this to one of the antique dealers on Clark Street. It appraised at fifty thousand. That was ten years ago." He said it as casually as if he were handing me a book to read.

I was in shock when I left with the pipe in my coat pocket. In my daze, I forgot that my car was parked outside Mr. Piyaratna's house. The fall air was brisk as I walked to my apartment. My financial problems were solved. The loss of my fellowship was immaterial now. I would have enough to complete my last year of graduate school.

I wondered what would have happened if my father had given me a lump sum to start my future when I returned home with my engineering degree, instead of leaving me to deal with his death and a pile of debts and responsibilities.

The pipe seemed lighter than I had noticed before, and I was afraid I might break it. I sniffed its sour odor and thought about my father putting his head in his hands on the verandah of our house. I wondered how long he had struggled with his gambling addiction and how he had managed to make our financial situation seem relatively normal for so long. Why had he not spoken to me about his anguish when I had been old enough to understand? But then I had never asked. I had barely known him, it seemed.

My mind was so muddled with questions that I pushed the Stop button of the elevator in my apartment building after it had risen a foot off the ground. I stepped out between floors, realizing I had been so caught up in my own problems that I had not understood Mr. Piyaratna's concern that I was avoiding my responsibilities. There was so much I did not understand about him: why he had never married, why he filled his magnificent house with garage-sale clutter, what reasoning had led him to decide that the time had come to help me with my finances. I was thankful that I would have many Fridays before me to visit him. I wanted to get to know him better, to ask about his family, and how he had got his scars. I did not even know if his family had ever owned a tea estate.

Today is the Day

THE FOURTH house on the Meals on Wheels route was in a complex Kalpana had not previously visited. The complex was called Myrtle Tree Gardens, which was a misnomer because there were no myrtles there, and few trees of any kind. Most of the plants visible in the mobile homes' yards were azaleas, weeds, and unevenly cut boxwood hedges.

A plastic pot of crimson geraniums was hanging from a hook by the front door of number 77 Willow Way. Kalpana noted from her delivery list that she was to drop off one meal, for a Mrs. Leela Subramanium. Immediately after she knocked, an elderly woman in a flowered dress came to the door. Her bearing was upright, but her head was moving back and forth in small jerky movements. It gave her an air of uncertainty that was undercut by her tightly pursed lips.

"You, who are you?" she said, when she saw Kalpana.

"Kalpana Fonseka," Kalpana said, proffering the packet of food she had taken from the crate in her trunk. "I will be bringing your hot meal Monday through Friday."

"What happened to Madeline?" Mrs. Subramanium said, looking Kalpana up and down. "She decided to go for that operation after all?"

Kalpana straightened the collar of her shirt with one hand. She was still holding the food packet in her other hand. She wondered how long this woman had been getting meals delivered. Kalpana had been doing a route for Meals on Wheels for two years, since her daughter Usha had entered high school and started needing her less. "Your mother thought about doing that," Lionel Fonseka, Kalpana's father, had said, when Kalpana told him about her new volunteer job. "But the arthritis was already making it hard for her to hold the steering wheel. That is why I told her better not." He had ruffled his beard the way he did when he got into territory he would rather forget, so Kalpana had gathered that there had been an argument about it. "Good thing she is able to do reading for the blind instead. Important to do *pin*."

These days he talked as much about doing *pin*, merit to ensure good in future lives, as he did about his Christian notions of doing penance for past sins. It was not that he had become a Buddhist. He remained as devout a Catholic as he had been throughout Kalpana's life, going quietly out on Sundays to Mass at the local church. But maybe the Buddhism the rest of the family practiced had leaked slowly into his thinking. When Kalpana was growing up in Colombo, the two religions seemed to coexist mostly peacefully in the family, although Kalpana suspected they had sometimes led to secret quarrels between her parents. Once, as teenagers, she and her brother had found several religious knickknacks in the garden outside their parents' bedroom window: a small stone Buddha statue that had smashed against the trunk of an araliya tree, a rosary with its white beads scattered, a brass oil lamp that her mother used to light in front of the living room Buddha statue, now dented on one side, a wooden cross embedded in the mud under a bougainvillea bush. Kalpana had asked who had thrown them out. But her parents had not wanted to discuss them. Don't take any notice of those things, was all they said. They had always been good at brushing difficult subjects under the rug.

"I said, did she go for that operation?" Mrs. Subramanium said.

"That could be," Kalpana said. "All they told me was that the person doing this route was out of commission for a few weeks."

Mrs. Subramanium sniffed. "Well, obviously. I told her. What else can you expect with bunion surgery?" The jerking of her head increased. She put out a hand and steadied herself on the door frame. Her hand was shaking. "And today of all days, she is not here." She turned and walked stiffly into her living room.

"Is there a problem?" Kalpana asked. She waited at the door, the packet still warm in her hands. She was ready to do whatever had to be done. Many times, she had retrieved medicine bottles from behind dressers, changed light bulbs, and lifted heavy objects for the seniors on her route. Once, she had even chased a squirrel out of a kitchen trash can.

Mrs. Subramanium lowered herself into an armchair. She sat rigidly, not leaning against its cane back. Her sparse white hair was pinned neatly at her neck. She seemed to be staring at a glass dish of Life Savers candies sitting on the coffee table in front of her. "You can put the meal on the table," she said.

Kalpana went inside, noticing the smell of lavender in the room. She was about to place the meal packet on the coffee table when Mrs. Subramanium barked, "Not there!" She pointed to a very small dining table set in the alcove to the right of the armchair. "There is where I eat."

Kalpana put the meal down on a tablecloth that was not only stain free but also pressed free of wrinkles. The room was narrow, with hardly any furniture. There was no television and nothing on the walls except for a framed studio photograph hung behind the armchair, of a middle-aged Mrs. Subramanium with an older man who stood a head taller than her. Next to them were two unsmiling young men in plain ties and a girl who looked as though she could have been in high school. Everything in the room was in perfect order. The books on the two-shelf bookcase had their spines lined up straight. Five pewter boxes with ornate lids stood on the shelf, also lined up. On the table, a white ceramic tea pot and a tin of Lipton tea stood on a small plastic tray next to an outsized glass shaker of crushed red pepper.

"Kalpana Fonseka, you said?" Mrs. Subramanium's voice had softened. "So they sent me a Sinhalese?"

Kalpana turned, startled. "You are also Sri Lankan? I thought you must be Indian." She saw the frown that wrinkled Mrs. Subramanium's forehead.

"Tamils are still ten percent of the island's population, let me remind you," Mrs. Subramanium said, her head jerking so rapidly that Kalpana wondered if she should offer to help. "Even after you've killed off so many."

Kalpana took a step back, her hand to her mouth. She told herself that age could sometimes be misunderstood for rudeness. Mrs. Subramanium was surely not accusing her personally. "I have plenty of Tamil friends," she said in as placid a tone as she could manage. "I just didn't know. Subramanium could be an Indian name also. There are so few Sri Lankans around here."

"Sit," Mrs. Subramanium said abruptly, waving a trembling hand at the other armchair, a chunky item covered in bruised maroon leather. When Kalpana hesitated, she added, "If you can manage to be cordial to an old Tamil lady."

Kalpana sat, trying to ignore her sudden uneasiness. Mrs. Subramanium pushed the dish of candies toward her. Kalpana took an orange Life Saver.

"Today," Mrs. Subramanium said, crossing her feet and clasping her hands together in her lap. "Today is the day I am going to die."

Kalpana felt her breathing stop. She inhaled deeply and reminded herself that she had a knack for helping the senior citizens on her route feel more cheerful. She had been told this several times. She leaned forward in her chair. "Are you ill, Mrs. Subramanium?" she inquired.

"Of course I'm ill," Mrs. Subramanium snapped. "I am only seventy-five. So why would I be getting meals delivered—these tasteless meals—if I was not ill?"

"What is wrong, may I ask?" Kalpana said. Mrs. Subramanium's finger nails were haphazardly cut, she noticed, although she was well groomed in other respects.

Mrs. Subramanium's head wobbled on her neck. "Can't you see?" she said, pointing at her head. "And not only that. My heart, my liver, my bladder, my bones. What is not wrong is a better question."

"Would you like me to take you to a clinic?"

"Clinics. Doctors!" Mrs. Subramanium muttered. "What can they do? When the time comes, it comes. And I can tell that today is the day." She clasped her hands tighter, as if to stop the trembling. Then in a softer voice, she said, "I want you to stay until I go."

Kalpana searched for something to say to that. In her hand, the Life Saver had become sticky.

"I don't want to die alone," Mrs. Subramanium said into the silence.

"But . . ." Kalpana started to say. She could not see how a complete stranger could be saying this to her.

"My daughter, Devika, lives in Maryland now," Mrs. Subramanium said, as if she had read Kalpana's mind. "She wanted me to go there. But after my husband died here, I couldn't leave this place. Two years now, he's been dead." Mrs. Subramanium looked around the room. "He'll be waiting for me, so I'm not afraid of dying. Leaving everything." She gestured at the candies as if they were the only thing she cared about leaving. "I just want someone here with me when I go."

"I can understand," Kalpana said, trying to keep her face serene. She struggled to find the words that might help Mrs. Subramanium. "But who can know when we will go?" She knew she should say more, but she could not think of anything. She edged forward on the chair, wondering whether to rise.

Mrs. Subramanium waved her back with her shaking hands. "Oh, *I* know," she said. Her voice had turned tremulous too. "Today is the day. May 17. I can feel it."

Kalpana looked at Mrs. Subramanium sitting there with her back upright. She did not look as if she were about to die. But what if she did?

"Is there someone I can call?" Kalpana looked at the photo on the wall. "Your daughter? Your sons? A friend?"

"No, no, no. Devika is too far away. It will worry her too much." Mrs. Subramanium pressed her trembling fingers to her cheeks. Kalpana thought she would say something about her sons, but all she said was, "And there is no one else." Then she looked at Kalpana, her eyes suddenly sharp. "Would you have stayed if I had been Sinhalese?"

There was a tight feeling in Kalpana's chest. She drew a calming breath. "Please, Mrs. Subramanium. Tamil or Sinhalese, Japanese or Chinese, has nothing to do with it." She glanced at her watch and realized she had a real reason to leave. "I have eighteen meals cooling in my trunk. People are waiting for their lunch. I am sorry, but I really have to go." After she rose, she added, "I hope you will be okay."

Mrs. Subramanium looked up at her. "Come back after you have finished the deliveries," she said. "Maybe I will still be here. All I want is for you to stay with me until I go." She looked smaller from this vantage point, Kalpana thought. The shaking of her head seemed more pronounced.

Maybe that was why she blurted, "I will try," before pocketing the candy in her hand and hurrying to the door. She pulled it shut, leaving Mrs. Subramanium sitting in her armchair, waiting to die.

The remaining deliveries took an hour and fifteen minutes. Kalpana drove from Myrtle Tree Gardens to Pinewood Point to Magnolia Terrace. She drove faster than she normally did. She almost ran over a cat on El Dorado Road. She was not as forthcoming as usual with her customers. She inquired after Mr. Garcia's grandchildren only cursorily, and she declined Mrs. Lee's customary offer of a glass of lemonade.

She could not get Mrs. Subramanium's words out of her mind. Her question was too absurd to take seriously. It was insulting that Mrs. Subramanium would even ask it. She had been doing volunteer work

since her college days. Until she had Usha, she had been a very energetic
volunteer. She had been involved in literacy projects, homeless shelters,
book collections for prisoners, food banks, and clothing drives. She had
not discriminated against anyone in any of her volunteer positions. Here
in the Sacramento area, Kalpana did not have any Tamil friends, but that
was not by design. Most of her Sri Lankan contacts were through Usha,
and the few Sri Lankan friends Usha had were all Sinhalese. Kalpana
had never asked Usha whether this was by chance, nor had she wanted
to discuss such matters with her.

Growing up in Colombo, Kalpana's closest friend, Indra, had been
Tamil. They had known each other since the age of six. When they
graduated from pretend games—policeman-thief, grandma-grandpa,
doctor-patient—to reading, they had traded their Tintins and Asterixes,
Enid Blytons and Nancy Drews. Indra had been the sympathetic one,
the one who could be counted on. Indra had cried when Sister Margaret
caned Kalpana for spitting at Myrna Peiris in grade four. Indra was the
one Kalpana had told when she got her first terrifying menstrual period
in Sister Helen's grade six class. Indra had whispered in Sister Helen's ear,
and then shielded Kalpana's bloodstained skirt from curious eyes as they
hurried to the office to phone Kalpana's mother. In grade eight, it was
with Indra that Kalpana had eavesdropped after school on the couples
who stood too close together at the bus stop, hidden under umbrellas.

The last time she had seen Indra had been in 1983, on the last day of
their time together at St. Catherine's. They had walked down Convent
Lane toward the sea, eating mango pickle from plantain leaf cones they
had bought from the vendor outside the school gate. Kalpana's emigra-
tion to the States was imminent. Indra's family had also been planning
to emigrate, to the UK.

"Wherever we are, we'll stay friends," Kalpana had said. She could
still remember the sour-sweet smell of the mango slice she had in her
fingers, and how sweaty the collar of her school uniform had been under
her plaited hair. There had been no clouds to block the afternoon sun.
The sea had stretched before them in an endless dazzling sheet.

Indra had turned to her, wiping a squirt of pickle juice from the black rim of her glasses. Mango pulp had already dripped onto her school tie, staining one of the white stripes yellow. "You better not forget to write," she had said.

Two weeks before Kalpana's family left for the States, race riots had erupted in Colombo after Tamil Tigers killed thirteen Sinhalese soldiers in the north of the island. Gangs of Sinhalese thugs had gone on looting sprees, destroying Tamil shops and houses in Colombo. When rumors of violence began spreading, Kalpana's father had brought his Tamil colleague, Andrew Selvanayagam, home with his family. The Fonsekas had hidden the Selvanayagams in the cellar under the front verandah of their house.

The cellar was a damp, cement-walled cave chockablock with broken furniture and cardboard boxes full of old records and files. It was rarely entered, so cobwebs hung everywhere in thick, sticky drapes. When Manu, the youngest Selvanayagam child, who was four years old, was lowered into its musty interior, he began to cry loudly. *Shhh*, they all said, the Selvanayagams and the Fonsekas, afraid that his crying would attract the thugs. He didn't stop, so Kalpana was sent to fetch the glass jar of Star toffees from the dining room sideboard. She handed the jar down into the cellar. The red, lemon, and green of the toffees caught the light from the single bare bulb in the cellar. Manu's cries faded to a sniffle. But the bulb had to be switched off so that light would not be seen through the small air slits in the cellar wall. When Kalpana's father shut the cellar trapdoor and darkness fell inside, Manu had started wailing again. The Fonsekas had concealed the cellar door with a black rubber mat. Kalpana's father had arranged the rattan verandah chairs on the mat, and the Fonsekas had sat on them. Kalpana had heard Manu sobbing underground while mobs of her fellow Sinhalese chanted threats on the main road. She remembered the fear she had felt, of both the sobbing and the shouting.

Days later, Kalpana had heard that Indra's house, where she had spent many afternoons, had been burnt to the ground. Indra's family had fled to safety. She had not heard from or seen Indra again. Her parents did not speak of what had happened. They had never believed in dwelling on ugly events. Kalpana herself could not bear to focus for too long on the painful details. Wasn't it enough that Indra and her family had escaped? The past could not be changed. She preferred to focus on the people she could help now.

At twenty minutes past noon, her deliveries done, Kalpana returned to number 77 Willow Way.

She knocked on the door, but Mrs. Subramanium did not come to open it. She knocked again, louder. She waited, watching the leaves on the hanging geranium stirring in a light breeze. There was only silence. After another series of knocks and more waiting, she turned the doorknob with a panicky feeling in her chest.

The living room was empty. The meal packet Kalpana had laid on the dining table was gone, and the table was as neat as before. Kalpana prepared herself with a deep breath and walked toward the open bedroom door.

The smell of lavender was stronger inside the bedroom. The small bed was painted white. Mrs. Subramanium was lying on it, her head propped on two thick pillows. A red floral comforter was pulled up to her neck. The only other piece of furniture was a bedside table that looked too fragile to bear the weight of the lamp and water glass that stood on it.

Kalpana had reached the age of forty-five without seeing a single dead body in real life, although there had been plenty of times when she had switched channels too slowly and seen dead victims of violence on TV. She had never gone to view bodies at the few funerals she had attended.

Now she moved hesitantly toward the bed. She could not tell if Mrs. Subramanium was breathing. She could feel her own heart pumping. She was about to place her hand on Mrs. Subramanium's forehead when Mrs. Subramanium opened her eyes.

Kalpana gasped, drawing back her hand.

"Ah, you are here," Mrs. Subramanium said, as if this were an everyday occurrence. She closed her eyes and, after a pause, opened them again. "Any time now. I can feel it. Wait with me." And she closed her eyes once more before Kalpana could say a word.

Kalpana did not know what to do, so she simply stood by the bed. She became aware of holding her breath. She let it out slowly. The window above the bed was open. Through the old-fashioned lace curtains, she could see the sky, bare of clouds. She could not hear any birds, perhaps because there were so few trees in Myrtle Tree Gardens. Number 77 was set quite a way back from the main road, so there were no traffic sounds either. Kalpana wondered how Mrs. Subramanium could stand this much silence. Did she listen to the radio? Did she think about her husband? And what had happened to her sons? Had they been Tigers? Been killed?

Mrs. Subramanium seemed to have fallen asleep. Her head was turned to the side, and Kalpana was thankful to see a few of the white hairs on her pillow fluttering rhythmically with her breath.

She wondered if Mrs. Subramanium might really die. Perhaps she should have considered the situation more. She could not wait indefinitely, standing there. But maybe Mrs. Subramanium would have a nap and wake up. Then they could talk about what needed to be done. She stepped cautiously forward to sit at the foot of the bed. But before her weight could settle completely on the mattress, Mrs. Subramanium bolted upright. "What are you doing?" she barked. She had taken down her hair, and it was lying in stringy waves on her shoulders. "No one sits on my bed."

Kalpana sprang off the bed. She wished she did not feel guilty. She had done nothing wrong. "I'll bring in a chair," she said. "Or maybe you feel better now?" She looked at Mrs. Subramanium sitting with her back like a ramrod, and thought she did not look at all near death.

Mrs. Subramanium sank her head back on the pillows. "Bring the chair," she said, and closed her eyes again.

There was only one wooden chair in the dining alcove. Kalpana brought it in and sat by the bed. She was wondering whether she should call the Meals on Wheels office when Mrs. Subramanium said, "We escaped because our daughter spoke perfect Sinhala." Her eyes were still closed.

Evidently she was talking in her sleep. Was she talking about the same 1983 riots that had been on Kalpana's mind? Or was she talking about a recent escape from the conflict in Sri Lanka? The civil war between the Sinhalese majority and the Tamils fighting for a separate state had gone on for more than two decades and only come to its bloody end a few years ago. Kalpana realized she did not know when Mrs. Subramanium had come to the States. Was she a recent refugee? But she seemed too acculturated for that. Her accent was not heavy, and her manner suggested she had been in the US longer than a few years.

Mrs. Subramanium opened her eyes and looked directly at Kalpana. "Devika was in the Sinhala medium in school, you see. Even though she was Tamil."

She was talking about her daughter's school days, so this had to have been a long time ago. Why was Mrs. Subramanium bringing this up? Perhaps there was a burden she wanted lifted, Kalpana thought. Seniors sometimes talked for that reason. She did not mind listening if it helped them. "I had Tamil friends who were in the Sinhala track with me," she said. "Was Devika in a Colombo school?"

"St. Catherine's," Mrs. Subramanium said. "My old school also, that was."

"Ah," Kalpana said. "That is where I went. I don't remember a Devika. But I finished in 1983. So maybe she was after my time."

"1983 is when I am talking about. She was in grade six. A twelve-year-old is too young to have to protect her family."

Kalpana thought of Indra, and she was afraid to hear the story. But what she might imagine could be worse than what she heard, so she said, "What happened?"

"My husband didn't go to work that day because of the rumors about rioting. There were so many of us in the house. My in-laws had come, and my parents. And the children were there. The boys were older than

Devika and their Sinhala was not as good. Everyone was afraid. It is hard to wait for something that you know is coming but you don't know when. It must have been after six when we heard all the shouting. It was getting dark. We could smell smoke from down the lane. We didn't know whose house was burning."

"Where was this?" Kalpana said.

"Wellawatte. Jeya Lane."

Kalpana let out her breath. Indra's house had also been in Wellawatte, where most of the riots had been, but she had lived on Castle Lane.

"You see, someone had put a cross on the garden walls of all the houses with Tamil occupants. In chalk," Mrs. Subramanium said. She lifted her head off the pillow. The effect of having rested must have worn off, because her head had started bobbing again. "Then a mob came to the gate, shouting and demanding to see who was there. Someone was carrying a torch. We could see the flames through a crack in the curtains." She rubbed her eyes. "We had to send Devika out to talk to them. She was the only one who could convince them. To this day, I dream about the terror of seeing her walking out to the gate alone."

"She must have been terrified herself," Kalpana said, and realized her voice had fallen to a whisper. She could see Indra in her mind, walking toward a crowd. She remembered the Selvanayagam boy sobbing under her feet.

"She didn't show it," Mrs. Subramanium said, joining her trembling hands together. "She was confident. We could hear her. She said her family was Sinhalese. But the thugs at the gate wanted to know why there was a cross on the wall. They tested her. They asked her to say 'bucket' in Sinhala. You know we have trouble with that *b* sound. But she had no problem saying *baldiya*. All her classes were in Sinhala and it was in Sinhala that she spoke with her friends. Only at home we spoke Tamil. That is why our house was saved."

"What a terrible thing," Kalpana whispered. Whether or not they were saved had hung on something as small as a single consonant. She tried to remember if Indra's Sinhala had been Tamil-accented. She could not recall hearing her using a *v* sound in place of a *b*, but then she had never thought to listen for it. She did not want to think about what had happened to Indra or how she had lost touch with her so completely.

Mrs. Subramanium lay back on her pillows. "That is nothing compared to what others have lived through these past twenty-five years. Or died in. Libraries burned. Houses destroyed. Limbs blown off. Every horror imaginable." She turned her head away from Kalpana. Then she added, "But you wouldn't understand."

Would Indra have said the same thing? Kalpana said, "I am sorry for everything you went through." It makes me ashamed to be Sinhalese, she thought, and then realized she had said it aloud. She did not want Mrs. Subramanium to think she had not intervened, so she added, "We sheltered a Tamil family during the riots. In our cellar." But not Indra's family, she thought. She did not say it aloud. Regret lay in her mind like a cloud.

Mrs. Subramanium was silent and still for so long that Kalpana wondered if she had fallen asleep. Or worse, she was thinking, when Mrs. Subramanium said, "Our Sinhalese neighbors were also very sympathetic. People brought us bread and tinned fish in case we had to hide. Some of them also had casualties. One neighbor was killed in a bomb blast in Pettah. And another one's son lost his leg because of a landmine in the north. I am not saying our side was free of blame. The terrorism and the violence, I didn't condone."

Some time passed before Kalpana could bring herself to say it. "I had a good friend who was Tamil. Indra was her name. Back when I was in school, no one thought of all these differences. Who even thought Sinhalese, Tamil?"

"That is true. Devika said the same thing. And in our generation also. Who said Tamil this or Sinhalese that?" Mrs. Subramanium turned her body around to face Kalpana. She had pulled her hands free of the comforter. Her head did not shake when it was resting on the pillow. "But still underneath there were the dissatisfactions and the inequalities. Who was getting the jobs and the promotions, who was making more money. Wasn't that what this was about? And now the young people have a history they can't forget." She frowned at Kalpana. "But why bring all this up now?"

"I . . . ? But it was you . . ." Kalpana started to say.

Mrs. Subramanium folded her hands under the pillows in a gesture that looked suddenly resigned. "Enough. Now all that is past for me," she said, and closed her eyes.

Kalpana stared at her. After several minutes, she saw that Mrs. Subramanium had finally fallen asleep. Air whistled from her mouth in soft rhythmic toots. Her expression was peaceful.

Kalpana walked out to her car and called Frances, the woman at the Meals on Wheels office.

"I can't stay any longer. My daughter will be home soon from school," Kalpana said, after explaining the gist of the situation.

"That's no problem. Mrs. Subramanium will be fine," Frances said.

"But don't you think someone should . . . I mean, what if she . . . what if something happens?"

"I'm pretty sure she won't die, if that's what you're worried about," Frances said. "She does this all the time. She's always convinced every day is her last. She wants to talk. Madeline was used to it and she knew how to get out of there quickly."

"So she's not ill?"

"Sure she is," Frances said. "But nothing's going to kill her right away. I can change your route, if this is too difficult for you to handle. There's another route that goes by the river."

Frances began describing the route, but Kalpana's mind wandered to the troubling memories that she usually took pains to avoid.

On the day after the Fonsekas had sat above the cellar door, Kalpana's father had driven the Selvanayagams to safety in a rickety white van borrowed from a neighbor. While her father was gone, Kalpana had sat at his desk, his old rotary phone heavy in her lap. She had thought about Indra sitting in her living room next to the Ganesha statue garlanded with flowers. Where were Indra's mother and grandmother? Praying? Crying? Was Indra trying to read, or was she trying to divert Aruna, her little sister? Why hadn't she called? Was she waiting for Kalpana to call? Kalpana lifted the phone from its cradle and dialed the first digit of Indra's number. But she could not get Manu's wailing and the thugs' shouting out of her mind. Only that morning, her parents had been discussing a Sinhalese family that had been attacked for sheltering some Tamil friends. The Sinhalese family's house had gone up in flames, all their belongings lost. That was why Kalpana's father had driven the Selvanayagams to another place.

Maybe if Kalpana had phoned Indra and described the Selvanayagams' sojourn in the cellar, and how Manu's sobbing had endangered everyone, Indra would have understood that Kalpana could not offer shelter. But Kalpana had, after several false starts, placed the phone back in its cradle. She knew the Star toffees would not help Aruna, at eight years old, to tolerate the cellar. Indra would be safer with her own family, she decided. When Kalpana's mother asked if she had news of Indra, Kalpana had shaken her head. Kalpana's mother had looked away at the bright zinnias lining the garden path. "They'll be fine, I'm sure," was all she had said. That had been further reassurance for Kalpana. But that night, she had lain awake, biting her nails and listening to bats swooping outside her bedroom window. In the morning, she had dialed Indra's number again and again. There had been no answer. It must have been several days later that Kalpana had heard about Indra's house burning, and Indra's family's flight from Colombo.

"Kalpana?" Frances said. "Do you want me to change your route?"

Kalpana thought of the last time she and Indra had eaten pickle together by the sea, and Indra's grin as she said, "You better not forget to write." But she had been too ashamed to write.

"Kalpana?"

Kalpana struggled to return to the situation at hand. She took the sticky Life Saver out of her pocket and put it in her mouth. She pictured Mrs. Subramanium sitting upright in her armchair, waiting day after day for her meals to arrive, with the dish of candies ready to offer on the table before her. Did the others who delivered meals stop to talk or watch her sleep? Probably not, Kalpana thought. Why should they feel responsible for Mrs. Subramanium's well-being?

"No need," she said to Frances. "I can handle it."

"Good of you," Frances said.

Kalpana bit into the candy and felt it break apart in her mouth. She was thankful for its tang, for it distracted her from an image of Indra's face, her eyes terrified inside the black frames of her glasses.

Sunny's Last Game

ON THE DAY OF the last game, Sunny climbed into the car with a black eye. The discoloration was barely noticeable on his skin, which was only a couple of shades lighter than mine, but I could not miss the bruise because of the puffiness of his right eyelid.

I pretended nonchalance, although there was a compressed sensation in my chest. Sunny tried to heave his backpack onto the back seat, panting, his breath smelling of orange soda. It took seven attempts because the pack was heavy and almost as big as his torso, and because he had to contend with his coordination skills. I gripped the steering wheel to curb my urge to help.

When the pack finally landed, Sunny attached his seat belt without making eye contact, even with the good eye.

"Good to see you, man," I said. "How was the day?"

"Great," Sunny said, staring through the window to where two kids were waving to him in slow motion. I recognized one of them: Bryan Scardino, also a sixth grader, a boy with dirty blond hair that fell in a perfect bowl around his head and teeth that seemed determined to push past his braces. Bryan was of nondescript height, and quite slender, but he had a pugnacity that made him vicious on the basketball court. I gunned the engine. As the car moved toward the two waving boys, I noticed that Bryan was mouthing something.

Sunny turned his face to them as the car moved past, and then he clasped his hands together above his head in the Brown School salute.

"What was he saying?" I said. In the rearview mirror, I could see the two boys laughing.

"Oh, Bryan. That kid," Sunny said. "He's a riot."

"Was he the one that made the black Hindu comment?" Ayomi and I had been speculating about this possibility for a while, given the child's behavior on the basketball court, but there was nothing we could do without confirmation from Sunny.

Sunny squeaked his fingertips across the dashboard. "I don't exactly remember," he said.

This had been the standard response to any probing question since Sunny had started middle school, or rather, since the black Hindu incident.

I decided I would do less harm if I let it go for the moment.

There was still the other, and possibly related, matter. "So we got a call from school," I said, as casually as I could manage. "We heard you got hurt."

"Yeah," Sunny said, presenting me with a waft of orange soda breath and a full, and distressing, view of his face. "See? Black eye. But it's minor."

"Exactly how did it happen?"

"I fell down against the music room doorknob."

"Did anyone . . . ?"

"No, Dad," Sunny said, turning his face to the window.

"Okay, but can you tell me who was with you?"

Sunny shrugged.

"Sunny? Was anyone with you when it happened?"

"Maybe," Sunny said. "Maybe not."

"Ms. Rienzo said you insisted you were alone when it happened."

"If I said someone else was there, you'd go and talk to Ms. Rienzo and Mrs. Langley, and tell them someone pushed me." His voice had gone high-pitched; that should have been warning enough.

"Sunny, I'm just trying to find out if someone else was with you."

"I don't exactly remember," Sunny said. "I think I was alone. I was carrying my trumpet."

"How can you not remember if anyone was with you?" The words rushed out before I could stop myself.

I knew the conversation was over before Sunny said, "I just don't," in a voice that seemed squeezed from a tight space, before he crossed his thin arms across his chest with an air of finality and pressed his lips closed, sealing in the orange soda smell.

Sunny still did not know that we planned to move him from the Brown School to Loyola, a private school not far from where Ayomi worked. Moving Sunny to a new school was the only way we could protect him from what seemed to be happening at Brown, but I knew that convincing him of this was going to be a near-impossible feat.

For some time, Ayomi and I had been second-guessing our relocation to Sandhill, despite its proximity to both our new New Jersey work-places, and the shining reputation of its public schools. On the Friday before the school year began, at an ice cream social for incoming middle-schoolers and their families, I had noticed how poorly named the Brown School was. I saw two or three children apparently of East Asian origin, but only one child besides Sunny with skin darker than the beige walls of the school corridors. I was relieved to see her: a girl with thick kinky hair and an air of supreme confidence who I thought might be African American.

Sunny seemed to see nothing amiss. Insisting on independence, he had roamed the unfamiliar school hallways ahead of us, examining the travel routes of Magellan and Vasco da Gama displayed in smudged glass cases outside the library, trying to slide over the varnished blonde flooring of the gym, and admiring students' artwork, which appeared to be tributes to the styles of Monet, Van Gogh, and Picasso, pinned to the walls.

When school began, Sunny's enthusiasm calmed my apprehension, at first. Every day, he came home full of talk about Ms. Portenoy, his language arts teacher. This was a woman who regaled her classes with the ostensibly true exploits of her two cats, suspiciously named Mettie and Allie, short for Metaphor and Allegory. Within the first month, a passion for writing burgeoned in Sunny. In elementary school, he had procrastinated over homework assignments for hours, sitting at the dining table drawing stick figures doing jobs he claimed needed no writing: chefs, carpenters, shoe-store clerks, rangers, video-game testers. But under Ms. Portenoy's influence, he scrawled page after page in his awkward cursive. Sunny tended to write about bullies and feeling left out, but he said his stories were all fictional. Most of the books he read were about things like that, he said.

Even Sunny's aversion to science disappeared. This seemed due to the fact that his science classroom opened onto an inner courtyard, where two bird feeders swung from a small maple tree. One was filled, a little at a time, with seeds, and the other with a sugar solution for humming-birds. The science teacher, Ms. Marasco, rewarded attentiveness and hard work with trips to the courtyard to fill the seed feeder; if kids were lucky, a hummingbird would come by to the other feeder while they were outside. Sunny, intent on winning this privilege, worked harder than he ever had before.

I only began to worry when Sunny mentioned, over dinner one evening, that someone kept calling him a black Hindu.

"Well, isn't that something," Ayomi said. She ladled a heap of fish curry onto Sunny's rice. Since Sunny had started at Brown, she had been making more Sri Lankan meals, filling the house with the insistent smells of curries she had previously made only on special occasions. Meatloaf, spaghetti carbonara, and macaroni and cheese, formerly dinnertime favorites, had been given a back seat.

"It's an insult. But that's not right, is it?" Sunny said.

"I can't count the ways that's not right," I said.

"Those words are not insults," Ayomi said.

"But he says it like an insult. And we are not Hindu, right?" Sunny said. "Hindus go to the temple, like the one Arjun Uncle took us to. They don't go to church."

"Right," Ayomi said, pushing Sunny's bean *mallun* to the center of his plate, despite his protests.

"But we are black," Sunny said, sounding unsure. "Even though you and Dad are blacker than me."

"Well, we are all dark," Ayomi said, trying to frame things right. She took the Goldilocks approach to race: you needed to think about it, but not too much and not too little. "But our race is not black."

I floundered for a while, trying to answer Sunny's questions about what exactly race was, until Ayomi said, "Race, well. It has to do with where people are from."

"More or less," I said.

"And you know where we're from," Ayomi continued. I wondered why the discussion seemed so much more uncomfortable than the dozens of others we'd had about the origins of our family.

"But we're American," Sunny said.

"Sri Lankan American," I said.

"And that means not black Hindu," Sunny said.

"I'm not surprised someone at Brown would say this. The level of ignorance," Ayomi said, *sotto voce*.

"It was just some clueless kid," I said, although I had been thinking the same thing.

"But that means the parents . . ." Ayomi said. "I told you, we should look around at other schools. What if this is only a small symptom?" And to Sunny, "Who said this, anyway?"

"Just some clueless kid," Sunny said, looking at her over his water glass. Then, "Why do you want to look at other schools? Brown is the best school." He clasped his arms over his head in the Brown salute. He did it at least once a day, it seemed. "Ignorance is like a headache. If you give it enough time, it goes away."

That made me laugh. Sunny was like a sponge; I never knew where he picked up the statements he would let out.

"True, sometimes a headache just goes away," I said. "But sometimes it means something more serious."

"Brain cancer," Ayomi muttered, too softly for Sunny to hear. "That's why we need to know who said this," she said more loudly. "So we can make sure he understands."

"Remember the thing about bullying?" I said. "You have to tell us so we can help. Or put you in a more suitable school."

"I am a man now," Sunny said, licking a curry splatter off his wrist. "I can deal with things. And Brown is the best school."

"Sure you can," Ayomi said. "And Brown is pretty good. But we need to know."

"So who said it?" I said.

Sunny swallowed the last of his rice and curry. "I don't remember exactly."

After that evening, Sunny's daily reports about school became less detailed, or rather, more positive. On several occasions, he came with injuries, a weal here, a bruise there. Getting nothing from Sunny, Ayomi and I went to see the principal, Mrs. Langley, a gray-haired woman with a placid demeanor and, under her frilly clothes, the physique of a wrestler. She wore white ankle socks with her black pumps, which made her look incongruously childlike.

"There have been no reports involving Sunny," she said, evening out a stack of papers on her desk. "But kids and accidents, you know how they are." She hesitated. "And some of the kids—I am not sure about Sunny—they're still developing their coordination. You know, sometimes I'm walking behind someone on the stairs, or even in the corridor, and then they'll trip. Just over their own feet." Mrs. Langley laughed. "It's that age, isn't it?"

I was sure Mrs. Langley had walked behind Sunny on at least one occasion. Sunny had a knack of tangling on his own feet and falling flat.

"Sunny's getting a lot better, though," Ayomi said. I could see she was not buying the principal's placating attitude. "Which is why we were wondering why he still has so many scrapes and bruises."

"He participates in the games, right?" Mrs. Langley said.

"Oh, he loves the basketball," Ayomi said. The YMCA that adjoined the school had after-school sports programs for children from Brown. Sunny was on a basketball team. "We've tried to persuade him to wait for the soccer season instead, because then height won't limit him, but he says basketball is what he wants."

"Well, good for him for sticking it out," Mrs. Langley said, rising to her feet. "And don't worry so much. He's doing great. The teachers would know if there was a problem."

But Ayomi and I both knew it was not that simple, and that a kid could be ostracized or even bullied without teachers having a clue. We knew this because we had grown up as first-generation immigrants, Ayomi in Tennessee and I in Alabama. We had met in the San Francisco Bay Area, where we had gone to college to escape our school histories and where we had remained until coming to Sandhill. In the Bay Area, we had only had to go to the market to be instantly surrounded by people speaking in the languages of five continents.

Sunny said helicopter parents were a pox on kids, and that stunted independence could follow a kid forever. I reassured him, but I worried, watching the way Sunny emerged alone at the end of the school day, the way kids like Bryan Scardino did stupid things like wave in slow motion or laugh after Sunny walked by, the way no one passed him the basketball at the after-school games, and the way the welts and bruises continued, unexplained.

· · ·

At the YMCA's entry door, Sunny keeled over, apparently tripping on air, before bouncing up and rocketing indoors. His lime-green T-shirt had the name of the team sponsor, "Hefty Hal's Hauling," on the back. The shirt looked like a mean joke on his small frame, and his black eye, purplish now and more visible, did not help his appearance.

"He could very well have got the shiner on his own," I whispered to Ayomi.

"Or not. I wish we could ask the parents. I bet they would have heard something," Ayomi said, but we both knew the other parents were not going to tell us anything. A clannish backwater, Ayomi called Sandhill. Being less than an hour from Manhattan, it was not a backwater, but it was clannish. Most of the parents were at least second-generation Sandhillers, and they roved in cliques that were closed to newcomers.

The game had already begun when we entered the crowded section of the gym where Sunny's team was playing. The place reeked of Doritos.

"Aagh. Red again," Ayomi muttered, as we hurried past the packed bleachers to the end area where we usually sat. This was the fourth time in the twelve-week season the greens had played the reds. I felt the same disgust. Bryan Scardino was on the red team, along with a friend of his, Cameron Wilder, a child with a loutish build and muscled calves that could have belonged to an eighth or ninth grader. When those two were there, I never stopped anticipating trouble. I perched on the edge of my bench, determined to call out the perpetrator if I saw another foul.

Sunny was the shortest kid on the court. The next shortest was a slightly bow-legged but outstandingly athletic child named Grayson, also on the green team, who could leap high enough to knock the ball from the tallest players' hands. Sunny not only did not have that ability; he seemed barely able to stay on his feet. What he lacked in athleticism, he made up for in enthusiasm, though. As soon as the whistle blew, he was ready, his knees bent, prancing, and occasionally wobbling, from foot to foot, his arms outstretched. He kept screaming, "Here, over here!" This was how it always was. His eagerness was painful to watch.

As usual, I kept willing someone to pass him the ball. On one level, I could understand why no one did; they were competitive little twerps, future stockbrokers and corporate lawyers, no doubt, and they wanted to win. The two or three times Sunny had managed to snatch the ball off the floor, he had lost it within seconds. His dribbling skills left a lot to be desired, and his throwing aim was pitiful. But I wanted someone to give him a chance. He was barely eleven, for Christ's sake! Couldn't they see he had to mess up a few times to learn to play?

The parents nearby were yelling instructions and encouragement as they always did, not only to their own kids, but to those of others as well. They seemed to know everyone's names. I had never heard any of them call Sunny's name, but then Ayomi and I did not call his name either. We sat in our corner of the Doritos-scented bleachers, Ayomi biting her nails and me with my back tensed, our eyes fixed on Sunny and the ball that never went to him.

"How's the eye?" Ayomi said in the halftime break, when Sunny came to get a drink of his orange soda.

"Mom!" Sunny whispered, looking around surreptitiously. This embarrassment had only appeared recently; before Sandhill, he had wanted to describe every ache and pain he had. "It's fine."

"Feeling tired, man?" I said. "You're really moving out there."

"I wish someone would pass me the ball," he mumbled.

"You can't keep waiting for it," I said. "Go after it. Knock it out of someone's hands."

"I'm trying, okay?" he said, and I realized he was about ready to cry.

In the back of my mind had been the idea that a bad experience at the season's last game might catalyze a readiness to leave Brown. Loyola kids had their own after-school programs, so they did not play at the Y. But now, I wanted Sunny to get passed the ball at least once, and I wanted some child to make a jackass of himself trying to bully Sunny in full view of everyone. Sunny could leave Brown vindicated.

Sunny had to sit out the third quarter; with eight kids on each team, some had to sit out a quarter. I could see he was livid about it. He sat cross-legged courtside, his hands clenched between his knees.

The game was getting heated. The green team coach, a rangy guy wearing a Knicks hat sideways and track pants too low on his hips, was no more than a kid himself, probably a high-school senior. Clearly, he was determined to win. He sprinted by the side of the court, hollering directions. Whenever a kid missed an obvious opportunity, he clutched his head in both hands as if it were about to explode.

At the third-quarter time break, the score was eight to ten, with red leading. Sunny was already pacing, waiting to get back on the court. I called to him, waving the soda bottle as an incentive. Clambering reluctantly up the bleachers, Sunny tripped on some unseen obstacle. For a second, he lay there, ignoring the hands of two nearby parents who had reached out to him. I could see how discouraged he looked. When he got up, there was a bleeding, dime-sized scrape on his knee, the pink easily visible on his skin.

"Okay, man?" I said, when he reached us and grabbed the soda bottle.

"Yes, fine," he hissed, although his eyes had filled with tears. Then after glugging soda and swatting at the orange stream of it that cascaded down his T-shirt, he said, "It doesn't even hurt."

"Okay, you listen to me," I said in his ear. "Go out there and play. Remember, that ball is yours. Don't wait for someone to give it to you."

Sunny nodded and clomped off, his face set. He tripped on the bottom step but managed to catch himself before he fell.

When the game resumed, Sunny kept trying to grab the ball, although his efforts came to nothing. Even when half of the quarter was gone, when I thought he had to be tiring, he jumped at the ball in Cameron Wilder's hands. He could have been a gnat for all the trouble he caused Cameron. But Sunny did not give up. He ran after the ball, tripping over his own feet and springing up, clawing crazily at the air whenever the ball was in someone's hands.

The problem, besides the lack of coordination, was that he did not have the reach he needed.

When the ball reached Bryan Scardino, Sunny leaped high, trying to bat it away, and Bryan elbowed him aside. Sunny fell as easily as if he had been a cardboard cutout, but when he landed on the floor, there was a resounding thwack that echoed across the gym.

"Foul! That's a foul!" I shouted, and only then realized I was on my feet, my fist raised. There was a lull in the parents' chatter. In the hush, I heard my heart racing, and the crackle of my shirt sleeve as Ayomi tugged at it, trying to get me to sit down. Bubble gum popped nearby.

"Don't go nuts," Ayomi whispered.

But I stayed standing. "Are you going to call it?" I called, raising my voice further.

The coaches, green and red, were staring up at me. The referee waved as if he had already been moving forward to call the foul. Sunny was on his feet, pretending he did not know who I was, although that was futile since Ayomi and I were the only people there who matched his skin color.

"Good on you," one of the parents sitting near us said. He was a beefy gentleman with the look of an aging skinhead. His ears stuck perpendicularly out of a head shaved smooth.

"I think he would have called it anyway," said another parent, a woman with ropy arms and dark hair scraped into a high pony tail, who seemed too painstakingly dressed for a kids' basketball game. "That one, he couldn't have missed."

"What's your son's name?" the woman sitting next to Ayomi asked her. The bubblegum was hers; she popped it again. Its smell, strawberry, drifted over to where I was standing.

I went back to watching the game rage on. The green coach had got more excitable, and the parents were yelling from every direction. Sunny was hanging back now. Instead of sitting back down, I ran down to the side of the court, ignoring Ayomi's attempt to hold me back.

"Sunny, get in there!" I yelled. "Move up, over there."

Sunny turned, looking horrified at my intervention, and then he ran into the thick of it, swiping energetically at the air near the ball. The ball was passed, but to Grayson, not Sunny.

There were chants of "Shoot, Grayson, shoot!" from the parents.

Sunny was yelling too, with his fists pumping, so I joined in, shouting, "Grayson, shoot!"

Grayson shot and made the basket and the parents began to cheer and howl. Sunny sped over to thump Grayson on the shoulder, although he could barely manage it with everyone else's long arms in the way. The grin on his face was as wide as when he beat me on the Wii, playing *Super Smash Bros.* He ran in a little circle, pumping his fist and saying, "Yes! Yes!"

When there were only three minutes left on the clock, I realized we had lost the chance for a win. The red coach had whipped the reds into a single-minded ferocity, and they dribbled and passed with a feverish focus, moving ever closer to making the final basket that would win them the game. All the green team had to do was keep them from doing that, I thought. Sunny would be okay with a draw. I stood courtside, and joined the other, seated, parents in shouting directions to every kid who had an opportunity to get in the reds' way.

Ayomi came down from the bleachers to stand beside me. "Calm down," she said, but then she got caught up in the urgency of the moment too, and started screaming to Sunny and Grayson and the rest of the boys whose names we knew from the parents' yelling.

When there was less than a minute left, amazingly, the green team got the ball. They started to pass it to each other. Sunny, Sunny, pass it to Sunny, I willed those boys. But it was to Grayson that the ball went. He was almost under the basket. No reds were around. Grayson took aim carefully and shot. The ball headed straight for the basket. And hit the rim. It bounced and went rolling away, amid a collective groan from the parents and the kids. Only ten seconds were left, not enough time for another try, but I was confident that Sunny would at least be pleased the reds had not won.

People had begun rustling in the bleachers, laughing and consoling each other about the draw and gathering their things, when a slow thudding began. Then I saw Sunny. He was hunched awkwardly over, dribbling with low careful bounces, moving slowly toward the basket.

Time took on a different meaning. Nothing else seemed to move, not the coaches or the referee, not the boys on the red team or the boys on the green. Only Sunny moved, slowly, bent over like a feeble old man, and the ball, with its heavy thuds. Yards away from the basket, Sunny straightened with the ball in his hands and aimed. The ball sailed through the air, seemingly in slow motion. There was no time left for it to reach the basket, but it did. The sound of it sliding in was lost in the long beep of the clock hitting zero.

A dumbfounded quiet descended. It lasted only a moment, and then the place erupted with a roar that rose to a deafening pitch. Behind me, parents were on their feet, cheering and applauding. The green team rushed Sunny; in seconds, he was teetering on their shoulders, beaming, his teeth stained orange from his soda, his hands raised in the Brown School salute. He was only there for a moment, and then he toppled down, giggling, scattering the group of kids.

It was Bryan Scardino who reached to give him a hand up. "Hey, good job," I heard Bryan say.

I climbed the bleachers to gather our belongings. Ayomi was wiping her eyes.

"That was fantastic!" the pony-tailed mother said, squeezing Ayomi's arm.

"I've been waiting all season for him to do that," the egg-headed man said, extending his hand. His name was Dudley, it turned out. He said his family owned the bakery on the corner of Pinecrest Road.

"And with that shiner," another man, who introduced himself as Bruce, the father of twins, Dean and Grace, said. "Grace said she saw him fall against the music room door today. Acted like a tough guy, she said. Not a peep out of him."

I nodded. "That's Sunny," I said, watching Sunny doing the Brown School salute. I slipped Sunny's orange soda bottle into my jacket pocket. I had a feeling that Sunny had been right about Brown; sometimes headaches were not worth too much thought.

The Lepidopterist

Mom got me a pair of green rain boots with painted eyes. She said they were like frogs. I didn't like them, so she took them back to Target. Boots aren't like frogs just because they are green. It's true that frogs could be green, but they could also be any other color. The poisonous ones are the brightest. Bright colors keep these frogs safe from creatures that might eat them: birds, snakes, dogs. Frogs have a pair of long legs, folded up, and a pair of arms. They have wide heads with bulging eyes. Boots don't have legs, or arms, or heads, or bulging eyes.

Now I have regular boots, with no eyes. I walk in them through the long grass, past my old playhouse with the shelf for importancies. I haven't sat in it since my sixth birthday, since Sammy said, *Check you out, dudette. Growing up.*

I like it when Sammy hugs me. Sammy's smell reminds me of our living room couch, where I sit and watch *Tom and Jerry* on Sunday mornings from seven to eight fifteen. At eight sixteen is when I put two slices of Oroweat whole wheat bread in the toaster, left slot first, then the right, so that Mom can push them down when she comes downstairs to make my scrambled eggs. Then I take two eggs out of the tray on the middle shelf of the fridge. I hold the eggs in my hands, knowing how easily the smooth crackable shells could spill out the mess inside. When the oven clock turns to eight nineteen, I line them up on the black countertop, pointed ends toward the wall. Dad doesn't know how to turn the mess inside the eggs into the right kind of scramble, warm and wet, with a tablespoon of reduced fat cream liquid and one handful of cheddar cheese. When he makes breakfast, I prefer to have buttermilk pancakes, which he knows how to make into perfect circles.

Sammy can make scrambled eggs the right way, and also circular pancakes. Sammy can do many things perfectly. This is because he is twelve, he has told me. He gets As on all his tests. He knows about motivation and aspiration. He reads a lot of books with only words. He also reads comics, but the pictures make no sense. He talks to Mom and Dad's grown-up friends. He laughs at jokes they make. Sometimes he tells jokes, and they laugh. He has told me that when I am twelve, these pictures, these books, these jokes, will make sense. Sammy is beautiful when he is on his skateboard. He holds his arms out so that his open jacket flaps around him, flashing blue, maroon, and silver. He jumps the skateboard over planks he sets up in the driveway. He zooms over the curb and away before I have time to yell bye. *I'm off to get a soda with Lee*, he says. I wait for him to come back, sitting on the stone bench in the front yard. The shade under the orange tree shrinks until it's almost gone. Then he is back, and we go in for lunch.

I walk over to the corner of the garden to check my chrysalis. It has been there a long time. Sammy showed me the caterpillar last summer. *Look at that eating machine*, he said. What I saw was a very small yellowish creature on the white flowers near the fence. The flowers had holes chewed out of them. I told Sammy the caterpillar didn't look like it was a robot, or any kind of machine. Sammy said he had been joking about it being a machine. I checked the caterpillar every day after that. It was always on the flowers. The flowers got more chewed up, and the caterpillar got bigger. Then in October, it wasn't there anymore. But there was a blue chrysalis on the stem of one of the eaten-up flowers. It has been there all winter. The caterpillar is safe inside, waiting until it's ready. When it comes out, it won't have to sit on this flower stalk. It'll be able to fly off to find flowers with nectar for drinking. I love butterflies: the fanciness of them, the way they flit around and disappear whenever they want, the way they are hidden inside waiting caterpillars.

Out here, in the back garden, there are a lot of flowers. I walk over to the stone birdbath, which has water in it. There are two pale hydrangea petals in the water, and also some fern leaves and twigs. I lean against the birdbath and wait for the butterflies to come by. It is one week after my birthday. Mom hung a banner on the fence that says *Happy 8th Birthday, Radhika!* It is still there. There are still shrunken balloons hanging in bunches from the branches of the plum tree. Dad brought his work-table out from the garage and covered it with a plain white tablecloth because he knows I don't like the ones with patterns. He hasn't taken it in yet. Mom, Kumari Aunty, and Dee Aunty cooked until evening, when people came home for the party. There is still leftover food in the freezer, even though I've been eating it every day.

I see movement. A butterfly lands on one of the pink flower spikes next to the birdbath. It's a Monarch, with orange and black wings. Sammy wore a Monarch costume for his third-grade play. After he sang, people stood up and clapped and whistled, and he bowed with his wings held out. *Just look at him,* Dad said to Mom. *How lucky we are*, Mom said.

The butterfly has gone off to the corner of the garden. I walk over slowly. I see it is resting on the yellow flowers, fanning its wings.

Dee Aunty's voice drifts out faintly. "How is she doing in school now? Has she improved?"

The glass doors to the garden slide open all the way. I hear Mom say, "Yes, yes. She's doing very well." Then she calls out to me. "Radhika! Forget about those butterflies of yours for now, will you? Bring your presents for your Aunty to see."

· 2 ·

We are at Dee Aunty's apartment, in San Francisco. We have to take the elevator to the sixth floor. I like elevators. "Let's take the elevator down to the tunnel," I say, when I see it.

But Dad says, "What movie is that from?" His lips are in a straight line.

Mom says, "You know what Jerry says. You're not supposed to repeat lines from movies."

"I just thought it was funny," I say.

Sammy puts his arm around me and laughs. Sammy is sixteen and a half. He is the only one who doesn't make a big deal about lines from movies. Jerry, who I go to see once a week at his office in Oakland, says I should use my own words, not words from movies. I've told him that movie lines are funny; they make me laugh, which makes me happy. He nods when I say this. Using my own words is much harder because then people don't understand what I mean. Jerry says I have to work at explaining what I mean. "Language is a shared system of communication," he says. He leans forward toward me when he says *shared* and a little spit sprays out of his mouth. "I understand," I say, because these are the words that make him lean back in his chair. I'm not sure why he says *shared* like that, or what *shared system of communication* means. People say strange things. It's like *opened his mind*. The book the sixth graders had to read over the break said that Weng Lin opened his mind. I asked Mom what *opened his mind* meant. *Stopped being afraid*, she said. Then why doesn't the book say Weng Lin stopped being afraid? Books would be easier to read if there weren't things in there that didn't make sense.

Outside Dee Aunty's apartment, there is a polished brass nameplate with the words *Deepika & Nissanka Gunaratna* in thick cursive, and under that *Consultants*. I am familiar with the word *consul*. I've seen it on another nameplate, along with the name *Mr. Joseph Edirisinghe*. A consul is a person who puts a stamp on your passport so that you can go to another country, like Sri Lanka, where we spend some summers. Consultants are a consul's assistants. This is part of why I like Dee Aunty and Niss Uncle: they help consuls. They are good at what they do. I have heard Mom say this.

Because it is a special occasion, Dee Aunty is in a sari. The sari is purple with a thin blue border. She has red lipstick on, and her hair is flying out around her face. She reaches out to give me a hug. I move back because she has the same smell as the school cafeteria. In the cafeteria, I sit with my friends, Michelle, Suzy, and Hadley. They are nice, but their jokes make no sense. Also, it is hard to hear them talk because there is always too much noise in the cafeteria. Dee Aunty has looped her sari end around her shoulders, so when she reaches out, the sari material falls down from her arms to her hips on both sides like scary wings.

"How about a hug for Dee Aunty?" Mom says, smiling.

So I let Dee Aunty hug me. I put my hands on the sides of her sari while she does it. It feels okay, a little slippery. The sari is silk. Niss Uncle is nowhere to be seen. Possibly he is in the kitchen, eating. Mom says he is a big eater. It is true that he is big around the middle. His feet and head are much smaller than his middle part. He has the same shape as the wooden wibble-wobble that sits on my bedside table. It is also true that he is an eater, of course. If he didn't eat, he would die.

"Still a real tomboy!" Dee Aunty says, patting my hair.

"Of course I'm still real," I say. There is something scary about this, though it is an odd thing to think. She thinks that at some point I am going to turn into a tomboy robot.

Dee Aunty looks at Mom. Mom holds my hand. "Dee Aunty meant to say you are a tomboy."

It is confusing because that is not what Dee Aunty said. "I don't like to wear dresses," I say, even though Dee Aunty knows this. I like jeans, T-shirts, and sweatshirts, like the clothes Sammy wears. I know I can't do everything Sammy does, because I'm not like him. For example, he's a boy and I'm a girl. There are also other reasons. I don't like to think about things that make me sad. I like my clothes to have bright colors. In bright colors, I am strong.

Dee Aunty's apartment has smooth dark floors that are like the passageway that the Incredibles have to run through when they are trying to get away from Syndrome. I've watched *The Incredibles* seventy-two times. Mom put it away for watching later because she says I shouldn't watch the same movie over and over again.

I flatten myself against the wall to avoid Syndrome's traps and enter the living room. In Dee Aunty's living room, there is a wide window with a seat in the windowsill. The material of the seat is rough, but it is comfortable. I sit there so that I can watch the cars going by outside. Looking out makes the sound of voices all talking at once less unpleasant. In addition to the cars outside, there are people, most of them carrying bags.

Niss Uncle has appeared in front of me, holding a silver tray. "Hello, hello, Radhika," he says. I like the way he looks. He has on a green sweater that covers his belly smoothly. On the tray there is a white paper lace doily. On one side of it are small rectangular pieces of cheese pizza. On the other side are cutlets, fried dark brown. "Do you feel like pizza or cutlets?" he says.

I have heard the question about pizza before. It is a strange question. "No," I say. I don't have any idea how pizzas feel, or cutlets. Niss Uncle nods and starts to move away. "I'd like to have a cutlet," I say. "Please. And also a pizza." The conversation has stopped. Niss Uncle looks over at Dee Aunty. She shrugs and smiles. Her smile is okay. "Some cream liquid would also be nice," I say.

"Milk," Sammy says.

"That one I don't remember," Niss Uncle says. He hands me a plain white ceramic plate and holds out the tray again. I take a pizza, which is warm and doughy, and a cutlet, and place them on the plate. Niss Uncle puts the tray down and goes to the kitchen. He brings the cream liquid back in a glass and hands it to me. I take it, but I can't drink. The glass has two stripes around the edge, yellow and red. It should be clear, or one color. I wait until Niss Uncle eases his body on to the sofa cushions. Then I set the glass down gently on the side table, sliding it around the small potted geranium so that I don't have to see it. When I look up, I see Sammy watching me. He comes over and ruffles my hair. Then he picks the glass up and takes it to the kitchen. The glass he brings back is clear, cylindrical, and full of cream liquid, which is thick and cold. Refreshing. I tip the glass up so that the cream liquid forms a nice mustache. I can feel it. I can picture myself with it. "Got milk?" I say to Sammy, standing with one hand behind my head like Kelly Clarkson in the milk ad. Sammy stands between me and the others. He puts his finger to his mouth. "Don't say lines from ads here," he says softly.

Outside, the wind is blowing a piece of paper around on the street. It flies up and then falls, over and over again. The awning of the café across the street flaps hard, but it doesn't get away. The wind whistles against the closed window. I can hear Dee Aunty talking to Mom, and Niss Uncle talking to Dad.

"Business has picked up a lot," Niss Uncle is saying. "But still, I am not thinking of this as a permanent solution."

"This is too frustrating for Niss," Dee Aunty says. "He's not living up to his full potential."

"The first thing to do is get a different location," Niss Uncle says.

"Niss always thought of this as a temporary situation, no?" Mom says.

"There are advantages to working at home," Niss Uncle says. "But it's time to move into a proper office building, even if it isn't in the best area. Get a good security system to keep out the thugs."

When I turn around, Niss Uncle is pushing his plate away. There are only a few cutlet crumbs on it. He wipes his hands on a napkin and tosses it, crushed up, on to the table.

"But will you still stamp passports?" I ask.

They all turn to me. They don't say anything. The wall clock ticks. The crushed napkin falls to the floor, but it doesn't make a sound.

"What passports, Radhi?" Sammy says.

"Isn't Niss Uncle still going to be doing the same job?" I say.

Sammy pauses. He nods. "Yes, he's still going to be a computer consultant. And Dee Aunty also."

Dee Aunty and Niss Uncle look at each other. Mom shrugs and smiles at Dad. They all seem to like the fact that Niss Uncle and Dee Aunty will be doing the same jobs. I didn't know passports stamps were done through computers.

They start talking again. It is too difficult to listen to all the voices. The room is small and crowded. I wander back behind the living room to the guest bedroom and shut the door. There is no noise inside, which is peaceful. This is a room I like. It is neat. The walls are plain, pale blue, and the three square pictures on the wall are photographs of San Francisco. The Golden Gate Bridge is in the middle. On the left are people hanging out of a tramcar. On the right is a plane flying away over Alcatraz. I go over to the dresser on which Dee Aunty keeps her lotions and creams. There are many to smell. Some jars and bottles are marked with the name of the smell and others aren't. I start with the containers on the left and work to the right. I smell lavender, sandalwood, shoe, roses, Bengay, dried spit, clay, phone, rosemary, and vanilla. Sandalwood is my favorite. It smells like the soap Mom uses. I rub on a little of the sandalwood lotion. It makes my skin feel silky. It has been a while, so I know it's time to get back to the living room.

When I open the door, I hear Dee Aunty saying, "So why don't you try taking her to someone else?"

Mom says, "I don't think that'll do much good. There are some things that she just doesn't understand."

"Takes everything literally, no?" Dee Aunty says.

"Problem is that she won't admit to needing any help. Insists her ideas are correct, however much you point out. Really, it's impossible to get through to her these days."

"It can't be easy for her, being different," Dee Aunty says.

"What would be the point of everyone being the same?" Sammy says.

This is the point at which I turn my head and see the framed picture on the wall next to the door. It is big, about one foot across, with malevolent green and black eyes, on a khaki green background. I can't move for a second, and then before I can think, I am screaming. There is a crash as something falls over, and Mom and Sammy come running. "What? What?" Sammy grabs my arm. I point at the picture of the butterfly with the terrible, perfect eyes on its wings. Sammy rubs his cheeks, and then he hugs me. "She got scared of your new picture," he says to Dee Aunty, who is standing behind Mom. "It's just a phase."

· 3 ·

It has been a month since Jude and I have been back here. I only got back from Fort Myers yesterday, and just before the Fort Myers conference, we were both in Malaysia. Mom and Dad have put in a new brick deck, but already it's messy with pulped fruit from the plum tree. They won't mind, I know, because the red admirals like it. There are dark-blue grapes on the trellis vine between the deck and the garden where I used to spend hours waiting for butterflies. The St. Catherine's lace is flowering, and I can see two Acmon blues hovering over it. The yellow of the rabbit brush I planted two years ago contrasts nicely with the light-blue sage near the fence. There will be some buckeyes nearby and maybe some swallowtails. Once I even saw two California dogfaces up close on the sage. One was a female, with a slightly asymmetric black dot on its yellow forewing. On the other one, the misshapen poodle's-head pattern that marks a male was clearly visible. What luck to see two together; they are normally so hard to find. As I walk toward the stone birdbath, I smell the horsemint. The mint attracts *Danaus plexippus.* Mom likes

Monarchs around. We have brought her two species of milkweed plants, *Asclepias eriocarpa* and *Asclepias fascicularis*. More food for their caterpillars means more Monarchs for the backyard. Mom can recline in her deck chair and watch them flying.

Mom appears through the sliding glass door. She is smiling. A folded newspaper is in her hand.

"You've seen this, no?" she says, when she reaches us. She hugs Jude and me together. Her sandalwood mixes pleasantly with the smell of Jude's shaving cream.

I nod, but she opens the paper out anyway to last week's "Living" section. "Good idea to wear a sari," she says. "Looks nice, with all the butterflies in the background like that."

I look again at the photo. The newspaper is the *Cupertino Sunday News*. The article will help to ensure business will continue to be good. The sari I wore for the picture is blue with orange flowers. Under the photo is a caption that reads, *Lepidopterist Radhika Seneviratna in her garden*. The article is titled "Butterfly Expert Helps Locals Beautify Gardens." The article describes my company, Butterflygarden.com. Sammy's name is in the article too, because I told the reporter, Megan Lepore, that I couldn't have started the company without him.

At the bottom of the Butterflygarden.com homepage is Sammy's name: *Samith Seneviratna, Webmaster*. I had the ideas, and Sammy designed the website to match them. He had to do it in his spare time, which was meager because his veterinary practice had already become busy. He had some help from Niss Uncle, who has a computer consulting company with eight employees.

There was a time when I had a butterfly phobia. The worst was the summer after I finished my difficult ninth grade year, the year when I had to deal with Samantha Taylor and her cheerleader friends bullying me. I refused to go outdoors for the entire month of July because I didn't want to see any butterflies. Sammy was in Ann Arbor then, in college. He talked to me on the phone every evening, trying to convince me to leave the house. I didn't want to though. But this is what he told me, day after day: *You've got to face the thing you're scared of, and then you'll stop being afraid.* He explained about Pavlov and his dogs, Little Albert and the white rat. So eventually, I did what he said. I sat at the uncovered dining table with his old Collins science encyclopedia in front of me for hours, opened to pages 261 and 262, which were on butterflies. It took me a while to get over the choking feeling in my throat, but then I read the two pages over and over again. That's how I started to get interested in Lepidoptera. The first trip I made outside in August was to the public library, on my bike. I brought home *The World of Butterflies and Moths* by Umberto Parenti. On the front cover was a creature that I later realized was an *Anthocharis cardamines*, looking curiously out with its compound eye. I stared back at it. It had a hairy body, skinny legs, and antennae that stood upright. There were faint imperfections on its orange-edged wings. I read the whole book from cover to cover, including the glossary, in three days. By the time I came to the tiger-striped *Arctia caja* on the back cover, I'd begun to see how different lepidopterans were from each other. I've seen them up close for fourteen years now, but I'm still amazed by their peculiar habits and the way they transform so patiently. I've studied the way they use mimicry and camouflage for so long that I can identify them easily. I understand how flowers use scent and color to signal them, so I am good at finding the food plants each species needs.

Jude and Mom talk while I dig a hole near the pond for the milkweed plants. The earth is soggy from the recent rain. The milkweed will grow well here. I can imagine them grown thick, with Monarchs flying around them. Butterflies love this garden, with all the sunlight. Sometimes a customer can attract butterflies just by cutting back some trees to let in the sun and lessen a garden's shadows.

"Dee Aunty and Niss Uncle are coming for dinner tomorrow. Niss Uncle's running his second marathon in the morning. Not bad at his age. Will you and Radhi come for dinner also?" Mom asks Jude. She doesn't wait for him to answer. "I'll make fried rice and the beef pepper curry you like."

Jude nods enthusiastically.

"He misses your food," I tell Mom.

Jude came with me to Penang because he isn't teaching summer classes this year. I suppose the whole family knows we're going to get married soon, even though we haven't made a formal announcement. I've known him for two years and three months, which is only a year and a week less than I've had Butterflygardens.com. We met at a conference in Boca Raton, where he was giving a talk on the migration patterns of Monarchs. We do many things together: hiking, butterfly watching, and traveling, which we both love. He has mostly taken over the customer service end of the company. He answers customer questions on the phone and deals with marketing issues that don't interest me much. He's more neurotypical than I am, so he helps me with the things I find puzzling, like figuring out what people really mean.

"Are you staying for dinner today?" Mom asks.

"What are you having?" Jude says.

"Only barbecue. Shrimp kebabs."

"We can't," I say. We wouldn't be done until maybe seven-thirty, and I like to eat at seven. "I have to go and see a garden in Tiburon. The people just moved in, and they want to redo their backyard. Jude's coming to help." This is what he calls *sussing out*, when I visit a customer's garden for the first time to see what kinds of plants would work best.

"Always working," Mom says, smiling. A figure of speech.

The truth is I like my job so much that I could work almost always. I like to show people how to attract butterflies and, especially, how to grow them. That's where all my years of experience come in. A few weeks ago, a teenager emailed me: *Imogene, 17 years, from Menlo Park*. There had been a chrysalis in her backyard, hanging insecurely from the bottom of a leaf. It was the same color as jade, she said, and smooth, so it was probably a Monarch, although I couldn't be sure without seeing it or knowing what kind of leaf it was on. The butterfly hadn't emerged, although she had watched it for many months. What, she wanted to know, should she do? Give up on it? Do something to it? Stop watching it, in case it was like a kettle on the stove? I am not sure what she meant by that, but I told her she could make sure there was shelter from the wind, warmth, and of course, enough sunlight. After that, it's a question of waiting. Even within a species, there can be variation in the duration of the caterpillar or chrysalis stage. Genes play a role in this, but transition to the next stage is sometimes delayed until the creature has the environmental conditions it needs.

Hopper Day

ON THE DAY OF the party, Sunethra awoke early, as usual. The floor was comfortingly solid underneath her. She only slept on the floor when Alex was away.

Alex had proposed the party to celebrate the anniversary of the day they still called "the Hopper Day." Three years had passed since that day. She had moved stealthily in the dim kitchen, mixing the hopper batter slowly with a wooden spoon, being careful to keep from knocking the spoon against the edge of the bowl, so as to not wake the sleeping household. She had jumped, splattering a drop of the batter on her blouse, when she found Alex suddenly next to her.

"Did I frighten you?" he asked softly, in the Sinhala that she was always surprised to hear him speak. His accent was not too heavy to understand.

"Yes, Alex *mahaththaya*, I thought everyone was asleep," she said.

"No need to say 'sir' to me. Just call me Alex," he said.

She did not know how to respond to that, so she just stirred the batter.

Alex reached for the glass on the counter, the one she kept aside for her own use. She pulled it away from his hand, letting go of the batter bowl.

"I can get you water in a clean glass," she said, taking one down from the shelf where the household glasses were stacked in orderly rows.

"No, I can use your glass. One glass is just the same as another," he said, putting the fresh glass back on the shelf.

"*Aney, mahaththaya*, that is not right, no?" she said, holding her glass clasped to her chest.

"This heat makes me thirsty," he said, prying the glass gently from her fingers. He filled the glass from the stainless-steel, boiled-water pitcher and drank. She felt uncomfortable seeing his lips pressed to the edge of her glass, so she went back to stirring the batter.

After he put the glass down, he asked her what she was making.

"I am preparing the batter for tomorrow morning's hoppers," she said. "But it is finished now." His mouth was slightly open as he looked at her. She turned away from him to place the bowl, covered with a damp cloth, next to the sink. The thick knot of hair at the base of her neck loosened, and her hair, freed, uncoiled down her back.

"Such lovely hair," Alex said. He reached out and touched a strand, so lightly that she barely felt it, but goose bumps stood out on her arms.

"I will go to sleep now, *mahaththaya*," she said, and walked past him with her eyes averted, feeling her untied hair moving from side to side over her hips.

She only started calling him Alex six months later, on the day when she woke him at dawn, wiping her hair away from his face, moving his long, pale arm and leg off her body onto her woven straw floor mat, so that he could return to his bed in the guest room before Nalini *nona* and Sena *mahaththaya* awoke.

. . .

Sunethra remembered that there were still many tasks to complete for the party. There would be a few other Sri Lankans there, some that she knew, and others that she did not. Of course, none of them really knew her. She felt heavy, thinking about it.

Rising to her feet, she gathered up the thick braid of hair that fell to her hips and twisted it into a bun. She rolled up the blanket she had slept on into a tight, neat cylinder and tucked it away in the closet. She plumped her pillow and placed it on the bed, then pulled taut the coverlet.

Peering through the window, she saw turgid gray clouds outside that looked like they would tear open any minute, spilling out rain in great gushes. She pushed open the curtains to let in the faint light. The curtains were new, a surprise for Alex, stitched from a sari she had bought at the Indian store on Meredith Street. She knew his tastes well and had picked colors he liked.

Sunethra was an efficient housekeeper. Nalini *nona* had always been happy with her work. "Such a good worker," Sunethra had heard her say to her friends on many occasions. "So clean about everything." She did not know about the business of the brassieres; that was one thing Sunethra could keep to herself. "Not a hair out of place. What I would do without her, I don't know."

Alex was appreciative too. "Just like my mother," he said. "How I love a tidy house." Sunethra understood that this was what held Alex and her together despite their differences, now that his early longing had settled into a quiet comfort. She did not mind because there was affection too.

Sunethra still talked to Alex in Sinhala sometimes, so that he would not forget. But her English was quite good now. She still had difficulty with short *o* sounds. Bottle. Not. Pot. She practiced every day as she straightened Alex's papers in the living room, chopped carrots and cabbage, and swept up sticky fallen grains of rice. But it was hard to remember to open her mouth wide, make a pig snout out of her lips, when she used these words, the way Alex had taught her. Sometimes she used the pig snout *o* sounds when she said words like "potato" or "go." Alex understood her anyway, but other people often did not.

She also had occasional trouble with idioms, but this would improve now that she was watching more television. Knowing more people would help too, Alex said.

That was the problem, Sunethra thought. Knowing more people. She liked Alex's American friends. Mostly they were Alex's colleagues from the university. Paula and Henry, for instance. She had talked to them many times about the spices in her prawn curry, the sales at Target, blocked drains, the Grand Canyon, getting rid of ants, and flowers that bloomed in the California winter. But when they sat down to dinner and got into a conversation with Alex, Sunethra was lost in language she did not understand. Their expressions shifted quickly from one to another, their hands flew around like hungry birds over a bread crust, and the words fell dizzyingly around her. Sociological analysis. Implications. Dialectic. Microdynamic. Subordination. Liberation. Emancipation. Marginality.

Alex's Sri Lankan friends were people he had met in the course of his research. Over the years, they had found him a Sinhala teacher in Los Angeles, introduced him to friends in Sri Lanka, given him the names of good restaurants in Colombo and supplied him with information about class differences and servants they had employed. None of them knew Sunethra's employers in Colombo, Nalini *nona* and Sena *maha-ththaya*. Alex had met Nalini *nona* through a colleague in the sociology department at the University of Colombo, and she had offered him the hospitality of her home. Of course, Alex did not have any contact with Nalini *nona* now.

From the kitchen, Sunethra had heard Nalini *nona*'s voice spluttering out on the verandah, when Alex had finally told her about his interest in Sunethra. "*Chee*, shame on you! What are you thinking? Coming here and acting like you are in your America! So much we liked you. I can't even believe. Sitting here like a saint in our house and the whole time doing this thing. Corrupting this innocent village girl. This is also part of your research project or what?"

Sunethra had packed her things in her old cardboard suitcase that same day. When she knelt down to touch Nalini *nona*'s feet as a sign of respect, Nalini *nona* had stepped back, her lips pushed together. Then the words had burst out. "No need of all that," she had said. "This is the way you repay us, no, *aney*. Fifteen years we looked after you."

Sunethra had slept in a white-sheeted bed with Alex in the Galle Face Hotel, eaten meals other people cooked, and used a gleaming bathroom that other people cleaned, until she got a visa to the US. Alex had written to Nalini *nona* twice after he returned to California with Sunethra, but Nalini *nona* never wrote back. Sunethra thought about Nalini *nona* often and with affection, but she never wrote to her because she knew Nalini *nona* would not respond.

Alex's Sri Lankan friends here were curious about Alex's Sinhala wife, what brought them together. Alex had agreed not to reveal details. At Sunethra's request, he had introduced her to them as a distant rural relative of a family he had stayed with in Sri Lanka. He gave the family a fictitious name. He understood Sunethra's uneasiness about telling the truth.

After Sunethra had been in California for more than a year, loneliness had led her to conceive the idea of getting a part-time job. A job as a maid, she had thought, would be possible, given her housekeeping expertise. Most other jobs would be inaccessible without written English skills. One day in February, as they were finishing their dinner, she had mentioned her idea to Alex. It would be easy to advertise in their small university community, she had pointed out. But Alex had laughed, wiping her chicken curry off his lips and handing her his used plate and fork.

"There's no need for that. You are the wife of a professor now," he had said firmly, re-folding his napkin into a neat square. "Not that there's anything wrong with being a maid. But there are so many other ways for you to meet people. You could take that ESL class, for instance."

. . .

When Alex called from San Francisco at one o'clock, Sunethra had already dusted the furniture and swept and mopped the smooth yellow wood of the floor. She had eaten a meal of rice, fish curry, and coconut sambol, washed down with a cup of hot tea. She had scrubbed the bathroom tiles to make the pale leaf pattern stand out against the blue background, and cut up the vegetables for dinner. Alex had asked for eggplant *pahi*, spicy fried potatoes, chicken curry, vegetable buriyani, and a salad with cucumber and onions, leaving out the green chillies for their guests.

He had loved her food from the beginning. When they first came to California together, she had been startled by the amount of food that his long body could accommodate. But now she just made bigger portions. Even the chutneys that were supposed to be eaten in small quantities, she made in big pots and stored in great glass jars in the fridge. She had got used to the gurgling sound of his spit as it went down the waiting tunnel of his throat, when she brought the dinner dishes to the table.

Sunethra took the cordless phone over to the sofa and then decided to sit in the striped blue-and-green velvet chair by the window instead. Besides the three seats on the sofa, there was a matching love seat, the striped chair, a rocking chair, the short-backed seat attached to the phone table, the swivel chair at the desk in the office, and the old arm-chair in the bedroom. Not to mention the eight dining table chairs. Seventeen chairs, all told, all of which were hers to use whenever she wished. There had been many more chairs in Nalini *nona*'s house, of heavy carved wood, bamboo, woven cane, and painted wrought iron. But custom had decreed that she not sit on any of them. There had been a low stool for her to rest on in the kitchen. When she wanted to sit down anywhere else in the house, she had just sat on the polished cement floor.

When Alex called, she sat cross-legged in the velvet chair and leaned her head back against the snug curved head rest.

"Hallo?" she said into the mouthpiece.

"Hello, sweetheart. What are you doing?"

"Just sitting. But I have not finished cooking for the party."

"Oh, you have a lot more time. I'll be there in a couple of hours to be your taster," Alex said. "But everything is okay?"

"Yes, yes, fine, okay," Sunethra said.

"Good, good," Alex said. "But can you do me a favor, Sunethra. Call Amali Herath, her number's in my phone book. She sent me an email asking if I could give her a ride to and back from the party. I forgot to tell her I could. Could you tell her?"

Panic rose inside Sunethra. *"Aney*, Alex. I can't do that," she said, reverting to Sinhala. "You can call her, no, when you come."

"That might be too late," Alex said, still in English. "You can do that, Sunethra. Remember, you're the lady of the house now. You'll be one lady of the house talking to another. No more saying *nona* and *mahaththaya.*"

Sunethra did not want to refuse, so she said goodbye and hung up the phone. She sat for a while with the phone in her lap. How long to hide like this? she thought.

Sunethra looked at the clock on the wall. Time was passing, and she had to call Amali Herath soon. She picked up Alex's small leather-bound address book, which was lying on the phone table. She looked inside the book for Amali Herath's number, under A and then under H. She could read words in English, but only slowly and with difficulty, especially if they were unfamiliar.

On and off over the course of the past two years, Alex had suggested that she take a class for South Asians, in English as a second language. He had pointed out that it would be a good place to make new friends from her part of the world. But her stomach fluttered when she thought about it.

The evening of Sena *mahaththaya's* sixtieth birthday kept coming back to her. There had been twenty guests for dinner. She had taken a tray of beef patties and fish cutlets out to the guests in the sitting room.

They had been gathered around, listening to Hema *nona*, Nalini *nona*'s sister.

"Seetha. You remember her, Ivy's servant," Hema *nona* was saying. "Ivy had her for so many years, since the children were small. Big woman, black as the middle of the night? How many times I've seen her at Ivy's. She was there at that party. Can you believe? All dolled up, lipstick and everything. She married that white man. How she met him, I don't know, but she went off to England. And she was there in London, at the embassy party, as if she belonged there. And do you know, when she saw me, she came straight up to me, and said, 'Hello, Hema.' Just like that she called me. 'Hema.' No shame or anything."

There had been murmurs after that. Guests had said, "*Chee*, really," and "*Aney*, true?" and "Can't even believe," as they selected patties and cutlets from the tray Sunethra held out to them. She had gone back into the kitchen then, so she had not heard the rest of the story.

Sunethra left the address book open on the phone table and went into the bathroom. She loved this bathroom, with its glossy blue wall tiles, the unmarked mirror that covered an entire half wall, and the floor that was as clean and dry as that in any other room of the house.

She removed her skirt and blouse, and stepped out of her cotton panties. She looked at her white nylon brassiere when she took it off, sniffed it to determine if it had a bad odor. It did not, although the underside of the straps, where they touched her skin, was discolored to a pale beige with her sweat, and a darker beige streaked the seams. Since she had first begun working at Nalini *nona*'s house after her mother died, she had worn a brassiere day after day, often for more than a week, switching it for a fresh one only when she feared that its odor would be offensively heavy. Even after coming to California, she had continued this practice of brassiere retention, unknown to Alex. She did not allow the sweat, evidence of her daily exertions, to accumulate on other items of clothing, changing them scrupulously every day.

She stepped into the bathtub and drew shut the etched glass door.

She washed herself, rubbing her thin shoulders with her index and middle fingers held together, as if sloughing off dead skin could make her feel lighter.

She looked around the bathroom afterward, wrapped in a towel. She did not mind the thin drip from the taps in the sink, which could not be shut off completely, or the fact that she had to push the cistern handle several times in order to flush the toilet. The bathroom she had shared with Sirisena, the elderly gardener who tended Nalini *nona's* overgrown bougainvillea bushes and swept up the daily influx of leaves that fell from the ancient mango and neem trees, had been nothing like this. There had been cracks in the wall, under the peeling paint, and her reflection in the small, spotty mirror had been distorted. The floor had always been muddy, because Sirisena had never been one to wipe the garden soil off his feet before entering the bathroom. And Sirisena's aim had seemed rarely precise, judging from the splatters of urine that often lay on the floor around the ceramic squatting toilet.

Ultimately, it was the bathroom that made her take action. She dressed in a clean brassiere, panties, and dress and went into the living room. She sat at the phone table and picked up the phone. She dialed Mrs. Herath's number slowly. Mrs. Herath had recently come here from the University of Colombo, where she was a professor of economics, for a year-long fellowship at Alex's university. Sunethra had not yet met her but had learned from Alex that she was in her late fifties.

Mrs. Herath answered the phone. "Hallo? Mrs. Herath? This is Sunethra speaking," she said in English. "Alex Wilton's wife."

"Ah, yes, yes, yes," Mrs. Herath said. "Of course, Alex told me. I am waiting to meet you."

"Yes, at the party today, we will meet," Sunethra said.

"Ah, okay, good," Mrs. Herath said. "Where are you from? Colombo, Alex said. But where?" she inquired, switching to Sinhala, inquisitiveness sharpening her voice.

"Colombo 7," Sunethra replied, taking a deep breath. "Flower Road."

"Aha, aha, right, right. So your family is there still? What's the surname?" Mrs. Herath asked.

"Surname? Surname is Abeyratne," Sunethra said, taking another deep breath. "They were like my family, for fifteen years I was with them. I cooked the meals, kept the house properly clean and neat."

"So you are a relative of theirs, no?" Mrs. Herath said, her voice pleading.

"No, no, but like a relative almost they treated me. I was the servant only," Sunethra said firmly, so that there would be no more need for explanation.

For a few seconds, there was no sound from the phone. Sunethra saw thin threads of rain unraveling outside. She took the phone over to the window and opened it to let in the sound of the drops plopping on to the concrete path. The faint smell of wet earth drifted in.

"Ah, true." It was a statement, not a question, from Mrs. Herath.

"Now, so, about today," Sunethra said, still in Sinhala. "Alex said that he can come and pick you up, no problem. So I will see you in the evening, no."

There was more silence then. Sunethra, unsure whether Mrs. Herath had hung up, said, "Hallo?"

"Ah, yes," Mrs. Herath said and paused. "Here, wait, I just remembered this minute. I have to be at home today. My husband is supposed to phone at eight. Ten in the morning in Colombo. Won't be able to come for dinner."

"No problem. Alex can drop you back before eight. You can just come and eat something, no," Sunethra said.

"No, no, no, too much trouble for Alex," Mrs. Herath said.

"No trouble," said Sunethra, just as Nalini *nona* would have said. "I'll tell him to pick you up at six, right." There was nothing more for Mrs. Herath to say.

Sunethra placed the phone back in its cradle. She stood up, feeling the light fabric of her dress slide softly down her legs, and looked around the room. The room would look nice if the potted palm from the front porch, with its gracefully pleated leaves, was brought in, she thought. She would ask Alex to bring it in when he got home. It looked too heavy for her to lift. Tomorrow, she would call about getting into a class to improve her English reading and writing.

Therapy

WATCH HER stroke the arm of your red leather couch. Let her talk. Just nod and stretch your lips and scribble on your pad. Make a to-do list. Think about what you'll do when the minute hand moves to ten. You'll wait for her to get off the couch Jerry gave you as an office-warming gift seven years ago. You'll escort her to the door. You'll shut out her wagging hips and write the shortest case note in the history of your practice. There'll still be light when you walk home. You'll clean the refrigerator, wash a load of whites, and sanitize the kitchen sink. You'll cook a chicken buriyani, mild, the way Jerry likes it, and cover the dish with the tea cozy you bought for him in San Francisco.

Watch her big red lips and listen to the words spilling from her mouth. You need to interpret them carefully. Watch her crossing her legs on Jerry's leather couch and remember the expensive education that prepared you for this lucrative practice. Don't flinch at the name of her man. There are many Jerrys in Palo Alto, and no doubt, several of them are artists and married. Your Jerry likes wasabi seaweed and novels about the zombie apocalypse. And your Jerry doesn't have a nickname. He would never call himself JJ.

Remember how you'd hold his hand over a cold wine glass and ask how his day at the studio went, whose portrait he painted that day. You'd remind him it was worth the time and money you put into your training to be able to support his artistic work the way he deserves. You'd tell him that you had another session with your newest client, and that she has been in love for months—that would be all you could say because you would, of course, respect her confidentiality. But then you remember that there will be no one to hear you. You can talk aloud about your client's problems, even mention her name. Jerry's painted ladies will watch you from the walls, but there will be no need for secrecy.

Let the client talk about how much she enjoys the bath salts in JJ's studio, the drives in JJ's Camaro to Half Moon Bay, the takeout orange chicken from Ho King. When she describes her mornings and the tea she drinks with JJ, stifle the thoughts of the chai tea you bought for Jerry from the Teavana store on Market Street. Observe the way she twists locks of her red hair in her fingers, the way she rubs her forehead, the way she jiggles her legs, the way her eyebrows twitch. You cannot help her with her fear of losing her man. She needs more help than you can give.

Listen to her describe JJ's studio on Embarcadero. Watch the way her bell sleeves fall back when she shows you how big the bay windows are. Watch her toss her red hair back when she tells you the studio's curtains are striped like a stand of bamboo trees. Don't think about the saris you used to make curtains for Jerry's studio windows.

Take the tissue box from your client's hands, with their French-tipped nails and silver rings. Turn away when you wipe the moisture from your eyes.

When she leaves, silence the phones and lock the door. Give up on keeping your crying quiet. Let go and sob. Don't go home to your empty living room. Turn out the lights and curl up on Jerry's red leather couch until you fall asleep.

The Rat Tree

WHEN I DECIDED to take the job, my friend Monica tried to dissuade me.

"You know what that intern who worked there said. It's like another world. If you're trying to prove something, you're going too far," she said.

I saw Mr. Ratnapola for the first time two weeks after I began working at the jail. He was shuffling down the hall of the Rehab Ward toward me, his hands clasped together below his handcuffed wrists. He was a small man. His hair was gray and wispy, a little long in the back. I was surprised to see an inmate who was clearly from South Asia. I had not seen any others. It did not occur to me then that he might be from Sri Lanka too.

When he paused at the door, waiting for his guard to sign him out, he looked up and saw me standing there. Not much of me was visible because I had wrapped my black scarf around my head and neck, and hidden the rest of my body in my boots, gloves, and long navy coat. But even then, I saw the look of recognition that crossed his face. He did not smile though, or say anything. Instead, he walked past me into the cold wind, through the door the guard opened.

The encounter made me feel calmer than usual. Other days, by the time I walked the path through the jail compound to the door of the Rehab Ward, my heart was thumping and my hands were shaking. It was the walk that made my pounding on the locked Rehab door so desperate, and my voice so thin and high when I identified myself to the guard inside.

My dread about the walk had begun on my first day at the jail. That day, I hadn't been alone, but with the senior psychiatrist, Dr. Denton, who had hired me. He met me at the front gate and made sure that I had left my cell phone at home, as jail regulations required. He introduced me to the three guards who operated the locked gates and the metal detector. They were solid looking, maybe because of the batons, pistols, and other hardware that jutted conspicuously from the belts of their blue uniforms. They seemed to know Dr. Denton well. Dr. Denton appeared to be at home in the jail, despite his crisply ironed shirt and his immaculate leather blazer, which made me feel relieved. I had worn jeans and a short tweed jacket, although it seemed odd to go to work dressed so casually. During my interview, Dr. Denton had mentioned that the staff usually wore jeans. My jeans and jacket were new, because I couldn't bear to wear the battered clothes I wore around the house or to the grocery store to my job, even as an entry-level psychiatrist.

Dr. Denton led me out of the guard station into the jail compound and pointed out the Medical Ward, the kitchens, Women's Blocks A and B, the gym and basketball courts, Men's Blocks C, D, E, and F, and in the distance, the Rehab Ward. All the buildings looked the same: gray, boxy, and windowless. Dr. Denton walked me down a broad concrete path that lay between the buildings. The sun was out, and a pleasant breeze was blowing. This was not going to be so bad, I thought.

"This is the way most of us get to Rehab," he said. "But a few of the younger ladies, the ones who are newcomers, prefer the long way. You turn left here," he said, pointing to a road that branched off past the medical building. "And then you keep going straight to Rehab. If walking under the rat tree doesn't bother you, you might prefer to walk that way."

He said it casually, as if everyone knew what the rat tree was. I wondered whether it was a type of tree commonly found in the US, one I had not come across in my ten years here. I pictured a gardener pointing out tree species. Oak. Maple. Apple. Rat. Or maybe it was "wrat," or "ratte."

I decided to ask Dr. Denton, even if that might emphasize my novice status. "The rat tree?"

"Ah, yes. You can see the top of it from here," he said, pointing. There was a treetop visible in the distance, looming above the drab roof of the kitchen building. It must have been the only tree in the jail compound. It was some sort of spruce, and the top of it was thick with leaves.

"It's nice that there's such a big tree in here," I said. "It makes the compound seem more pleasant somehow."

Dr. Denton looked at me, his head tilted slightly. "That tree is full of rats," he said. "That's where all the rats from the kitchens go. They take shelter there. It's warmer in there than on the ground. There are no holes for them in these concrete walls."

"But rats don't climb trees!" I said. "At least, I've never heard of that."

"These do," Dr. Denton said, not argumentatively, but simply stating a fact. "They've jumped down onto people walking under that tree. Once, several jumped down onto Therese, our filing assistant. And Anne Chen, she's one of the nurses in Medical."

"Jumped onto them?"

"Jumped, fell, I don't know. They said jumped," Dr. Denton said, shrugging. "You aren't fond of rats, I gather."

"Not really, no," I said, wanting to seem professional. It was not easy because the thought of the rat tree had made my throat close up.

I couldn't even bear rats when they were dead and barely recognizable, preserved in formaldehyde. I had tried to dissect one once during a group project in a premed biology class. But the rat lying there in front of me, gray and leathery, had filled me with such revulsion that I couldn't cut into it. Each time I touched it with my scalpel, my hand jerked back involuntarily. The others in the group had stared at me, astonished and amused. I was embarrassed that my behavior was so irrational. Eventually, someone else had done the dissection, while I stood in the background, trying not to gag. I had been careful not to register for any more classes that required interacting with rats, alive or dead. It was difficult enough to suppress my disgust when I saw photographs of them in textbooks, their skin peeled back to display their slimy-looking insides.

"Well, then you can just take this other route. It's shorter anyway," Dr. Denton said. We walked on past the front of the kitchens and the women's blocks, toward the gym. Outside the gym, there was a basketball court enclosed by a high fence topped with coils of barbed wire. A group of male inmates in orange uniforms was playing basketball. About twenty or thirty other inmates were lounging around or seated on steel benches at the edge of the court.

As we came up to the fence, one of the inmates whistled. The sound stood out clearly against the diffuse noise of voices and laughter. Another inmate yelled, "Yo, baby! Where *you* from?" Others began turning around and whistling or calling out, and soon, a group of inmates had gathered along the perimeter of the fence. One of them, a tall, muscular man with a boxer's nose and a completely shaved head, looked me directly in the eye, cupped both his hands over his crotch, ground his hips, and said, "Take your clothes off for me, baby."

Before I could get over the shock I felt at this utterance, another man yelled, "Yeah, let's see what's under them clothes, huh?" Yet another man, whose smooth skin and baby-faced features made him seem much too young to be in jail, pressed his body against the wire of the fence and crooned, "Wrap that hair around me, honey! Wrap it around me, oh yeah, oh honey!" There were humming cries of, "Mmm-mmh!" Some of the men stuck their lips to the fence and made slurping, kissing noises. Others laughed.

I looked straight ahead, at the road, and tried to seem unconcerned. My ears and face felt hot, and it was difficult to fight the urge to run. Behind me, I heard a voice shout out, "Ooooh, that ass! I want some of that!"

Dr. Denton turned around and said, "Cut it out, you guys."

To me, he said, "Don't let it get to you. Ignore them. They'll be more respectful once they get to know who you are."

I heard one of the guards inside the fence say, "Back, back! Get back from that fence!" But there was not much enthusiasm in his voice, and the inmates did not respond to his order. The whistles and catcalls followed us until we were out of earshot.

My dreams that night were filled with men in orange suits chasing me around shadowy buildings, and heavy, hairless rats that leaped down onto me from fences, their writhing tails burrowing greedily under my clothes.

I had held other clinical positions before, during my training. They'd been at outpatient clinics in upscale Philadelphia suburbs. My patients had worn understated clothes and shoes polished to a high sheen. They had expected the best. Only one of my patients had questioned my credentials and asked to see a more experienced clinician. She was a stern middle-aged professor, a scholar of ancient Roman history. Her primary care physician had referred her to my clinic because of her constant concern over the possibility that she might accidentally swallow her tongue while lecturing to her students. I had not wanted to suggest that her worries were excessive. Most of my other patients had been eager to assume that I would not have been hired unless I was highly competent. Their confidence had rubbed off on me, and I had been relatively comfortable diagnosing problems and prescribing medication and psychotherapy.

At least, that was what I had thought until I asked my primary supervisor, Dr. Lockwood, for a recommendation. It was not that he wrote a poor reference. But he ended his careful evaluation with these words: "Although mild-mannered and not one to take risks, Dr. Peiris is an astute clinician, and will do fine in a safe and nurturing setting."

I sorted the walk-in closet in my apartment into two sections. In one section, I hung all the clothes that I could wear to the jail, and in the other section, the clothes I could not. The clothes I could wear to the jail were the ones that could cover and conceal: thick, long-sleeved shirts that buttoned high; baggy sweaters; long jackets and cardigans that fell over my hips; loose pants; and ankle-length skirts.

The cold wind that blew through the jail compound allowed me to wear an additional layer outdoors, usually my long navy overcoat. I started pinning up my hair so that it would be less visible too. But even with all that, I worried. Each day, when I came to the fork between the short road and the long one, I hesitated, trying to force myself to choose the road that led under the rat tree. I never could. The thought of the rats kept me on the path that ran past the basketball courts. I kept my eyes down and tried to keep my mind occupied by thinking about positions to which I could apply when the next job season arrived.

My fantasies did not sustain me, though. By the time I arrived at the door of the Rehab Ward, I felt completely exposed, my clothing stripped from me by the inmates' shouts.

I wished I had listened to my parents. "You can give up your apartment and come back home for a long vacation until you find a good job," my mother had said when I called about my new position.

"Ma, this is a good job. It will give me great experience," I said.

"You'll be fraternizing with the scum of society, Preethi," my father said. I could hear him tapping his pencil on his desk, the way he did when he was irritated.

"Fraternizing? I'll be seeing patients who need help," I said. "This is not Sri Lanka. The jails are decent places." At the time, I had never set foot in a jail in the United States, let alone in Sri Lanka. My interview with Dr. Denton had happened at a local hotel, during the American Psychiatric Association's annual convention.

I was uncomfortable when inmates were with me in the so-called consulting room, which was a small, bare-walled, windowless cube lit by two fluorescent bulbs. The regulation furniture was all plastic, designed so that no pieces of chairs or tables could be secretly removed and used as weapons or means for suicide.

Dr. Denton and Dr. Holmes, the other senior psychiatrist, saw the men who lived in dorms within the Rehab Ward, men who suffered from severe depression or who were in the early stages of recovery from drug addiction. Most of my patients were men who lived in other blocks of the jail. Each day, guards brought them to me for brief consultations. They came in groups of five or ten. They lounged on chairs in the starkly lit corridor, a few feet away from the open door of the consulting room, waiting their turn.

I sat by the door. It had a Plexiglas pane in it, so the guard who strolled along the corridor outside could see that I was not in trouble, even if I closed it. I left the door open. The inmates came in one at a time. I did not engage them in much conversation. I asked them what the problem was, keeping my eyes down as much as possible, looked in their file, and prescribed medication, mostly antianxiety drugs or antidepressants.

One of my first patients was Phil Simmons. He was the man with the boxer's nose and the shaved head that I had seen on the basketball court on my first day. Dr. Denton had already told me about his history. He was one of the regulars in the jail. This was his fifth incarceration, although he was only forty.

"He's the one to watch out for," Dr. Denton said.

"Why is he here?" I asked.

"Robbery, this time," Dr. Denton said. "I think he likes it better in here than out on the streets. Some of these men have an easier time in here than in the world. They have a safe place to sleep, plenty of heat, three meals a day."

He saw me grimace. "You don't like bologna, I see," he said, smiling. He handed me a small sheaf of papers. "Some things for you to look through," he said. "I don't know how familiar you are with malingering. There's a lot of that here. Save the meds for the men who need it."

I had never come across a case of malingering during my training. "You don't have to worry about that," I said. "You won't find me giving out medications to people who are faking."

Dr. Denton smiled again. "Good to have a capable clinician on-board," he said.

Mr. Simmons looked even larger in the consulting room than he had out on the basketball court. The plastic chair across from me looked absurdly small in comparison to him. He did not look like he belonged in the room. The sight of him sitting there reminded me of an illustration I had seen in a book when I was a child: a circus tiger balanced on a tiny stool, baring its teeth at a costumed tamer.

"How can I help you, Mr. Simmons?" I said, surreptitiously wiping the sweat off my palms onto my jeans. I wished I had not forgotten to get my white doctor's coat from the closet in the file room, where I had hung it up when I arrived that morning.

Mr. Simmons leaned back in his chair and grinned. His front teeth were stained brownish yellow, and the upper middle two were chipped. Reddish blonde stubble marked his ruddy cheeks, and a tattoo of a bleeding rose covered his forearm. His eyes were a surprisingly soft brown. He stretched out his legs. His hands were resting on his crotch. "I can think of a buncha ways," he said.

I wondered if he could see how hard my heart was thumping. I tried to breathe deeply. "I see you were on Valium the last time you were in jail," I said, looking at his file and avoiding looking at him. "For anxiety?"

"Yeeees," said Mr. Simmons, his tone mocking. "Thing is, I'm so tense I just can't get me to sleep. Keep having this dream and it wakes me up. This broad comes to see me. Takes off her clothes. Every fucking stitch. I'm staring at her bare ass and her tits. They're big, y'know, juicy. I'm just getting ready to get into it with her. Then she walks off. Ass swinging like nothing you ever seen. There's this big old knife in my hand. I run with it, huh? Almost get to her. Then I wake up. Every time."

I looked up from the file.

He was still grinning, picking at his teeth with a long thumbnail. "Bet you never had a dream like that."

"I can't say I have," I said, turning my eyes back to the file, wishing I sounded less apprehensive.

"Good soft bed you sleep in, I bet," he said. I could hear the smirk in his voice. "All covered up. You sleep naked under those covers?" His chair grated across the floor.

I drew another deep breath, nausea rising in my stomach. I did not respond.

He was quiet for a minute then. "No. Not your type a dreams," he said. "Not the type to be knifing anyone. What d'you dream about then? Books?" He laughed.

"I'll renew your prescription," I said. All I wanted was for him to get out of the room.

"And I'll see you next week," said Mr. Simmons. "I'll be waiting." He pulled himself out of his chair.

After he left, I went down the corridor and into the small staff kitchenette adjacent to the filing room. I locked the door and looked at myself in the mirror. I looked too young to be doing this job.

I thought about what my ex-fiancé had said in the note he had sent me from Colombia. In addition to informing me that he had chosen to continue his Médecins Sans Frontières position, he had denounced my inability to commit two years to working in a country he said was safe enough but which I knew had one of the highest rates of drug violence in the world. You can go on living your sheltered life if you want, he had said, but that's not how I want to live.

I wet a paper towel and wiped my face. Then I went back to the consulting room. My experiences with the rest of my patients that day did nothing to increase my confidence.

Monica called the following day, which was a Saturday, thankfully free of the jail. I was lying in bed, feeling anxious, and trying to read an article about malingering.

"Well, do you like it?" she asked. I could hear a little malice in her voice.

"I love it," I said, which was what I had also told my parents. "It's pretty different from Clarendon, of course. But I feel like I'm really making a difference. And the men are just, you know, people. Like you and me. Just people who happened to take the wrong path."

"I have to hand it to you," Monica said. "Honestly, I didn't think you'd be able to cut it. But you've adjusted so quickly."

"I know," I said. "I'm surprised I've been able to. But listen, I have to go. I was just rushing out the door. I'll call you."

The first time Mr. Ratnapola came into the consulting room, he called me "Mrs. Peiris," even though he knew I was a doctor. His handcuffs were off. He shuffled to the table and sat down.

I said, "I'm not married."

He looked at my bare ring finger and nodded, looking a little uncomfortable. He did not say anything else about it, but he stopped referring to me in any way at all.

I knew by then that he was from Sri Lanka. I had heard from Dr. Denton. We were the only people from Sri Lanka he knew. Mr. Ratnapola probably knew we were from the same country too, from my name, but he did not say anything about it.

"So, Mr. Ratnapola," I said. "How can I help you?"

"Sleeping," he said. "Can't sleep. Everything else is okay. Food also, I don't mind. The men are okay, they leave me alone. I help people with their cases. Read law books from the library. But can't sleep."

"I can give you some pills," I said. "But you will have to come back once a week. I can only give you a few at a time. And you can't keep taking these for long. It's a short-term solution."

He nodded as he came in the next week. "The pills helped," he said.

"You are sleeping well?"

"Yes," he said. "But you, you are not. Black circles under the eyes. Not a good sign."

"I've been staying up too late," I said.

"Worrying," he said.

I nodded and opened his file. "I can prescribe the same pills for another week," I said.

The following week, my morning staff meeting ran late. My patients were already outside the consulting room, leaning in a jagged row against the corridor wall, when I came into the Rehab Ward. As usual, my hands were shaking as I pulled off my gloves. The dreaded walk through the compound had been particularly taxing because, in my nervousness, I had dropped the files I had been carrying in front of the basketball court. The inmates on the court, led by Phil Simmons, had abandoned their games and lined up at the fence, whistling and cheering while I chased down papers and crouched on the ground, fighting my nausea, to pick them up.

Inside Rehab, I walked past the patients outside the consulting room without looking at them. I nodded to the guard at the door of the room and went in. Mr. Ratnapola was the first patient to come in.

"How are you?" he said.

"Fine, okay," I said. I was still trying to catch my breath, and the nausea was still lurking.

"You don't look so fine."

"I was hurrying," I said. "To get here."

"Not only that," he said.

"No." I realized my face was a little sweaty, even though it was cold outside.

"The men are bothering you?" he asked.

"The men? Yes, I suppose so," I said. "I still haven't got used to this place."

"Different from the world," he said.

"I hate walking past the basketball courts," I said.

"Simmons. That fellow is the ring leader," he said.

The guard looked in through the Plexiglas pane, and I realized that I had forgotten to wear my white coat again. Mr. Ratnapola's file was lying closed on the table in front of me. I opened it.

"The sleeping pills are working well?" I asked him.

"Yes, okay," he said.

I renewed his prescription for another week.

The next week, I asked Mr. Ratnapola where he was from in Sri Lanka.

Mr. Ratnapola clicked his tongue. "How can I tell you that?" he said, sounding irritated. "Next thing, it'll be all over the *Daily News*. 'Harischandra Ratnapola Talks to Jail Worker in States.'"

This had not occurred to me, but I could see the truth in what he said. Sri Lanka was a small country. Word spread quickly. I leaned over and pushed the door closed. The click of the latch sounded loud.

"Everything you tell me is confidential," I said. "Unless I get a subpoena. I can't talk about my patients with anyone. It's against the law."

Mr. Ratnapola snorted. "What law?" he said. "They're going to enforce American law in Sri Lanka also?"

"I suppose not. But there's also the ethics of it. I don't talk about my patients, here or there."

Mr. Ratnapola was silent for a while. Then he nodded. "Kandy," he said. "I am from Kandy. My brother is a doctor also. Internal medicine. He works in Kandy General Hospital. Srinath Ratnapola. Do you know?"

"No," I said. "I did college and medical school here. I only go back in the summers, to see my parents."

"What do your parents do?"

"Thaththi is a lawyer," I said. "Senior state counsel."

"Willy Peiris?"

"No, Denzil," I said. "Willy is my uncle. Thaththi's brother."

"Your mother? She is also working?"

"She's a dentist. Private practice."

"They are in Colombo?" he asked.

"Yes," I said.

"Ah, right," he said. "My wife's brother-in-law's cousins are all in Colombo. They might know them."

It was strange to be having this ordinary conversation with an inmate in the jail, one who was accused of no less a crime than murder. His file had told me that, and also that his bail was a very large sum of money. I knew no details about the allegations against him, but it seemed unlikely that he could be a murderer. I did not want to discuss the topic with him. I had been warned about the legal and ethical hazards of discussing the inmates' alleged crimes.

When Mr. Ratnapola came in the next week, I saw that his hair was freshly cut, very close to his scalp.

"A new haircut," I said.

He ran his hand over the stubble on his head and smiled. "Makes me feel more at home," he said.

"I don't know if that's a good thing," I said.

"Good to feel at home," he said, leaning back in the plastic chair.

"When do you think you'll get out?" I asked. It was only after I said the words that I realized I was getting into dangerous territory.

Mr. Ratnapola shrugged. "You mean, when I will go to prison?"

"No," I said, hastily. I did not want him to think that I believed he was guilty. "I mean, when is your court date?"

"Not for another month," he said. He seemed unconcerned.

"It must be hard. For you, and for your family," I said.

Mr. Ratnapola rubbed his cheeks with his hands. He had let his nails get overgrown. "They are in the world," he said. "My wife is with my daughter. She will look after her mother."

He covered his face with his hands for a moment and then rubbed his cheeks again. I saw that there were tears in the corners of his eyes. "She is at Yale University now. Law school. This is what she wanted to do. But before, she wanted to study women's rights. Now she is doing criminal law."

"You must be proud of her," I said. I could not think of anything I could say to make him feel better.

Mr. Ratnapola nodded. He pressed his thumbs into the corners of his eyes and then dragged them down his face, leaving wet lines on his cheeks. "Her husband was beating her," he said. "He wanted to know where she was every minute. He forbade her to apply to law school. Even get a job. See her parents."

I was beginning to feel uneasy. "I have to remind you," I said. "I don't talk about my patients. But if I was subpoenaed, I would be legally bound to answer questions in court, even if I didn't think that was the ethical way to treat my patients."

Mr. Ratnapola nodded again. He looked at the Plexiglas pane in the door. The guard was not there. "I am only telling you about my family," he said. "Nothing that you want to write notes about. You won't even remember any of this."

He did not wait for me to reply. I put down my pen. "He was a tourist," he said. "Can you believe? We were on holiday. In Galle. Coromandel Hotel. My cousin is the assistant manager. Eric was sitting at the next table. Having rice and curry. Even eating dried fish. Just like a local fellow. That's how we met. Got to be very friendly. We invited him to come home. Tilaka liked him. My wife. Nice fellow. Those days, he was nice. Nice-looking also. Skin was red like a boiled prawn, but nice face. Good smile. He started writing to Sumathi after he went off, back to the States."

"Sumathi is your daughter?" I wanted to hear his story, although I knew the inmates waiting outside would be getting restless.

"My only," Mr. Ratnapola said. "Tilaka had four miscarriages after that."

"I'm sorry to hear that," I said.

"What for sorry?" Mr. Ratnapola said. "Our karma. Sumathi is enough. Very good girl. Bright also. But she got fooled by Eric. We also got fooled. But can't say. Maybe he changed. Eight years ago, that was. Person can change."

"Yes," I said.

"Eric was the one who said we should come here. He was earning enough to sponsor us. Stockbroker. Good job. After we got citizenship, he helped to start the business. Shop, we have. Had. Now, of course, sold. Convenience store."

"It sounds like he was a pretty nice guy," I said.

Mr. Ratnapola hunched his shoulders. He put his head in his hands. He did not look up when he spoke. "Before, yes. But then all this jealousy. Always shouting at Sumathi. Twice she came with broken hands. We took her to the hospital. Bruises all the time."

"Why didn't she leave?" I asked.

"Not so easy. He said he would kill her. Find her and kill her. And us also. Who knows if he was telling the truth? Also, she was attracted to him. Even with all this. Sometimes everything was fine and dandy."

"It would have been more rational to leave," I said.

Mr. Ratnapola made a snorting sound. "Rational? We are all making irrational choices, no? But after we make the choice, then have to stick to it. Embrace it. That is what I always told Sumathi. When she was small. And she was trying to embrace her choice. Stay in the marriage."

"So what happened?"

"He died," said Mr. Ratnapola. "Hit on the head. Blood everywhere." He rubbed his eyes and then folded his arms across his chest. "But now Sumathi is free."

I nodded, not sure what I could say.

"It is hard to see what young women go through," he said. "You also. Something has to be done."

"I could leave if I am not happy here," I said. "But leaving in the middle of the year seems like a defeat."

He was silent for a while. "I have friends," he said finally. "They can send a message. Not hurt Simmons too much, you understand. Only get him to stop. But weapons, they don't have." I was not sure I understood what he meant.

He picked up the plastic coffee cup I had brought from the Rehab kitchenette. "A piece of glass would be enough. Small, so that no one would see." He slid the cup over to me. "Think about it." There was no expression on his face.

The realization of what he meant made me recoil from the table. "Are you telling me . . . ?"

He glanced at the shut door. "I am not saying anything," he said. "But you have to play with the rules in the place. And this is not the same world as outside." He pushed back his chair. "Think is all I am saying."

I did not tell Monica, my parents, or anyone else about Mr. Ratnapola's suggestion. Over the following week, I tried, from time to time, to think about what he had said. But my mind slid around his words. At first, they seemed simply ridiculous, and then too unpleasant to contemplate.

I had no intention of taking any contraband to work on Tuesday. Maybe it was frustration with my daily nausea that made me drop my nearly empty coffee cup shortly before I left my apartment. When I crouched over the ceramic fragments scattered across the kitchen tiles, I remembered how the inmates had called out and rattled the basketball court fence as I picked up my fallen papers, and the look I had seen on Mr. Simmons's face when I finally got to my feet. Before dumping the cup fragments into the trash can, I picked out one piece and laid it on my palm. It was a little smaller than my thumb and not particularly sharp. It looked like a tooth, I thought: long, brown-stained, and slightly curved, like a large rat's incisor. On impulse, I put it in my bag, tucked under my folded doctor's coat.

The guards at the gate knew me by then. I walked through into the jail compound without any trouble.

I kept my head down and hurried past the basketball court, trying to ignore the catcalls and the sight of Phil Simmons standing at the fence, massaging his crotch.

My doctor's coat, when I took it out of my bag, was stained with coffee from the cup shard I had pushed under it. I was dabbing at the stain with a tissue when Mr. Ratnapola shuffled into the consulting room.

"That will come out," he said. "No one will notice."

I nodded, feeling more anxious than I usually did in his presence. I pulled his file out of the stack on the table.

"That is not why I came today," he said. "Only to see if I can help. You have thought about what I said?"

I got up from my chair and shut the door.

"I can't talk about that," I said, but I could not help looking over at my bag, where the piece of ceramic lay hidden.

"There is no need to talk," he said. I saw that he had noticed my bag; I usually left it in the file room.

"I could leave," I said. "Or put up with it. It gets better, Dr. Denton says."

Mr. Ratnapola opened his hands in a small gesture. "That choice, you have to make," he said.

He watched me quietly while thoughts flooded my mind, about what crime I would be committing, about the Hippocratic oath I had taken, about how many people might get injured even with one ceramic tooth, and about what my parents might say. Then I remembered the reference Dr. Lockwood had written. Was this another instance of not being willing to take a risk? Was I so afraid to play by the new rules in this place that I would rather give up and leave?

I glanced at the Plexiglas pane in the door. The guard was nowhere to be seen. My bag was lying on the floor by my chair. It would be easy to take the piece of ceramic out and pass it to Mr. Ratnapola across the table, I thought. Or maybe I could drop it on the floor. It would barely make a sound. Dropping it could almost be accidental. He would pick it up and roll it into the waistband of his pants, perhaps, or tuck it into the hem of his uniform shirt.

I do not know how long I sat there with my thoughts and Mr. Ratnapola silent across from me.

Later, I thought there had been a fifty-fifty chance of deciding one way or the other. It did not seem implausible that I might have chosen to slip Mr. Ratnapola a light sliver of ceramic in those circumstances and in that world, even if that meant committing a crime that could have ended in someone's serious injury or maybe death.

But I did not do it. I bent and shut the flap of my bag. "All I can hope is that it gets better soon," I said.

Mr. Ratnapola did not speak for a while. Then he said, surprisingly, "You are tough." He rose abruptly from his seat. "No pills today. I am going to try without." He went out of the room without looking at me again.

When Mr. Simmons came in, a half hour later, I was swallowing the last of the coffee in my plastic cup.

He sat across from me, and leaned back, his thighs spread wide. "Spilt something right there," he said, grinning, his eyes fixed on the stained breast pocket of my white coat.

"How can I help you, Mr. Simmons?" I said, trying to ignore my discomfort.

"Just sittin' here is helping me no end," he said, covering his crotch with his thick fingers. "Y'know what I'm saying. And that Valium, that's the cream on the cake." There was a wet sound as he sucked air through his front teeth.

Maybe it was Mr. Ratnapola's offer of help, or the knowledge that the ceramic chip was lying in the bag next to me, or the fact that I had brought the chip to the jail, or simply the choice I had just made, that allowed me to look Mr. Simmons in the eye for the first time. "What problem do you have, Mr. Simmons, that makes you need the Valium?" I said.

A crease appeared in his forehead and then he showed his teeth in a sneer. "Well, now. Haven't I told you about them dreams that keep waking me up? This one broad, y'see, with an ass like a ripe—"

"Yes, I remember you told me several times about your dreams, Mr. Simmons," I said, forcing myself to keep my gaze steady on his face. "Is that the main problem?"

He dragged a nail across his front tooth. "Hmmm-uhhh. If I can't sleep, how can I get me some of that . . ."

I interrupted him again. "Well, I am sorry to hear that, but I can't prescribe any more Valium." I saw his mouth drop open a little as I slapped his file shut.

He planted his hands, bunched into fists, on the table between us and leaned his bulk toward me. "See here . . ."

I stood up as casually as I could. "I think you will get used to sleeping without the pills," I said.

Then I called out to the guard and informed him that Mr. Simmons had completed his visit.

It was only when Mr. Simmons was leaving the room that I noticed the resigned slump of his shoulders. It occurred to me that I had not seen him from any angle but head on. The years had not been kind to him, I saw; at forty, he was already bowed with the weight of them.

"Let me know how you fare," I said.

He left without glancing back.

Three weeks passed. The weather was getting warmer. I could no longer wear my long coat to work. I thought about wearing one of my baggy long-sleeved shirts, untucked over my jeans. Instead, though, I wore a light, fitted T-shirt, tucked in. I left my hair unconcealed, tied up in a ponytail. Instead of carrying my white doctor's coat to work in my bag, folded up, as I had in the past, I put it on over my clothes. Although the coffee stain had not washed out completely, it was only faintly visible.

There were puddles in the jail compound from the rain the night before. I wondered whether to take the road past the rat tree. I had walked that way a few times by then. Initially, it had not been by choice but because a construction crew jackhammering down to the plumbing system had closed off the path past the basketball court. I had clenched my jaw and given the tree a wide berth, alert to the risk of rats falling from the branches above. But nothing had happened, and since then, I had ventured that way a few more times. There had been no ill effects, perhaps because the rats were as watchful of me as I was of them.

But on this day, I chose the shorter path. The wind was gusting as I walked toward the basketball court. As I drew closer, I heard someone say, "Hello, Doc." It was Mr. Ratnapola. He was sitting on the bench by the side of the court. I had not seen him there before. It was hard to distinguish him from the others milling around, all in their orange uniforms.

I stopped and walked over to the fence. The men by the fence became silent. I could feel their eyes on me. "Hello, Mr. Ratnapola," I said. "How are you? Is everything going well?"

"Yes," he said. "Fine, everything is okay, Doc."

"Good to hear," I said.

I caught sight of Mr. Simmons some distance away.

"Mr. Simmons," I said. "How's it going?"

"Survivin', Doc," Mr. Simmons said, his tone grudging. "More or less."

Rain began to fall as I turned away, flecking my stained white coat and the orange uniforms of the men waiting by the fence.

I nodded to the men and walked the short distance to my consulting room, listening to the thud of the basketballs as they went back to their games.

Security

THE MAN WAS standing near a bronze reclining Buddha statue in the last room of the university museum's Asian collection. He caught Prasad's eye because he stood in front of the statue for an inordinately long time, his head cocked, his hands gliding over the lapels of his jacket. In profile, the man was handsome, with graying blonde hair and the frame of an aging athlete. He might have been in his early sixties. It did not occur to Prasad that the man might have ill intentions; the statue was securely encased in glass, and the man seemed too genteel to be any trouble. The only reason Prasad continued to watch him was that there was not much else to do besides look around and smell the perfumes of people passing by. Prasad performed his duties, which consisted mostly of patrolling the rooms, diligently, but he doubted anything would ever be stolen. A weapon seemed unnecessary, although he had a baton in addition to a flashlight and a walkie-talkie. Sometimes, when he studied the artifacts displayed in their generous glass cases, he reflected on their legitimacy; they were already stolen, he thought. He knew they had probably been purchased for far less than they were worth from desperate people in their countries of origin.

When the man finally began to walk toward the exit, Prasad saw that the first three buttons of his pale-blue shirt were unbuttoned. This fact seemed at odds with the man's upright bearing and his trim good looks. Near the door, the man pulled a set of keys from his coat pocket, and Prasad saw something small and silvery slip to the floor.

"You dropped something," Prasad called out, but his voice was drowned by the shrill laughter of a group of students just entering the room. The man, oblivious, stepped through the rotating glass exit door of the museum.

Prasad hurried over to the object the man had dropped. When he picked it up, his mind went blank for a moment; he could not understand how the thing in his hand could have been in the man's pocket. What lay on his palm was his sister's silver pendant. Under the loop that had connected the pendant to its chain, the name "Manik" was spelled out in a Sinhala font as straightforward as Manik herself: මැණික්. Prasad did not wonder whether it belonged to some other Manik. The edge of the last character had a slight defect, a warping of the metal, that he recognized. He was certain that it was the pendant their mother had given Manik the day he and his sisters had boarded a plane headed for the States. His other sister Varuni had got one with her name on it too. Varuni, not surprisingly, had requested, and got, an embellished font, the end of the "ru" curled, the top of the "ni" thick. Their mother had haggled with a jeweler at a small silver shop in Kandy town to get the pendants custom-made. After giving his sisters their necklaces, their mother had hugged Prasad close and whispered in his ear. She was the same height as he—both of them towered over the other members of the family—and so could do that easily. She reminded him to take care of his sisters. He had laughed; he expected they would be looking after him, their baby brother, as they had always done.

When the unexpectedness of seeing Manik's pendant receded, Prasad realized that his sister must have dropped it somewhere on campus. The man had probably pocketed it to take to a lost-and-found deposit. Prasad scurried to the exit to see if he could hail the man, to thank him, but the man was getting into a car parked some distance away. Prasad, as the only security guard on duty in the Asian collection, could not leave the museum, so all he could do was watch the man drive past in a sleek navy-blue convertible, his arm draped carelessly over the open window.

By the time Prasad got home that night, he had forgotten about the pendant. When he was cycling back from the museum, one of his tires blew out. He had to walk the bike home, his stomach growling during the three miles from the campus to the apartment he shared with his sisters.

The dented saucepan was still outside the door of his ground-floor apartment, its lid tightly fitted and filmed with dust. Prasad sighed. One of these days, he would have to clean it. He had given up hoping his sisters would take care of the problem.

Baila music, an old Gypsies song, was throbbing out of the open window, along with the unmistakable smells of his sisters' cooking. When he opened the door, fumes of burned garlic assaulted him. He realized how hungry he was when his stomach growled louder, even when he knew what he would be eating. All five of them—his sisters and their upstairs neighbors, Brad, Lal, and Imran, all members of the SLSA, the Sri Lankan Students' Association—were already sitting in the living room with their plates on their laps.

"Finally!" Varuni said, with a hand over a mouthful of food. "You couldn't have called if you were going to be late?"

Prasad noticed that Varuni was wearing the mustard-yellow blouse she had recently bought at the thrift store on Sepulveda Boulevard. He was glad that the blouse was not see-through in the light from the table lamps; it had been embarrassingly so in daylight, and his pointing this out had sparked an altercation. Prasad had had several altercations with Varuni lately. She was such a wild card. She saw nothing wrong with having lunch alone with boys on campus, some of them not even Sri Lankan. He had seen her several times sitting on the wall by the fountain or lounging on the grass in front of the student union, giggling flirtatiously with one or another doting fool. There was nothing Prasad could do to stop her. She laughed at him when he told her acting like that would give her a bad reputation.

"Flat tire," Prasad said. "And my phone ran out." He washed his hands, eyeing a pile of charred rotis. Even if they had not been burnt, he knew they would be hard enough to break a tooth. Thankfully, some tortillas had been heated in a pan as substitutes. He took two and added a few pieces of meat from a watery chicken curry.

"On Friday, the best rabbit curry you have ever had," Brad said, grinning, as Prasad settled on the ripped ottoman. It was comfortable but always the last seat anyone took because of the gaping tear that ran across its center.

"*Chee*, stop talking about that," Varuni said, grimacing. "I'm not going to eat it, I told you."

"Forget it, *machang*," Lal said. He pushed a lock of hair off his pock-marked forehead with the back of his hand. The hair had been sprayed or gelled again, and his shirt looked ironed. As usual, he was taking too much care with his dinnertime appearance and sitting a little too close to Manik, Prasad thought, although he was not too worried about it. Manik had good sense. She was friendly enough with all three of their neighbors, but there was something about her businesslike attitude that kept them at arm's length.

Prasad, chewing a leathery piece of chicken, was surprised when Manik said, "Fine, make your curry." She said it calmly, with her usual lack of drama.

The others turned to stare at her.

"You are encouraging this madness?" Imran said.

"People eat rabbits," Manik said, scraping up the last bits of curry on her plate with a shred of tortilla.

"Not those rabbits," Lal said. "Who knows what germs?"

"You engineers," Brad said, still grinning. "Germs won't live through autoclaving, *machang*." One of his curly yellow hairs had fallen onto his plate. Brad picked it off and flicked it to the floor. Prasad always forgot that Brad was not Sri Lankan until some small detail like that caught his eye. He didn't pay attention to how transparently blue Brad's eyes were behind his big square glasses, or to the way purple veins snaked under the pale skin of his wrists. And Brad's Texas accent was easy to overlook, maybe because he used the same Sinhala slang they all did, mingled with his English. He was as much a part of the SLSA as any of them. No one excluded him or pointed out that he was only an honorary member by virtue of having spent eighteen months in a village in Sri Lanka, teaching English.

"I'm not eating it," Varuni reiterated. "You'll have to make it as an extra if you're making it in your turn to cook. Lal and Imran won't eat. And Prasad won't." She looked at Prasad for confirmation, her face still screwed up in disgust.

"Just try it," Manik said to her. "Pretend he bought it from Albert-sons."

Varuni shuddered at this, a whole-body gesture that made her blue-painted toes twitch and her silver earrings chime. "No chance. If it's his cooking day, he'll have to make something else also. Dhal at least."

"But you and Manik are the dhal experts," Imran said, and then he broke into his cackling laugh.

"Very funny," Manik said, a frown gathering.

"Come on, they're getting better," Prasad said, because they were his sisters after all, but then he couldn't help adding, "On Sunday, they made scrambled eggs for breakfast and I didn't vomit afterward."

Varuni chucked the TV remote at him, and he ducked, laughing and snatching his plate out of the way.

"That dhal pot has been sitting outside for how long?" Lal said.

"Just throw it out, *machang*," Imran said. "No amount of cleaning is going to help that pot now."

Manik was the only one not laughing by then. Prasad was wondering if she was going to get into one of her black moods when Varuni said, "Don't change the subject. Our cooking is not the issue." She pointed a half-empty beer bottle at Brad. Until then, Prasad had not realized there was beer. Now he saw that there were several empty bottles on the two side tables, even though it was only Wednesday: Heineken, pricier than their usual weekend brand, and obviously a twelve-pack. He hoped their neighbors had bought it; otherwise, there was going to be a big dent in the week's grocery budget.

"Brad will get in trouble for taking the rabbits," Varuni said. "Lab assistants aren't supposed to take them." Again she looked at Prasad for support. "Right?"

Prasad shrugged. "How should I know? Maybe the profs don't care what happens after the hearts are taken out. They're dead, men."

"Euthanized," Brad said, wagging his finger. "They just get thrown out."

"Electrocuted," Imran said. "That's why I am not going to eat." He finished the water in his glass—he was the only one not drinking beer, for religious reasons—with a sanctimonious flourish.

"Think," Brad said. "Electrocution is better than what happens to cattle in a slaughterhouse. Instant. Almost instant."

"Who knows what shady things they feed them? In a lab. *Chikay*," Lal said.

"I know exactly what, *machang*," Brad said. "It's the standard diet. All natural. And I told you, all the experiments are behavioral, looking at what stress does to their hearts. No drugs, nada."

"Those poor, innocent rabbits," Varuni was saying, when Manik brought Prasad a beer.

"There's more in the fridge," Manik said.

Prasad was about to ask her, quietly, who had bought the beer, when she flipped her long plait off her shoulder, exposing her silver chain swinging without its pendant. Prasad remembered what was in his pocket.

"Did you know you lost your pendant?" he said, as she sat back down.

Varuni's hand went automatically to the neckline of her yellow blouse, but Manik only looked alarmed.

"What? No. No. I haven't lost it. It's in the bedroom."

She thought he was going to accuse her of carelessness, Prasad realized.

"Are you sure?" he said, trying not to grin. If he wasn't so tired, he would take a picture of her reaction when she realized she had lost it. He took a refreshing swig from the bottle. The beer was perfect for washing away the taste of burnt garlic, too much salt, and the cinnamon—who knew how many sticks his sisters had put in this time—in the curry.

"Positive," Manik said. "It came off the chain, so I put it in the coconut." This was a bowl, made from a polished coconut shell, that Prasad's sisters had brought with them from Sri Lanka, and that now sat on their dressing table.

"You better check," Prasad said. She was looking worriedly at Varuni, he noted. This was going to be funny. They hurried off to their room, muttering to each other.

Brad was still gushing about the rabbit he had brought home. Prasad had seen it in his neighbors' freezer. He appreciated the amount of work Brad had put into skinning the thing, but the sight of its rigid body had not provoked any desire to see it cooked, only disgust and pity. He was sick of hearing about Brad's plans to make lab rabbit a staple of their evening meals. He was sure none of them were going to eat it, however pressed for money they all were.

He was scrubbing the curry pot in the sink—after the dhal pot became defunct, he had started putting leftovers in the fridge, no matter how inedible the food was, and washing the pots right after dinner—when Varuni sailed back into the living room.

"Don't worry, we found Manik's pendant," she said, plopping down on the sofa.

"What? The pendant from Amma?"

"Otherwise?" she said, kicking her feet up onto the coffee table. "Of course that one."

"Are you sure?"

"Yes! What's the matter with you? Why are you asking such stupid questions?" She looked at him, her eyes wide. Both his sisters had big round eyes with heavy lids. When they had fought as kids, Prasad had called his sisters "froggies," but now he had to admit his sisters' eyes were beautiful: deep and filled with a Buddha-like innocence. At the moment, though, there was something in Varuni's eyes that made him wary.

"Never mind," he said. He checked to make sure the pendant was still in his pocket.

After his sisters went to sleep and the apartment fell silent, he tiptoed into their bedroom and carried out the coconut. There were two silver chains in it, one with Varuni's pendant, one without a pendant. He emptied the coconut onto the kitchen counter and scrabbled through its other contents: earrings, two plastic rings, a few pennies, a SpongeBob eraser, a pencil stub, and an assortment of hair ornaments. That was all.

Later, Prasad thought that if he had not agreed to help Brad, he might have remained ignorant of what was transpiring.

But on Friday afternoon, Brad, who was responsible for that evening's dinner, phoned Prasad as he was leaving his economics class.

"Can you come and give me a hand?" Brad said, sounding out of breath. "There's going to be a flood here. This damn dishwasher got messed up again, and I can't get it out by myself to do the fix."

"I have to go to work, *machang*," Prasad said. He pulled his bicycle from the rack outside Dupree Hall. "Until six. Call Lal or Imran."

"They've gone downtown," Brad said. "Won't be back until dinner. I can't cook sloshing around like this."

"So go to my place and cook," Prasad said, wheeling his bicycle down First Avenue.

"The girls won't let me make the rabbit there, you know that," Brad said. "Come on, *machang*. You said today is your extra shift anyway. You can do the Saturday shift instead."

"You are a bloody nuisance, men," Prasad said, exasperated. "I don't even know why you are making that bloody rabbit." He sighed. "Wait, will you. I'll call the museum and tell them and then I'll come."

When Prasad got to Tanglewood East, he passed by his apartment door with the pot of rotten dhal still outside, and went up the stairs to Brad's apartment. The place smelled like a wet dog. Brad's kitchen linoleum was littered with soggy towels and napkins, T-shirts and various other pieces of cloth. Even Brad's fabric wall hanging printed with Sinhala letters was on the floor, sopping wet. The right use for that wall hanging, Prasad thought. The sight of it on Brad's living-room wall had always bothered him. It was a trifle Brad had bought at a tourist shop in Sri Lanka. Prasad couldn't understand why anyone would hang an alphabet on the wall, except in a child's room. Even less comprehensibly, a lot of the letters were missing, as if only the ones considered most attractive or exotic had been selected for display. What if I picked out only fifteen or so letters from the English alphabet, the ones I liked the most, and put them up on the wall, he had said to Brad. How would that look? Lal and Imran, who also disliked the wall hanging, had agreed with Prasad, but Brad had only laughed. If you did that with the English alphabet, you would be putting up gibberish, but the Sinhala letters are so awesome, it doesn't matter, he had said.

"Still leaking," Brad said, pushing wads of cloth around with his bare feet. He looked as though he had fallen or lain down on the floor; his shaggy curls were sticking damply to the back of his neck, and his T-shirt was wet and grungy. Even his glasses were spattered with drops of water.

"Hell of a laundry job you're going to have, men," Prasad said. He took off his sneakers and waded into the mess, trying not to slip on the wet floor. "OK, let's pull the thing out. Ready?"

Once the dishwasher was heaved away from the wall, it did not take long to stop the water running. They had put the dishwasher back in place and started gathering the wet clothes when Prasad heard a door bang open downstairs, and then Manik's voice, sounding rushed.

"See you later!"

A moment later, Varuni's voice called out, "Be careful! And remember, six ten latest. Prasad will be home by six twenty for sure."

Prasad hurried onto the walkway outside Brad's apartment to remind Manik to buy a tub of yogurt if she was going to Albertsons. Manik was in the parking lot below, in jeans and a flowing batik blouse she had brought from Sri Lanka. Her hair was loose down her back, bushy the way it was right after she brushed it. She was wearing a pair of silver sandals he didn't recognize. They had thin heels that, although not very high, looked too uncomfortable for walking the half-mile to the grocery store. Prasad was opening his mouth to call out to her, to ask her if she was taking the bus to campus or downtown, when a navy-blue convertible pulled up next to her. He recognized it and the man inside immediately. He was too surprised to speak; by the time his mind registered the facts before him, the car had zoomed away.

Initially, Prasad had only been curious. His misgivings had not begun until he noticed how unforthcoming Varuni was being. She had refused to tell him anything about the man or where Manik had gone. Finally, when he threatened to call their parents, she had said plaintively, "He's just a friend. Why are you making such a fuss?"

"If he's a friend, why so secret? Why didn't she just bring him home? How come I haven't even heard of him? And why does she have a friend that old? Is he one of her professors?"

"What?" Varuni said. "Stop getting so worked up! Of course he's not a professor. And it's not such a secret. Brad knows." And then her face closed up as if she felt she had said too much.

Prasad had gone back up the stairs to Brad's apartment. He could feel the wrongness of the situation chafing him like a rip in his underclothing. What was going on? For a moment, he wondered if Manik could be trying to audition for a role in a film or for a modeling job. After all, they were in Los Angeles; Hollywood was not so far away. But surely that was too improbable; Manik would not try to do something that drastic without a family discussion.

Brad was wringing out a rag in the sink, his wet clothes stained with dishwasher grime.

"What, *machang*?" he said, when he saw Prasad's face.

"Don't *machang* me, men," Prasad said. "Do you know what Manik is up to? She's gone off with some old fellow. In a navy-blue Porsche."

A look of annoyance appeared on Brad's face. It was not what Prasad had expected, and it threw him off.

"Why do you care?" Brad said. "Your sister is a grown-up."

That stunned Prasad for a moment. "Grown-up or not is not the point," he said. "What about her safety? She hasn't even taken her phone. Who knows what could happen if she has gone off with some Hollywood type?"

"Calm down, *machang*," Brad said. He skated over the slick floor to the mop in the corner, leaving grimy tracks in his wake. "What's going to happen in broad daylight? From what Manik told me, all they do is go to a mall or a restaurant."

"Why would she tell you and not me?"

"Probably because you react like this," Brad said, gesturing at him with the mop. "This is nothing to worry about. They've gone to a public place."

"For what? And who is he?"

"He's an art collector, *machang*. Hans Reck is his name."

"You know him?"

"I sold him something recently. Something I found in my closet, a thing I brought back from Sri Lanka."

"What thing?" Prasad said, raising his voice over the sound of the dirty water Brad was squeezing out of the mop into the sink.

"Oh, you know, a piece of carved wood the Kaluwatte family gave me. An old thing that could go over a doorframe."

"*Mal lali?* An antique, you mean," Prasad said, thinking that the Kaluwattes, who had been Brad's host family when he lived in Sri Lanka and who considered him almost a son, had probably given him an heirloom, not knowing that it was illegal to take antiques out of the country and certainly not expecting Brad to sell it. "This fellow, Reck, buys these sorts of things?"

"He has a store off Sunset Boulevard. It's called Artasian. Mostly antiques from India, Pakistan, Bangladesh, Sri Lanka. He was very keen on getting more stuff from Sri Lanka. Underrepresented in his shop, he said. He asked me if I knew any girls who would be willing to talk to him, tell him about the country, that sort of thing, so I introduced him to Manik. Varuni said no."

Prasad was so stupefied by this that he did not realize he had stepped backward into the pile of soggy clothes on the floor until he felt their clamminess against his ankles.

"But didn't you think . . . Why did he want to talk to girls? Why not me or one of the other fellows? And why the bloody hell didn't you tell me?"

For the first time since Prasad had come into the apartment, Brad looked uncomfortable. Patches of red appeared in his cheeks. He put the mop down and adjusted his glasses with a jerky movement.

"He didn't give you money or anything, no?" Prasad said, although even asking the question seemed absurd. But then he saw the way the color in Brad's cheeks got brighter, until his face looked like it was burning.

"He gave you money?" Prasad said.

"Only for an introduction to the SLSA. Listen, *machang*," Brad said. He turned the tap on and wet his hands, ran them over the back of his neck. "The guy is perfectly safe. I checked him out thoroughly online. And I explained everything to Manik and Varuni. The guy just wants to be seen with a pretty girl in public, that's all. On Wednesday, he took Manik to a four-star Italian restaurant on Melrose Avenue for lunch, and then brought her right back home. Today they were going to the

H & H Center, just to walk around, Manik said. She said he is very gentlemanly."

"What is wrong with you?" Prasad said.

"What the hell is wrong with wanting to be seen with a pretty girl?" Brad said. "Every guy wants that."

"*Ado*, have you gone mad? He wants to be seen with a Sri Lankan girl? What kind of dirty fellow is this?"

"Relax, *machang*," Brad said. "You are taking this way too seriously. This guy thinks of her as a daughter, probably."

Prasad had an unpleasant tightness in the pit of his stomach, remembering the way the man had considered the Buddha statue in the museum, and the way his shirt had been unbuttoned. "I can't believe you would introduce him to them without telling me," he said.

"Look, *machang*," Brad said. He sounded angry now; his face was still red, and his forehead was sweaty, but there was a righteous tone in his voice. "This is a free country. They're grown-ups. Since when have you ever had a say in what they do? And it's not like they're some innocent village girls. You guys are from Colombo, totally westernized. What is the big deal?"

"Wearing jeans doesn't mean there are different expectations, men," Prasad said. He felt weary all of a sudden. He wanted to sit down, and to not have to worry about what could be happening to his sister.

He left Brad's apartment without another word and trudged downstairs to his apartment. He found Manik's pendant, which he had hidden behind the lamp stand by the coffee table. He had put it there thinking that he would try to find out why his sisters had lied about it, and then he had forgotten about it. Now he clenched it in his hand. Some peace and quiet were what he needed. He was sinking down onto the fleecy stuffing that spilled out of the ottoman when Varuni came into the living room. She had been crying, he could tell. Her eyes were red, and a small trail of watery mucus was visible under her nose. Just a kid, Prasad thought, even though she was a year older than him.

"Now you've made me worried," Varuni said, wiping her nose with her sleeve. "But it's not like she's doing anything terrible. She just goes out to eat and talks to him. Not like she's a prostitute!"

The word was like a slap to Prasad. "I don't want to talk about any of this," he said. He took the ottoman outside and sat down by the front door. Out of the corner of his eye, he could see the rotten dhal pot. He slid the ottoman forward a couple of inches so that the pot was no longer in his peripheral vision. Seeing the pot increased his agitation; it made him realize not only how irresponsible his sisters were, but also how blind he had been to their irresponsibility. Images kept rushing through his head, increasingly unpalatable: Manik strolling arm in arm with the man at H & H, the man putting his arm around her, kissing her, unknown people taking pictures with their phones, videos appearing on YouTube that ruined Manik's reputation, Manik lying injured, maybe dead, in a hotel room, police arriving to tell him, his parents' faces when they heard the news. Prasad pocketed Manik's pendant, pulled out the old iPod he had bought with part of his security guard paycheck, and plugged into his music, hoping to drown out his thoughts.

By six o'clock, Prasad had calmed down considerably. He realized he had overreacted, although he was not about to admit that to Brad or to Varuni. Manik was a sensible person and tough-minded, not someone who would be easily steamrolled. And he had to acknowledge there was nothing reprehensible about going to a mall or to lunch with an older man who wanted to learn about Sri Lanka. He supposed that it was the suddenness of finding out that had made him react the way he had.

He had been sitting outside on the ottoman, leaning against the wall of his apartment. It was cool enough that afternoon that the sunlight, when it slanted under the walkway above him, was pleasant. He was feeling faintly drowsy, lulled by his music and the swaying branches of the lone palm tree at the edge of curb, when Hans Reck's navy-blue car turned into Tanglewood East's small parking lot. Prasad recognized it from the *Road & Track* magazines he sometimes perused at Walmart: a Porsche Carrera GT, the car of a collector.

Through the windscreen, Prasad saw Manik's face register his presence with a look of dismay, saw her mouth form what he thought might be, "Oh, shit."

The car stopped several yards away. Prasad got to his feet as Manik opened her door. By the time he got to the car, she had walked around to the driver's side, and the man had got out as well.

"This is my little brother, Prasad," Manik said. "Prasad, this is Hans Reck."

"How do you do?" Prasad said. He extended his hand, but the man put his hands together in the traditional Sri Lankan greeting.

"*Ayubowan*," Hans Reck said, so Prasad had no choice but to reciprocate, although the gesture seemed oddly out of context in the dusty parking lot of Tanglewood East, with its rusted "Vacancy" sign and crumbling concrete border. Hans Reck was wearing a cologne that reminded Prasad of cloves; it was a subtle scent, nothing ostentatious or obnoxious.

"Very pleased to meet you," Hans Reck said. He stressed the word "very" in a way that grated on Prasad. "Your lovely sister has told me a lot about you."

The unnecessary adjective, more than the ingratiating tone, was what got to Prasad. "But my lovely sister didn't tell me anything about you," he said, ignoring the glare Manik was casting him. "Won't you come in and have a drink? We can have a chat." He pointed toward their apartment, noticing that the door was open and that Varuni was poised in the doorway as if ready to flee. His sisters always complained that he scared off any boys who showed an interest in them by interviewing them in detail, but this was different. This was an old man whose reasons for meeting with Manik were unacceptably opaque.

"Not today, Prasad," Manik said, the glare becoming more pointed. "Hans has something else he has to do."

"Hans?" The way Manik was addressing this man by his first name gave Prasad a bad feeling. The man was clearly older than their own father. His forehead had a papery appearance that suggested that he might even be as old as their grandfather, even though his cheeks barely sagged, and there was only a touch of gray at his temples. An oily sheen lay on his skin, as if he had recently applied some sort of face cream. Definitely the Hollywood type, Prasad thought, the kind of man who tried to look and act as if he were younger than his age.

"Don't be ridiculous, Prasad," Manik said. And to the man, she said, "He thinks I shouldn't call you by your first name because you are older than me."

Something inside Prasad recoiled at how familiar Manik was with the man. His thoughts began churning again. What was going on?

"Where exactly did you go, Akka?" Prasad said, looking at Hans Reck, although the question was addressed to his sister.

"H & H. Not that it's any of your business," Manik said.

"You went shopping?" Prasad said, looking at Manik's empty hands. Why would she go shopping with this old man? There was only one shopping bag inside the car, he saw: a bumpy brown paper bag standing upright on the passenger seat Manik had vacated.

"We walked around, and then we had some excellent Ceylon tea and scones at Chado," Hans Reck said. "Manik likes the cream they serve with the scones."

Prasad looked at the gratified smile that lingered on Hans Reck's pale lips and felt his heart drop. The man had pronounced Manik's name perfectly, without a trace of an American accent. How long had they known each other? And what was going on?

"You have known my sister long?" he said. Another car entered the parking lot and had to skid toward the curb, scattering gravel, to get past. They were still standing by the open door of the Porsche.

"Prasad," Manik said, as if she always called him that instead of Malli, little brother.

"Not long," Hans Reck said. Then, with his hand open as if he was offering Prasad a gift, he said, "My intentions are honorable, I hope you know. I want to get to know your sister, your family."

Prasad stood with his hip against the sharp edge of the open car door. There were words in his throat, but they were rude and inhospitable, not like ones his parents would have used to welcome a stranger into their home. He did not want to say them. But he also did not want to welcome Hans Reck or his supposedly honorable intentions; there was something wrong with what the man was saying, although Prasad could not put his finger on the problem.

A curry smell wafted over, and Prasad knew it had to be the rabbit cooking in Brad's apartment. Brad was an excellent cook. He was the only one among the six SLSA members at Tanglewood East who ground spices in a small mortar before cooking a curry. He pulverized whole cumin and mustard seeds with garlic and red chilies as if he were a village housewife.

Hans Reck's nostrils flared, and his eyes darted to where Varuni was still standing. "A wonderful aroma," he said.

Manik said nothing to this. There was impatience in her expression. Prasad was relieved that she did not invite Hans Reck to dinner, but the silence was awkward, broken only by the swishing of the palm tree rising incongruously out of the concrete and the hiss of cars zipping past on the main road.

Instead of getting into his car, Hans Reck indicated the Tanglewood East sign that loomed tall at the edge of the parking lot. "You like this place?

Prasad had no intention of telling the fellow about his likes and dislikes. Their apartment was fully carpeted, and there were newish lampstands, although it had its drawbacks: the dismissive management, the narrow windows, the malfunctioning appliances, the drains that clogged too easily, the indestructible roaches that populated the bathroom. But none of it was any of Hans Reck's business.

"Fine. Like any student apartment," Prasad said. He took a step back from the car to show that the conversation was over. He no longer had an interest in chatting with the man. It would be better to find out from Manik what this was all about.

"There are some very good places close to the campus," Hans Reck said.

Talking through his hat, Prasad thought. Was the man an idiot or just used to living in his bubble?

"Never mind, Hans, I told you, we can talk about all that later," Manik said. She looked anxious, Prasad thought.

"About what," Prasad said.

"Not now. Hans has somewhere he has to be," Manik said.

But Hans Reck said, "I have some friends in real estate. I can get you a very good deal on a nice three-bedroom apartment close to the campus if you're interested. The rent will be practically nothing."

Manik pulled at her earring, looking over at the door to the apartment. Prasad saw that Varuni had gone inside, but a chink in the window blind suggested she was looking out.

"Thanks," Prasad said. "But we're fine here."

"Think it over," Hans Reck said. "My pleasure to help out friends."

"I don't even know you," Prasad said.

"I know Manik a little," Hans Reck said. "And my hope is to get to know her and your other sister—and you—more. Take your sisters out to some good meals, to talk, that's all. I don't know anyone from Sri Lanka, you see. I'd like to learn about your country." There was a slightly defensive note in his voice, Prasad thought, perhaps in reaction to the expression Prasad was sure was on his own face.

Prasad did not know why the man's explanation made him so intensely uncomfortable. It was an innocent enough desire the man had. He breathed in the smell of Brad's rabbit curry and wondered how to get the man to leave so that he could talk to Manik in private. He put his hands in his pockets, preparing to saunter away from the car with feigned casualness, and felt the edge of Manik's pendant.

"Here," he said to Manik, pulling it out of his pocket.

A look of shock dawned on Manik's face.

"Where did you get that?" she said, glancing sidelong at Hans Reck, and Prasad saw that the man was also looking nonplussed.

"At the museum. Mr. Reck dropped it." To Hans Reck, he said, "I work there." He held the pendant out to Manik, but it was Hans Reck who reached for it. Prasad did not let go.

"I gave it," Manik said in response to Prasad's raised eyebrows.

"I was hoping I hadn't lost it. I hung it up there, but it fell off. I was sure I had put it in my pocket," Mr. Reck said. Prasad followed his gesturing hand and saw an elongated, ornate metal hook hanging from the driving mirror of the Porsche. Mr. Reck tried to take the pendant, gripping the thin metal between his index finger and his thumb. "Such beautiful shapes."

"They're letters," Prasad said. "Manik's name, not a car decoration." He yanked on the pendant, wrenching it from the man's hold.

"Give it back to him," Manik said.

"Have you gone mad?" Prasad said. He turned on his heel and walked away toward the open door of the apartment, the pendant clenched in his fist.

At the doorway, he stooped to pick up the dhal pot, to calm his seething thoughts. Varuni was sitting by the window when he went in. "You're going to clean that now?" she said, when he hefted the pot onto the kitchen counter.

Prasad did not respond. He took a deep breath and raised the pot lid, ignoring Varuni's comments and her exaggerated expressions of disgust. Green and white mold furred the sides of the pot and the congealed surface of the dhal his sisters had made almost two weeks previously. He began scooping the mess out with a spoon, throwing it into the trash bin. Then his breath ran out. He gagged at the stench and tried to cover his nose with his sleeve. But it was no use. He had to shut the lid.

"I told you, you shouldn't have opened it," Varuni said.

"How is leaving it closed going to help? We can't throw a twenty-dollar pot," Prasad said. "I'll have to put boiling water and vinegar."

He was about to fill the kettle with water when Manik came in, her expression grim. She was carrying the shopping bag he had seen inside Hans Reck's car.

She said nothing about the dhal pot. Instead she said, "You're making a big deal out of nothing. He's nice and respectful. All he wants is to be seen with us. It'll help the business at his shop, he said. And for that, one of those fancy apartments near campus for half the rent we pay here? What's the harm?"

When he said nothing, her tone got sharper. "You liked having beer on Wednesday. And good beer. We could afford a lot more things like that, just for going out for a few harmless meals here and there."

This stunned Prasad so much that he could barely get the words out. "That beer was from him?"

"So what? A present, and because it's the brand you like so much," Manik said. Then, noticing Prasad's eyes on the bag in her hand, "And this. Heineken and chocolates. For all of us. What's wrong with that?"

Prasad put the kettle away. All he wanted was to get out of the apartment, away from his sisters and their senselessness. The pot would have to wait until he had the will to clean it. He picked up the pendant lying on the counter and tossed it to Manik. "I'm going up to eat. There's that rabbit, but Brad also made dhal. You can decide what you want to have."

He left the apartment, leaving his sisters frowning at each other.

A Burglary on Quarry Lane

RASHMINI WAS so preoccupied that she only noticed the flashing lights after she had showered and put on her pajamas. The lights were reflecting off the shadowy living room walls. She balanced on the sofa springs and reached through the window bars to push against the cloudy pane. The window creaked open, inch by inch, to reveal a hubbub in the yard. The slumlords' back porch light was on. A police officer was taking pictures with a small camera, and another was combing the mulberry bushes with a hockey stick. Two more officers were talking on the porch steps. A police car was parked on Quarry Lane, in front of the slumlords' house. Rashmini could only see the car's front end between the side of the house and the boxwood hedge, but there was no mistaking the blue and red light streaming from it.

She changed out of her pajamas and hurried out, across the garden stones, to the porch.

"Something happened?" she said.

The officers turned. A few seconds elapsed before one said, "Who are you?"

"I'm Rashmini. Rashmini Hapuarachchi."

"Rush-a-ma-what-a-ma-who?" the officer said, predictably. "Where did you come from?" He had the weary appearance of a person who had experienced too many disappointments. His weathered skin was drawn over protuberant cheekbones, and his jaw looked as if it was carved from rock. Deep grooves ran from his nose to the corners of his lips. Something in his eyes suggested bitterness.

"I stay in the carriage house. Over there. Did something happen?"

"A break-in, a burglary," the other officer said, lifting his hat to scratch his stubble-covered head. He was a gangly man, easily two decades younger than the first officer, with hunched shoulders that indicated a discomfort with his superior height. His eyes drifted over Rashmini's boyishly cut hair and stretched-out white T-shirt, her old jeans, and rubber flip-flops. Rashmini drew herself up. Disregarding what others thought of her clothing was a habit she had learned young. Clothes only had to fit reasonably well and be clean. Everyone in the Colombo school she had attended had worn a white school uniform. The uniforms were supposed to erase distinctions of wealth and class, but of course, everyone had known who the scholarship girls were, from their carefully mended school ties, the frayed edges of their canvas shoes, the way their polyester uniforms were worn thin enough to be see-through, and the khaki-colored underarm sweat stains that no amount of washing could remove.

"Where were you this evening?" The first officer hitched his trousers higher on his muscular hips and studied Rashmini. She read the name printed on his badge: Kent McCarthy.

"I had dinner with a friend at the Francesca," Rashmini said. She looked around the empty porch and then through the slumlords' partially open back door. The billowing edge of a burgundy tablecloth was visible above the gleaming floor. She could hear the whirring of a fan. The slumlords were nowhere to be seen. Rashmini smelled cake baking. It was an unusual smell in the yard; until then, she had not thought either of the Hills the baking type. Now that she had thought of it, she realized that she had never heard the clanking of pots or the odor of cooking leaking from the house. She could not count the times Mr. Hill had supervised her progress across the yard, his girth wedged into the wicker armchair on the porch. Most of those times, he had been picking morsels from a plate and sipping from a teacup that looked too delicate for his gnarled fingers. She had never wondered who had prepared those snacks. Had the window and door to the backyard always been shut? Maybe that was why she had smelled nothing.

"The Hills. They're okay?" she said.

"When did you get back to your apartment?" McCarthy asked. He slid a notebook from his pocket.

There was no sense in being offended that he was ignoring her question, Rashmini told herself. There were routines to police business. "Nine fifty-five. I looked at my watch."

"You a student?" The younger officer, whose badge identified him as Howard Alistair, said.

Rashmini shook her head. "A data technician. In the economics department, in Ramsey Hall."

The officer brandishing the hockey stick jumped back as some small creature scampered out of a mulberry bush and rustled through the hedge.

"What did they take?" Rashmini said. "The burglars?"

Alistair fidgeted on his feet. "Well . . ."

McCarthy broke in. "See anything unusual?" He began scribbling in his notebook. He did not sound very hopeful. There was an edge to him that reminded Rashmini of her father. Perhaps McCarthy's dreams had been thwarted too. She considered the rigidity of his lips, wondering what his ambitions might have been: to move up in the ranks of law enforcement? Or had he wanted to give his children more than he had been able to?

"I saw a man when I came back," Rashmini said.

McCarthy's head snapped up. The officer inspecting the yard stopped walking around. The one with the stick dropped it and came over.

"Where? Who?" McCarthy said. The grooves on his face deepened.

"I've never seen him before. He was standing over there, between the carriage house and the alley. He was looking for someone called Miriam. Miriam Evans, I think he said. No, Marion Evans."

"You had a conversation?" McCarthy said. His eyes had narrowed to slits, accentuating the heavy ridges above them.

Rashmini backed away from the officers crowding around her. She could smell their sweat and, on one of them, a hint of onions. A childhood filled with one-hour rides on jam-packed buses to and from her Colombo school had left her with a distaste for having strangers' bodies too close. By the time she got home in the afternoons, her school uniform had usually smelled of the bodies against which she had been crushed, of sweat and coconut hair oil, and occasionally of men's cigarette smoke or the fresh fish in someone's market basket. "Yes, I told you," she said to the officers. "He said he was looking for Marion Evans. I told him there wasn't anyone by that name here, that there were some other carriage houses along that way. Then he left. He was very polite."

"What did he look like?"

"Youngish. Tall. Darkish hair. He was white."

"Not much of a description there," McCarthy said, sounding sour. He looked as though he had not expected anything more.

"It was dark. This porch light wasn't on then, and there's no light outside the carriage house." Rashmini had complained to the slumlords that she could not see enough to fit her key into the lock at night. They had suggested that she carry a flashlight. Maybe now, after a burglary, they might reconsider installing an outdoor light.

"What was he wearing?" Alistair said. He ducked his head further into his shoulders as he spoke, as if he were unsure whether to ask the question. He looked new on the job.

"A black cap. And something casual. I think jeans. Or maybe sweat pants. Darkish T-shirt."

The radio strapped to McCarthy's belt came to life. A voice grated over static. McCarthy stepped aside to growl into it.

"I wasn't paying attention," Rashmini added. "I was trying to turn the key in the front door lock. You have to keep jiggling it." This was another problem the slumlords ignored; they should have changed the lock, or at least oiled it.

"Witnesses don't always remember details," Alistair said, and Rashmini wondered if this was something he had recently learned, perhaps in college. He did not appear much older than she was. "Why don't you go home, Miss. We'll come and see you later if we need more information."

McCarthy grunted as he put his radio away and closed his notebook. He did not seem happy about the situation, but that was not Rashmini's problem.

When she got back to the carriage house, she bolted the door and tugged the creaky window closed. Then she began to worry again about her decision to remain in the States. Spending the whole evening talking to Josefina had not lessened her frustration. Josefina, an immigrant herself, from Ecuador, had advised her to forget Mason's question. It is a small thing, Josefina had said, and you will have to put up with such slights if you want to make a life here. Harden your mind, let these things bounce off.

Rashmini found it upsetting that Josefina could be so blasé after the incident at Hobson's Seafood Grill the previous week, when Rashmini had invited Josefina to dinner with her parents. A waiter had surveyed Rashmini's mother in her cotton sari and her father with his neatly oiled hair and asked for a credit card before taking their order. It was at Josefina's insistence that they had all walked out, leaving the waiter goggle-eyed and the embossed menus open on the table.

Now Rashmini was no longer sure she wanted to stay in the States, despite her dream of succeeding on her own.

Since graduating from college six months previously, she had been working in Ramsey Hall, one among a pack of workers who sat glassy-eyed before computer screens, scrolling through columns of numbers for minimum-wage pay. At first, she had worked under Professor Lambert. She had got accustomed to him mispronouncing her name and stopped feeling irritated or thinking of a small skin disease every time he said her name wrong: Rash-mini. But now, she had been passed on to another boss as if she was a dinner dish, and she was supposed to learn new tests. What was Rasch analysis anyway? And worst of all, Mason wanted to call her Jane.

After they had walked out of Hobson's the previous week, her father had shaken his head. "So this is the price you are paying for independence," he had said. "Is it worth it?"

Rashmini had taken in his grim expression and remembered how much of his softness and humor he had lost when he sacrificed his own dreams in order to give his children a good future. She wondered if seeing his children get an education abroad had been worth what he had given up. But all she had said was, "This kind of thing happens once in a while. Not a big deal."

When Rashmini heard the knock at the door, she had already unpacked the cushions. The cardboard boxes that had held them were flattened and stacked neatly in the corner next to a pile of wadded plastic wrap.

Mrs. Hill was standing outside, the late afternoon sunlight brightening her dyed chestnut hair. Today, it was waved at the sides and pinned stiffly back. Her mauve linen dress was belted around her still trim waist. Her crocodile pumps, with their three-inch heels, were ridiculous for an evening at home.

"Yes?" Rashmini said. Her last conversation with Mrs. Hill had been two days before the burglary, on the day her parents had left. Not even a week had passed since then, and the unpleasantness of the interaction had not yet faded from Rashmini's mind.

Mrs. Hill's eyes, purple-shadowed and magnified by the thick lenses of her glasses, fixed themselves on Rashmini's face. "We were robbed on Monday," she said, without preamble. It was an exclamation, accusatory, but that was the way Mrs. Hill always spoke.

"I know," Rashmini said. "Did you lose a lot?"

"Money," Mrs. Hill said.

"Sorry to hear," Rashmini said. There were so many things that could have been taken, she wanted to say, thinking of the sleek bronze horse heads on the slumlords' living room mantel, the sculpted alabaster lamp stands, Mr. Hill's state-of-the-art audio equipment, and the jewelry Mrs. Hill wore. "I wanted to ask if you both were alright. But you haven't been home the past few days." The truth was she had enjoyed lingering in the yard without being scrutinized by Mr. Hill or getting into an argument about being careless with the premises. She had strolled barefoot across the lawn on several occasions, rebelling against the slumlords' insistence that she restrict herself to the garden stones and reveling in the feel of the grass underfoot.

Mrs. Hill's stare was so flinty that Rashmini added, "The lights weren't on, so I assumed . . ."

"I suppose you saw the burglar alarm we had put in," Mrs. Hill said. She pulled her belt tighter around her waist. A pale stone, an amethyst perhaps, flashed on one finger.

"What? No. After the burglary?"

"You know quite well we didn't have one on Monday," Mrs. Hill said.

Rashmini, rolling these words over in her mind, saw that Mrs. Hill was peering past her, at the new peach seat cushions padding the hard sofa springs. Piled against the sofa arms were the five new textured throw cushions, patterned apricot, fuchsia, and white, startlingly bright in the dingy interior of the carriage house.

"New cushions," Mrs. Hill said. She pressed her lips together, and Rashmini saw that her lipstick had crept into the wrinkles around her mouth.

"My parents thought the place needed spiffing up. And this way people can sit comfortably on the sofa." Rashmini could not resist adding, "I mean, who really sits on a sofa without seat cushions?"

"The previous tenants were happy to have the sofa," Mrs. Hill said. She patted the waved hair above her ear. Rashmini wondered, as usual, how often she had manicures. The color of Mrs. Hill's nails changed frequently, and they were perfectly maintained.

"Right. The same ones who were happy to build shelves and make their own improvements."

Mrs. Hill's glare grew more piercing. "They didn't sit around complaining."

The woman was too much. "I've told you where I work. Just because I can't afford the time or the money for improvements the landlords—you—should be making doesn't mean I'm lazy." Rashmini felt her blood pressure rising. It was Mrs. Hill who probably sat around all day, flipping through *Vogue* or the old people's version of *Seventeen*, whatever it was. Did Mrs. Hill ever pore over data sheets? Had she ever had to figure out how to do a Rasch analysis? It had taken three days to learn how to begin. Thinking about work reminded her of the casual way Mason had asked if he could call her Jane. At first she had laughed, thinking it was a joke.

"Look at that. You must have found a good garage sale," Mrs. Hill said. Rashmini saw that she was still peering into the carriage house, her gaze fixed on the cup and teapot lying on the side table.

"My mother sent me a china set," Rashmini said. The cushions and the china could have been peace offerings, she thought. Her parents had spent too much of their visit trying to convince her to leave the States and return to Sri Lanka. "She didn't want me using the crockery you had put in the kitchen."

Rashmini left the door standing open and covered the five steps it took to cross the length of the living/dining room and enter the kitchen. The good thing about a kitchen this size was that she could stand at the two-burner stove and reach the sink, the squat dorm-style fridge, the single stub of Formica countertop, and the metal overhead cabinet, just by turning her body around. The three chipped mugs and the mis-matched plates that had been in the cabinet were now in a cardboard box she had placed on the fridge. She carried the box to the door. "Here are the old cups and plates."

Mrs. Hill's nostrils flared as if she had suddenly smelled a sharp odor. "How generous of your parents. Cushions. Such nice china. A whole set? Plates too?"

"How to eat without plates," Rashmini said. She held out the box, but Mrs. Hill made no attempt to take it from her.

"What did they do, sell a kidney?" Mrs. Hill said.

Two bees buzzing behind Mrs. Hill landed on a foxglove by the box-wood hedge. This was why she lived here, Rashmini reminded herself: the garden was glorious, even if she had to walk across the stones when the slumlords were around, and the carriage house was self-contained. At any time, she could shut the door and be alone.

She advanced onto the shredding plastic door mat and thrust the box at Mrs. Hill, forcing her to take it in her arms. Rashmini hoped the bottom of the box was dirty, so that it would spoil the fussy mauve dress.

"For someone your age, you really are an ignorant lady," she said, before retreating into the carriage house and shutting the door.

The tea in the pot was lukewarm, but Rashmini poured some into her cup and took it into the bedroom.

A double bed with a corroded iron headboard almost filled the bed-room. Next to it was a gouged wooden plank attached to the wall by means of three metal brackets roughened with rust. The plank served as a desk. It was against a door that had been nailed shut. Above the desk were two bracketed planks for holding books. A few planks next to the desk acted as a dresser, holding stacks of clothes. To reach the bathroom, which had the only mirror in the house, she had to walk sideways between the bed and the shelves.

There was only one picture in the room, a blurry photograph Rash-mini had pinned above the desk, of the small, run-down bungalow in

Yakkala, Sri Lanka, in which she had spent the first twelve years of her life. Those had been the years her father had believed he would make a success of his writing. In the foreground of the photograph, near the mussaenda bushes with their velvety flowers, were two scrawny hens. There had been several that roamed free in a patch of overgrown garden. It had been Rashmini's task to collect their eggs for the family each morning. Looking at the photo, Rashmini remembered the incessant tapping of her father's fingers on the keys of his gray Remington typewriter. The machine, and its suede dust cover, had been a present from Rashmini's grandmother, the only extended family member who had not disapproved of Rashmini's father's writing ambitions. The sound had been a constant in Rashmini's childhood, along with the thready feathers that she tended to find in unexpected places: floating in the water tub in the small brick outhouse, clumped on the coconut husks used to light the cooking fire in the kitchen, stuck on the nylon saris her mother wore to her sales assistant job, or snagged on the stitching of her brother's scratched old cricket ball.

Rashmini contemplated the photo as she sat at the desk and ate one of the Lemon Puffs her parents had brought, licking off the yellow filling before dipping the sugared biscuit into her tea. The Oreos she bought regularly were poor substitutes for these, she thought. She wondered if her father had been right. Would it be better to go back home? He had offered to relieve her of the obligation of working at the farm if she wanted some independence. She could work in Colombo and stay with Maureen Aunty and George Uncle during the week, he had told her.

Still, she would not have independence, at least not the kind of independence she could have here. She might just as well ask for winter in Sri Lanka; the most she would ever get was an air-conditioned house. But there were upsides to returning home. For one thing, she would not have to tolerate the kind of ignorance she encountered in the States.

The day her parents had left, Mrs. Hill had come to the door. When Rashmini opened it, Mrs. Hill had craned forward, peering inquisitively into the gloom of the carriage house. "Your parents are still here?"

Rashmini had taken her time answering. She had pressed the defunct doorbell repeatedly, pointedly. The slumlords' refusal to replace it was another sore point. "As a matter of fact, I dropped them today at the airport. They are going to Arizona to see my brother before going back home. Why are you asking? There's a problem?"

Mrs. Hill showed no evidence of noticing the doorbell. "I was curious," she had said.

"They said that you came yesterday, when I was at work. That you walked right inside when they were sitting in the bedroom. So was there a problem you came about?"

Mrs. Hill had shrugged. "I heard voices. The door was open. I came in to see who was here."

Rashmini had waited, watching Mrs. Hill purse her lips.

"This is a small house," Mrs. Hill had gone on. "It's meant for single occupancy."

"The rental agreement doesn't say anything about not having guests. What it says is that the landlord has to get the tenant's permission to enter the premises."

Mrs. Hill had blinked. "Three people in here. The fire department wouldn't have been too happy about that."

Rashmini had lounged against the door frame. "The fire department. Hmm," she said thoughtfully. "What would the fire department say about a carriage house with only one exit and bars on all the windows?"

Mrs. Hill's irritation was clear on her face. "The bars are there for safety. You're welcome to remove the desk and open the fire exit. We thought you'd like the desk there, so we didn't take it down when the last tenant left. He built it." She smiled, but Rashmini could see how contrived the smile was. "He was such a nice young man. A graduate student in the German department. He was German himself. It's a pity he left. He was always adding something to this house. His parents came to visit him once too. Of course, they stayed in a hotel."

"They didn't want to stay with him?" Rashmini shook her head pityingly. "So sad. They must have not been close. My parents wouldn't dream of it."

Mrs. Hill frowned as if Rashmini had suddenly made a loud, unpleasant sound. "How could they have fit in here for six days? Where could you have possibly slept?"

"Obviously not on the sofa springs," Rashmini said. "I have a sleeping bag and look, there's so much space here"—she indicated the narrow stretch of floor between the door and the sofa—"I was very comfy."

"There are some hotels around here that are very reasonable. I realize your parents are used to small spaces, but they would have been more comfortable in a hotel. They wouldn't have needed a grand place."

"I didn't realize you knew them so well," Rashmini said. "You must have stayed a while to chat. Funny, they didn't mention."

Mrs. Hill had recoiled. She had taken a few mincing steps away on her high heels before turning around. "Your rent is due in eight days. Don't forget."

"For sure, I'll drop it off." Rashmini had stretched her lips into a smile and shut the door.

On Saturday morning, Rashmini was woken by two knocks, far too loud to be made by Mrs. Hill. She staggered to the door, her legs stiff from sleep. Dew was still visible on the yarrow flowers opposite the doorway. Officer McCarthy was pressed against the honeysuckle vine by the door, his uniform crisp. Officer Alistair was standing three feet back with an official-looking red folder in his hand.

"Remember us?" McCarthy said. He hitched up his belt buckle and looked past Rashmini at the dim living room. "We need to ask you a few questions."

Alistair coughed in the background. "Sorry to disturb you, Miss," he said, stepping forward. "Can we come in?"

Rashmini crossed her arms over the thin cotton of her pajama shirt. "I just have to get changed."

After getting into her usual jeans and T-shirt, she invited them into the living room.

"Wait, no, don't!" she said as Alistair prepared to settle his weight on the chair by the fold-out board that served as a dining table.

Alistair stopped short, his lanky legs bent, his rear end suspended over the seat. "What happened?"

"That chair's broken. Try this." She drew the other wooden chair forward.

Alistair folded his awkward length on the chair, smiling shyly. "You must eat alone."

"When I have people to dinner, they sit on the sofa or the floor. Once, a friend of mine sat down in that chair, and the legs collapsed."

"Have you thought of repairing it? Or giving it back to your landlords?" Alistair said, casting his eyes around the cramped space.

"The slumlords? I haven't got around to it. I don't talk to them much."

Alistair said, "What did you call them?"

"Private joke," Rashmini said. "Just the way they act. You know he used to be dean of the business school. And she was a marketing person. A successful one, apparently. That fancy house, with all that amazing furniture, but look at this place they rent out."

McCarthy, incongruous next to a fuchsia flowered cushion, said, "Not on good terms." He made a note in his little book.

"This used to be where their son hung out. His den," Alistair said.

"What son? I didn't know they had one," Rashmini said.

"He had hopes of being an artist, I heard. Years ago, that was. I bet the place looked different then," Alistair said, his eyes still roaming around the room.

"They never said anything about a son living here," Rashmini said.

"He doesn't have anything to do with them is what I heard," Alistair said, suddenly more animated. "Used to be a tweaker. You know, methamphetamine. Lived on the street at one time."

Rashmini stared. "The Hills' son?"

McCarthy broke in, his tone impatient. "Cut the chat," he said to Alistair. "What is this, a social call? We need to get to the bottom of this burglary."

"What is this about?" Rashmini said to him. "Did you find the man?"

"We'll ask the questions," McCarthy said. "Rasha . . . Rasheem . . . How do you say your name?"

"It's pronounced Jane."

"Jane?" Alistair said, and McCarthy looked confused.

"It's a joke," Rashmini said.

"You're full of jokes," McCarthy said.

"I just started working with a new professor at my job," Rashmini said. "He asked me if he could call me Jane because my name was too difficult for him to pronounce."

"Not a bad idea," McCarthy said. A grin appeared, the first Rashmini had seen on him.

But Alistair shook his head. "People like to stick to what they know. Even if it's wrong."

"Well, Jane, Rasheem, whatever," McCarthy said. "We are here to ask you a few questions."

"At Mrs. Hill's request," Alistair said, sinking his neck again into his shoulders.

"About the man I saw?"

"Plenty of valuables in that house, plenty to take. But only money was taken. Who would know there was that much money inside that kitten?" McCarthy said, pinning her with his disappointed eyes.

"What kitten?"

"Mrs. Hill said it was where she put the rent money. The kitten she had on the mantel in the living room," McCarthy said.

"Oh, that black kitten? I've seen it when I've gone into the house to pay the rent. I didn't know there was money in it." Rashmini said.

"Mrs. Hill is more upset about losing the kitten than all that money," Alistair said, looking at his finger nails. There was an apologetic note in his voice that Rashmini found odd. "It used to be her son's. He slept with it, she said, when he was a kid."

"Wait," Rashmini said. "You must be talking about a different thing. The kitten I saw on the mantelpiece wasn't a toy. I'm sure it wasn't soft. It looked like it was made of stone. Not the kind of thing a kid would take to bed."

"That was it. Marble. She showed us a picture," Alistair said.

How could anyone sleep with a marble kitten, Rashmini was thinking, when McCarthy said, "That's the one she wants back."

"I can understand that," Rashmini said. She needed coffee, she thought, rising from the sofa. Nothing made sense before she drank a cup. "You wanted to ask me something? Although I told you, I don't remember anything else about the man."

"Maybe there wasn't a man," McCarthy said.

Rashmini turned from the doorway to the kitchen nook to see McCarthy examining the label on the fuchsia cushion lying beside him. Alistair was wringing his hands and examining the tip of his own shoe.

"What?" Then she realized what he meant. "Oh, you mean it wasn't him. You talked to him? Or you found it was someone else?"

McCarthy lifted the cushion and sniffed its nubbly surface. "Smells new," he said. "You did some shopping recently looks like. And not at Walmart or IKEA."

She wished McCarthy would get to the point.

"Mrs. Hill said you bought some things recently," McCarthy continued. He thumped the cushion with the flat of his hand.

"What are you . . . ? Why do you keep talking about . . . ?"

"She mentioned some problems," Alistair said, his fingers worrying his collar. "Conflicts." His eyes went to a red tulip Rashmini had placed in a jar filled with water. Its stem was still straight, but the edge of one petal had begun to wither.

"This is about the lawn?" Rashmini said. "I ruin the grass by walking on it? Well, now they should be happy. Now I only walk on those stones."

"She said you steal flowers from the garden," McCarthy said, jerking his head at the tulip.

"Okay, this is too much," Rashmini said. "Steal? I live here. So that's my yard also! They cut armfuls of those flowers all the time. I take maybe one flower a week."

Alistair cleared his throat. It was an uncomfortable sound, the sound of dry tissue abrading. "Well, Mrs. Hill has a notion . . . ," he began.

"Look, Rasheem," McCarthy said, tapping his pen against his notebook. "Mrs. Hill thinks you stole that money from their living room while they were upstairs."

"What!" Through the fog in Rashmini's mind came the thought that she had uttered that word several times since the officers had entered the carriage house. It was not like her to be at a loss for words.

"She says she won't press charges if you return what you took and move out," McCarthy continued. "A pretty good deal, I'd say."

Rashmini raised her hand, trying to order the thoughts crowding into her mind. "Are you joking with me?" she said.

Alistair cleared his throat again. "What Mrs. Hill said is that you know their comings and goings, so you had the opportunity," he said. "And the motive."

"Why would I take their damn money?"

McCarthy cast his eyes around, at the dirty white walls and the scratched floorboards. He prodded the fuchsia cushion with his pen. "You got to buy some pricey things. These, some good crockery, we heard. And what else?"

"My parents sent me those," Rashmini said. "They ordered them online. The stuff just got delivered. Same with the china." Then she wished she had not said all that as if an explanation was required.

"Your parents. They came to visit you from Sierra Lanka and couldn't afford a hotel, but this . . ." McCarthy thumped again on the cushion. "These must be what, a couple hundred a pop?"

Rashmini drew herself up. "Sri. Sri Lanka. What makes you think they couldn't afford a hotel? They stayed here because they knew that was what I wanted."

"Rasheem," McCarthy said. He rested his cheek on his hand and shook his head.

Alistair's face had gone red, his embarrassment obvious in the way he rolled his neck.

"Are you accusing me?" Rashmini said. She dredged her mind for information. This was America. There were laws about these things. Were they allowed to come into her house and make such claims? Should she call someone? Who could she call?

"We are reasoning with you," McCarthy said. "Return the money you have left. The kitten."

Alistair untied his shoelaces and retied them. Rashmini's blood boiled, looking at him. He seemed so uncomfortable. Maybe he saw how ridiculous all this was. But why did he not say something?

She leaned for a minute against the doorway to the kitchen area. Its surface was sticky with grease. On warm days, when the windows were closed, she could smell the rancidity in the air. The place had not been painted in years. The kitchen in the Yakkala bungalow had smelled of grease too, and smoke from the cooking fire. The walls had been covered with soot. If her father had not given up his writing ambitions and agreed, finally, to join his brothers in the family farming business, her parents might still have a kitchen like that.

It occurred to her that fuming about people's ignorance did nothing. "Just wait a minute," she said.

She marched past them into the bedroom, a matter of a few steps. Alistair mumbled something in the living room as she yanked her photo album off the plank above the desk.

When she took the album back to the living room, McCarthy was on his feet, looking toward the bedroom doorway. Did he think she was trying to abscond? Escape somehow through a barred window?

She opened the album and thrust it at him. "This is my parents' house," she said, pointing at a picture in which she and her brother stood with their parents on the long front verandah of their current two-storied house in the Colombo suburb of Ja-ela. The picture had been taken on a summer trip back home from college. The wall behind them was studded with smooth amber stones, and the floor was tiled in pale marble. The clay pots suspended by chains from the high ceiling were overflowing with ferns that were freshly watered. The pots were still beaded with moisture. Three scarlet crab claws formed a striking flower arrangement in a hip-high vase by the French windows opening onto the verandah. Rashmini's mother tended the house carefully now that she no longer needed to work long days as a sales assistant. She could afford to keep her own hours as the bookkeeper for the family business.

"We don't all live in thatched huts in Sri Lanka," Rashmini said. She watched McCarthy's expression change from condescension to confusion. She waited while he passed the book to Alistair.

"My family owns a poultry farming business in Sri Lanka," she went on, as they flipped through the pages of the album. "My parents came here to try to persuade me to come back, now that my studies are finished. They think that if I stay here, I will be a second-class citizen. And maybe they are right." She took the album back from Alistair and snapped it shut. "You can tell that woman I wouldn't steal even if I was poor. I grew up poor, and I didn't steal anything then. I didn't take her damn money." She jerked her head toward the slumlords' house as she opened the front door. "Also, you can tell her I have a lease and I am not leaving."

McCarthy opened his mouth to speak.

Rashmini said, "Please. Have you talked to their son? Maybe he took the bloody kitten, if it was his. Maybe it was him I spoke to that day."

Alistair's fingers fluttered over his shirt buttons. "I thought of that. I wanted to ask Mrs. Hill for a picture of her son," he said. "But she insisted you had taken the kitten."

"So you don't even have a picture I could look at to see if I recognize him?"

The officers moved to the door, silent.

Alistair turned on the doormat to raise his hat, but Rashmini shut the door without saying anything more.

She sank down on the sofa cushions and listened to their footsteps receding across the garden stones. Outside, the flowers, with their variegated colors, were in bloom, she reminded herself. She surveyed the living room. Perhaps small changes would make living there more pleasant. She could change the place gradually, tackling problems one by one. She could oil the lock on the door, hang more pictures on the walls, and cover the ruined floorboards with a fleece rug. She would paint the place herself, instead of waiting for the Hills. The walls would be pale coral, she decided, to remind her of the soft mussaenda flowers that had grown outside the bungalow in Yakkala.

She wished she knew whether the man she had met had been the Hills' son and whether he had burgled his own parents. There had to be a lot that lay behind the Hills' wealth, behind Mr. Hill's critical comments and Mrs. Hill's stony stares. She wondered what kind of childhood their son had had. If he came by again, she would invite him into the carriage house for a cup of tea; maybe she would find out what had made him sleep with a marble kitten.

Leisure

THERE IS PINE oil in the air, but dirt has blackened the grout between the floor tiles. Uncaring fingers have left their mark on the once-white curtains. Dust clouds the windowsill. It's quite a change for Aunty Rani. She liked her house pristine. Her skin is unkempt now too. It hangs loose; she has stopped using her imported Oil of Olay.

I haven't seen Aunty Rani in twenty years, since I last visited Sri Lanka. She is old, eighty-three or four. She'd worn Kanjeevaram silks and bordered chiffons in reds and oranges, stylish sari blouses even past the age of sixty. It's disorienting to see her crumpled under the gray bed sheets, wrists bare of bangles, nails stubby, unpainted.

Kamalawathie is here again with her. My mother says she comes every Sunday, after her weekly worship at the Buddhist temple in Maradana.

She stays for an hour, my mother says, but doesn't say much. Today it's the same. Kamalawathie is silent after greeting me and nodding to my aunt. She watches and waits, relaxed in the chair next to me. The way she does it, you'd think she was quite used to sitting in chairs in Aunty Rani's house. Aunty Rani looks away. She looks displeased, but doesn't comment.

It must be hard for her to bear this, although her mind is feeble now. I remember an afternoon in August. There was a power outage. Tempers are short in the heat, when the fans don't work. But that was no excuse. I remember the water flying from Aunty Rani's tumbler, the way it seemed suspended before it made impact. Kamalawathie gasped when it struck her blouse. Her mouth was pinched tight as she pulled the soaking cloth away from her skin.

"*Iced* water, I said!" That's what my aunt shouted, leaning back in her antique recliner.

I heard what Kamalawathie muttered then, though not to Aunty Rani's face. "Bitch. A curse on you."

Kamalawathie used to wake early, slam pots and spoons around to make Aunty Rani's bed tea. At night, she only snapped her sleeping mat open when Aunty Rani had gone to bed, her feet massaged and her face creamed. The pristine house was Kamalawathie's doing. The furniture, passed down through generations of aristocracy, was never dusty. Aunty Rani sat and ate the meals Kamalawathie cooked her. Roti for breakfast, or hoppers. Rice and seven curries every day, spices ground fresh. String hoppers from scratch. They didn't have takeout meals then. Aunty Rani entertained on weekends. The guests adored Kamalawathie's dishes. Aunty Rani had it hard when Kamalawathie went to visit her family in her village twice a year. Sometimes she wasn't sure if Kamalawathie would return.

"All these luxuries she has," Aunty Rani said to my mother once. "Big house. Good food. A fan in the kitchen even. Doesn't have to chop wood to cook. The thing is, servants these days don't appreciate. But how can you expect gratitude from them? Not civilized, no?"

The times have changed. After three decades at Aunty Rani's house, Kamalawathie has made enough to pay the village employment broker. She has got her daughter a lucrative maid's job in the Middle East. That's why Kamalawathie looks Dubai-rich. There is a gold chain around her still muscled neck. There are three thin, rolled-gold bangles on one arm and beaded slippers on her feet. She carries a new plastic handbag. Her sari is printed in red and green, and oddly, she has on nail polish.

"Can you believe?" I can imagine my aunt saying. "Cutex! Who does she think she is!"

The maid comes in with a lunch tray, places it on the table by the bed. Aunty Rani raises her head off the pillow and stares at it for a moment: boiled rice, lentils, a small dish of fish curry.

"Ring the bell when you finish," the maid says, businesslike. She won't take any nonsense, I can see. It's hard to find live-in servants to work in Colombo houses now, my mother says. This maid is from an employment agency. Her job is nine to five. She gets two days off a week.

Kamalawathie rises to leave. She pats Aunty Rani's hand, embraces me with her robust arms. Aunty Rani looks confused. I am taken aback by Kamalawathie's familiarity, but then I remember what America has taught me: we are all equals. I am not sure that I understand Kamalawathie though. In her place, revenge is what I would come here for. *See my independence*, I would breathe silently. *Feel my health*. I would rattle my bangles. *Hear my wealth*.

"Why do you come?" I have to ask. "Are you so fond of her?"

"Fondness is another thing," she says, shaking her head. Up close, it's easy to see that the white stones in her earrings are not diamonds. I wonder if she's simply waiting, and watching, for Aunty Rani's karma to play itself out.

Kamalawathie holds my arm in her hands. "You, even with all your time in America, you should know things are not so simple," she says. "Thirty-three years, we were under the same roof. She needs visitors…" She looks down at her fingernails. I see the red paint is inexpertly applied, but unchipped.

Accident

DAVID TRIPPED on Sonia Aunty's verandah steps and hit his face on our third day in Colombo. I worried that his bloody nose would affect his reception at the party that evening. I had persuaded Sonia Aunty to invite all the relatives, even the Matara crowd that had been blackballed for missing my grandmother's funeral five years ago. Persuading Sonia Aunty that the party would not offend my parents was harder, but I had managed that too.

"It's been months," I reminded Sonia Aunty. "Old news now. No one is going to be shocked."

The blood that dripped from David's nose was as dark and viscous as the molasses his mother had drizzled on cornbread while I sat stiffly at her dinner table, the time we visited her in Dallas. Drops oozed through

David's fingers as he clutched his nose, and coagulated on the red stone of Sonia Aunty's steps. He was grinning as if this were just another fraternity prank. It was the same grin he had had the first time I had seen him, when he had been in a tracksuit plastered with blue feathers and I had been wearing a bicycle helmet and filmy fins constructed from an old voile sari my mother had given me. That seemed eons ago now, although not much more than eighteen months had passed.

"Aiyo, aiyo, get him to the hospital now," Sonia Aunty said, as I pulled David to his feet. She tucked her sari *pota* around her plump middle and tried to steady David, which was difficult because she was easily a foot shorter than him.

"I still want to see the golden carp," David said, stumbling against the clay bird bath that Pedris, Sonia Aunty's gardener, had filled with fresh araliya flowers for the evening's festivities.

"Yes, yes, you can see after you get back from the hospital," Jith Uncle said. His words were slurred. They had been drinking Jith Uncle's whiskey for two hours by then. Jith Uncle had taken the day off from work to help with the party, but all afternoon, he had been watching movies with David. First it had been a World War II documentary, and then, after they started drinking and laughing, a flickering film of the Marx brothers.

I led David to the car. Sonia Aunty hurried into the house and reappeared with a frayed towel, which she spread across David's lap and the back seat. "To catch the blood," she said. The tone of her voice reminded me of the way my mother had sounded on the Friday evening she had seen David on TV, high-fiving his frat brothers in front of a smoking house.

Sonia Aunty looked at my dress, one of the comfortably high-waisted shifts I had been wearing to lounge around her house since we had arrived in Colombo. The dress stopped several inches above my knees. "Go and change, Dilini. You can't wear that to the hospital." I knew from the way her eyebrows were twitching that she was irritated about the whole situation. She looked very much like my mother in that moment, although Sonia Aunty was much more rotund than my mother, a fact my mother attributed, illogically it seemed to me, to Sonia Aunty's childlessness.

"Never mind that," Jith Uncle said. "For an emergency, it's okay to wear."

On Jaya Road, Jith Uncle swerved to avoid a black cat that darted out of a lantana bush, and nearly crashed into a parked van. When he accelerated too quickly off Circular Road, I realized his judgment was impaired.

I wondered if I should ask him to pull over. But he still thought of me as a child, and anyway, I didn't have a license to drive in Sri Lanka.

"Maybe we should go back and get Sonia Aunty to drive," I said.

Jith Uncle laughed. "Why, you think I am drunk after a couple of whiskeys?"

At the Pannipitiya junction, a woman stepped onto the road and Jith Uncle braked too slowly. One minute she was standing open-mouthed in her starched dress, holding a polka-dotted umbrella against the afternoon sun, and the next she had disappeared. The umbrella stood in the roadside grass like an oversized poisonous mushroom.

I jumped out with my heart pounding while Jith Uncle was still fumbling at his door handle and David was saying, "What? Why are we stopped?"

People were already swarming toward us, yelling and gesticulating. A tuk-tuk driver in a sweat-streaked khaki shirt reached the woman before I did. She was lying on the asphalt with her hair frizzed around her. A spangled red hair clip had got knocked off her head. One hand, with a wedding ring, was lying across her dress. It was difficult to focus with all the commotion. Thoughts were jumbled in my head: Is the woman dead? Need to try CPR. Could she be pregnant? Does she have children? How old would they be? Who should I call?

Then I saw the woman move. I ran around to where I could see her face. She was fleshy and middle-aged, with the marks of healed pimples on her cheeks and wide creases across her forehead. She was blinking as if she had something in her eye.

"Are you okay?" I said in Sinhala.

"I just fell," she said, sounding astonished.

"Does anything hurt?" I said.

The tuk-tuk driver helped her to a sitting position. "Let her stand up and then we can see," he said.

"See, see, you are fine," Jith Uncle said as the woman staggered up, clutching me and the tuk-tuk driver. Sweat was running down Jith Uncle's face, soaking his sideburns.

Nine or ten other people had reached us by then. One person, setting eyes on David, who was standing by the driver's door, said, "*Suddhek!*"

People started exclaiming over the presence of a white man. I thought of my father saying, "Whether you go to Colombo is your business now. Just don't let David drive. You know what trouble there will be if he has an accident."

Acrid fumes swallowed us as a bus screeched by, honking. Several schoolboys balanced on the footboard jumped off and came running over to join the crowd.

A man who had a plastic ruler stuck in an ink-stained shirt pocket said, "This *suddha* has got hurt also. Look at his nose. He must have hit his head on the wheel."

David was surveying the hullabaloo with the cheery befuddlement that appeared on his face when he was intoxicated. For the first time since we had arrived in Sri Lanka, I noticed how different he looked from everyone around us, with the blonde hair that straggled over his ears and his rosy, freckled skin. It made me think of how different I must have seemed to him, the night I first met him, at a Halloween party I had attended with my friend Fallon. I knew I looked out of place, not only because I was the only brown person there, but also because of my odd costume. Fallon had wanted us both to go as mermaids, in green-and-blue bikini tops and trailing skirts. We made fins out of one of my mother's old saris and attached them to our arms and the backs of our skirts. But when I looked in my bedroom mirror before leaving for the party, I thought the bare expanse of my midriff looked inappropriate, so I decided to go as a fish instead, to Fallon's dismay. I put on a lime-green Lycra shirt and on my head, a green bicycle helmet, decorated with scales painted on with nail polish. When we walked into the party, the first person we saw was David, who had also ended up in an unexpected costume, one amended at the last minute. In his case, it was not by choice, but because his fraternity brothers had squirted glue onto his black tracksuit and then poured a sack of bright-blue feathers over him. Instead of the panther he had wanted to be, he had ended up as some sort of impossible tropical bird. He still had whiskers painted on his face.

"The *suddha* knocked this woman down," another man said, jerking me back to the present. He had his hands on his hips in a way that seemed threatening.

"No, no, he wasn't driving," I said, but my words were drowned in the bellowing voice of a matronly woman standing next to David.

She said, "Didn't even look at where he was going." Perspiration had darkened the armpits of her flowered blouse. Her substantial bosom heaved as she glared at David.

"Driving as if this is England," another man said. He looked like a clerk in a government office, with his gray-checked shirt tucked over his hollow chest and pot belly.

Someone had seated the woman who had been hit on the dusty hood of the Peugeot. There was road dirt smeared on the back of her dress. She had knotted her hair into a haphazard bun, but it was coming undone and snaking across her shoulders.

Jith Uncle's hair was standing up in oily peaks. He raked his hands through it again. "Shall we take you to the hospital?" he said. "That is where we are going. They can check to make sure you are all right."

"Checking is not enough," the bosomy woman said. Her ponytail, smelling of sandalwood, brushed against me as she turned to face the thickening crowd. "This *suddha* here ran this woman down."

David had his arm on the open driver's side door. He fingered the caked blood on his face, looking dazed. The breeziness had gone out of his manner. "She's not hurt, right? What's going on? What are they saying?"

"He wasn't driving," I said directly to the bosomy woman, still in Sinhala.

But she did not seem to hear. She touched my sleeve, which was stained from when I had pulled David to his feet on the verandah steps. "*Aney*, Miss, you also got hurt?" she said.

"No, no, this is from before," I said. The heat and the noise, combined with the press of sweating bodies, were beginning to make me feel nauseated.

The pot-bellied man pushed his way to the front. "This *suddha* can't come here and drive as if he is in England," he said, his voice stentorian. There was a ripple of agreement from the crowd, and two teenaged boys in grubby white school uniforms cheered and slapped each other on the back, laughing.

"You are not England here," the pot-bellied man said to David in English, shaking his fist in David's face. David took a step back, looking puzzled.

"Ask him for money," the man said in Sinhala to the woman who had been hit.

"Call the police!" someone shouted from the crowd.

Jith Uncle inserted himself in front of David. "Look," he said, looking around the crowd. "I was the one who was driving. Not this fellow. This fellow is my niece's husband from America. What is all this nonsense? This fellow fell on our steps and I was rushing him to the hospital and that is why we had the accident. But the woman is fine. We'll take her and get her checked. Enough now of the nonsense." He rubbed his cheek, looking surprised at his own eloquence, although he was normally so garrulous, even when he was not drunk, that he sometimes drove Sonia Aunty to shut herself in the kitchen for the sake of quiet.

"See this, selling out his own people for the *suddha*," the bosomy woman said to the crowd.

There was hissing from the crowd, and cries of "*Ado*, go away!" and "Let the *suddha* pay!"

"Him telling lies, you think helping?" the pot-bellied man said to David in English.

David said, "What?"

"We'll make sure this woman is all right," I said to the bosomy woman in Sinhala. "My husband needs to see a doctor. His nose could be broken."

The woman looked me up and down as if she was seeing me for the first time, and I wished I had stopped to change my dress before leaving the house.

Two police officers arrived and forced their way to the front. When the older of the two took a pen and a notepad out of his breast pocket, people started hollering, offering disjointed pieces of the story.

"Right, right!" the younger policeman shouted, waving his hands and trying to silence the crowd, while the older one took a statement from the pot-bellied man, who had evidently appointed himself spokesman for the woman who had been hit.

"This is all wrong," Jith Uncle said. "I was the one driving. This woman was not hurt. Just ask her."

The older policeman looked at Jith Uncle's Peugeot, at David with the blood dried on his face, and at my kneecaps showing below my skirt. "Best thing is to go to the station," he said, smoothing his graying mustache with his pen. "We can discuss there."

By the time we got to the police station, it was almost five o'clock. Three young men were gathered around a telephone pole outside the station, their shirts psychedelic and open to halfway down their chests. When I got out of the car with David, they began hissing and calling out in Sinhala. One winked.

"Have you no shame? This girl is married," Jith Uncle said.

"Okay, okay, no problem, boss," one of them said, but when Jith Uncle turned away, the young man winked at me again.

"What? What were they saying?" David said.

"Never mind. Rowdies. It's because my dress is short," I said, even though I knew Jith Uncle had heard what they had said, how they assumed the worst because I was with a *suddha*. Even my own parents had assumed that my values would change if I was with David. That was why they had initially tried to get me to stop seeing him. They didn't start talking about how a marriage could be compromised by incompatibilities of religions and cultures until they thought I was getting serious. And after David appeared on TV, they had refused to have anything to do with him because of what they called his public indecency.

"I'll set them straight," David said. He turned back to approach the men.

Jith Uncle pulled him away. "Come, come, David. We have enough trouble here." He sounded worried. He was no longer slurring his words.

"What trouble?" David said. His hair, turned dark with moisture, was plastered above his ears. Irritation and the heat had sobered him too. "The accident? This is a simple misunderstanding. It will be easy to clear up. I'll talk to the police."

The annoyed way Jith Uncle shook his head made me worry that I might lose David's main ally. I wondered if we would have time to find a bathroom so that David could at least clean the blood off his face.

We entered a spacious room with windows open to a small yard overgrown with weeds. The woman who had been hit was sitting before one of the desks bordering the room. Behind the desk was Kuruvila, the gray-mustached police officer from the accident scene, talking to a sari-clad clerk who was writing in a ledger. When Kuruvila saw us entering, he hurried over.

"I informed the inspector about him," he said, jerking his head toward David, who was looking nonplussed. "Go there, to the inspector's office."

"What did you tell the inspector?" Jith Uncle said.

But Kuruvila had already walked away.

The cement floor of the inspector's office was streaked with the tracks of dragged chairs. A ceiling fan spun above an ancient desk. Meticulous piles of papers on the desk were pinned down by two large, bubbled glass paperweights. We sat in scratched metal chairs before the inspector, a short-necked man stuffed tightly into his khaki uniform.

"So Kuruvila told me your friend here ran over a woman," the inspector said to Jith Uncle in Sinhala.

Jith Uncle recoiled as if he had been struck. "What madness is this?" he said. "I was the one driving, and all I did was nudge the woman with the car. She is not hurt. And this man is my nephew." When the inspector smirked, Jith Uncle added, "In-law. From America."

The inspector's eyes flicked over me. I placed my hands on the desk so that he could see my wedding ring.

"Can you tell me what is going on?" David said to me. "What did he say?"

I put my hand on his arm at the same time that Jith Uncle said, "Wait, men."

"Yes, yes, you tell what happened," the inspector said to David in English, but he continued before David could speak. "You are coming here and knocking down one of our women." He leaned across the desk, his chest straining against his shirt buttons, and pointed a pencil at David.

"What are you talking about?" David said. "I wasn't driving."

"So. Just like that, your nose got blood." The inspector twirled the pencil in his fingers. His wedding ring flashed.

"The nose, that happened before," Jith Uncle said in Sinhala, but David interrupted.

"What the hell does my nose have to do with it?"

"We were going to the hospital," Jith Uncle said to the inspector, glaring at me as if I were to blame for David's outburst. "To get the nose checked."

"Look, there has been a misunderstanding," David said. "A simple matter. Let's not complicate it."

"In America, everything simple, no?" the inspector said, tapping his pencil on one of the blue glass paperweights. "But here, different."

"The woman who got hit is there in the hall," I said. "Call her in and she will tell you what happened."

The inspector tossed his pencil onto the desk. "So you also think, so simple, Miss? Living in America. But here, not so simple. This kind of incident has to be reported. So many forms have to be filled. Too much work when we have such a small salary." He took up the pencil again and pointed it at David. "You, but, must be making a good salary."

"He doesn't even have . . . ," I started to say to the inspector. But then I stopped because I did not want Jith Uncle to think of David as not properly employed. I had described David to him and Sonia Aunty as a writer working in book sales, which was a fair enough way to describe a part-time bookstore clerk with an English degree and writing aspirations. Sonia Aunty and Jith Uncle had looked uncomfortable when I told them that. Perhaps my parents had already discussed the subject with them: David's so-called lack of ambition, despite being the son of a successful real estate developer.

"For us, everything is hard because we have no money," the inspector said. He extracted a small, brown envelope from his desk drawer and blew into its empty interior.

"What is this?" Jith Uncle said, although I could see that he knew as well as I did where we were heading.

The phone on the desk rang before the inspector could go any further.

"Hallo? De Silva speaking," the inspector said. Then his offhand tone changed to one of attentiveness. He sat up and adjusted his badge. "Yes, sir, yes." His eyes slid over us. "Yes, yes, no problem, sir . . . No, nothing broken, sir . . . No, no trouble, everything has been sorted out . . . Yes, sir, no problem at all, only filling out an accident report . . . She is also fine, sir . . . Good, good, sir . . . Okay, sir." He slid the empty envelope back into his desk drawer as he hung up the phone.

"So yes," he said. He shifted some papers and handed Jith Uncle a form. "As I was saying, all you have to do is fill out the form for the accident." He tapped his watch face. "Getting late. It was only for you that I stayed late, after Kuruvila told me about the accident."

"What is going on?" David mouthed at me.

"Everything is fine," I said.

While we were at the hospital, waiting to be seen, Jith Uncle phoned home and discovered that our release from the police station had been engineered by Sonia Aunty. The owner of the banana shop at the Pannipitiya junction had seen the accident and sent his boy in a tuk-tuk to inform Sonia Aunty. She had dropped the deviled eggs she was stuffing and called her cousin Tressie, who had contacted her neighbor, the deputy high commissioner of the police.

"Go easy tonight," I said to David, picking a flake of dried blood off his cheek. I used my left hand so that the patients gawking at us in the waiting room could see I was married.

"It's a party, Dili. Sonia will want me to have a good time."

"I wish you'd stop using her name as if she is our age," I said.

When we visited Dallas two weeks before we got married, David's mother had told me to call her Lindsey, although her pinched lips and grudging tone had suggested that it would be better if I did not speak to her at all. I had not addressed her by name at dinner or when David and I said our stubborn goodbyes. She stood on her front porch as we drove away in the Toyota David had rented, past the neighborhood's carefully landscaped front yards and the sprawling houses in which the only brown-skinned people were domestic employees. She did not wave. I had not had to deal with calling David's father by his name either; he had not shown up for dinner. The fact that he had chosen to work late was a clearer signal of the family's disapproval than David's mother's attitude or David's married brother's refusal to return David's phone calls.

"Fine. Sonia Aunty," David said. "And look at Jith. Okay, Jith Uncle. He could drink me under the table. We're thick. Look how he whips out his whiskey for me every evening."

"Because you're his guest," I said. "Doesn't mean he'll approve if you overdo it. Everyone's going to be at this party. You can't blow this. We need family now." The pale tiled floor of the waiting room looked as if it had been mopped recently, and the smell of Dettol hung in the air, but I couldn't help wondering about what hospital germs might be transmitted from the blue plastic arms of our chairs, or from the people sitting across from us, watching us as if David was from another planet.

"Dili," he said. "Stop being so uptight. Everyone's going to come around. Maybe even my parents someday. And your family. Even your parents."

"They had one and a half years to get used to the idea and it didn't happen," I said, thinking of all the times my parents had pleaded with me to get to know a Sinhalese boy. But for all their pressured talk about marriages needing shared religion and culture, I knew they would have given in if I had insisted on getting married, if everything had not gone wrong because an unexpected mishap at David's frat house had put David in the spotlight when he had been at his worst.

"But now they will. It's just a matter of time," David said.

By the time we had got back to Sonia Aunty's house and changed our clothes, the lights strung on the rubber and breadfruit trees were lit. The garden was noisy with laughter and talking. My relatives were standing around with glasses or sitting on the chairs laid out on the lawn, the women in showy silk saris and armfuls of bangles as if this were a regular homecoming party, rather than one being held almost four months after the honeymoon and without the bride's parents present.

For a few seconds after we emerged, there was complete silence. Then Sonia Aunty took David's arm and mine. She had worn a crimson Kanjeevaram silk, as if to stand in for my mother. I hugged her.

I had counted on Sonia Aunty for support from my early days, when she had made excuses for my habit of pulling my older cousins' plaited hair. It was Sonia Aunty that I called from Virginia the week before my sixteenth birthday, two years after I immigrated to the States with my parents; Sonia Aunty convinced my parents that an American teenager should be allowed to have her eyebrow pierced. Sonia Aunty also talked my parents into easing the curfews in my senior year of high school so that I could occasionally go to parties with my friends, Mariah, Elise, and Fallon, whose parents were far more lax than mine. Bringing Dilini up with our values is one thing, but you can't insulate her from American society if she's living there, Sonia Aunty had once written in a letter to my mother. My mother listened to her because Sonia Aunty was her eldest and most rational sister. It was Sonia Aunty who interceded for me when I wanted to move in with Fallon during my college years. Maybe it was because Sonia Aunty had no children of her own that she had always been willing to plead for me. My mother had told me about the circumstances of Sonia Aunty's childlessness: how she had got pregnant at the age of twenty, soon after marrying Jith Uncle and before she felt ready to have a child. There had been complications during labor; the child had been stillborn, and Sonia Aunty had been pronounced incapable of bearing another.

"Finally, they are here," Sonia Aunty said, pulling us forward. She had worn perfume, for the first time since we came to Colombo.

People began clapping. Manju Aunty was the first to come up, the lights glinting off the pin in her old-fashioned hairpiece. She kissed my cheeks. "Look at you, all grown up," she said, as if it had been much longer than a year since I had visited Colombo with my parents. "And this is David? Not at all as I pictured," she said.

Sonia Aunty gave her a look. Manju Aunty was known for making gaffes.

But Manju Aunty laughed and shook David's hand. "I mean the nose," she said. "What an ordeal for you, no?"

Monty Uncle hugged me and said, "Came alone this time, we heard."

"Daddy is organizing a convention in Richmond," I said. "And Mummy won't come without him." These were facts, although they had nothing to do with why my parents had not come to Sri Lanka with us. I thought of the conversation I had overheard between Monty Uncle and my father during my family's visit the previous year. I had only been seeing David for a few months at the time. My father had been lamenting about my interest in David, and Monty Uncle had told him not to worry because I was only going through a phase, testing my limits. Of course, that had been long before the TV broadcast. I knew Monty Uncle had probably heard about the broadcast by now, from the Sri Lankan network in Virginia, if not from my parents.

"So you had a run-in with our police fellows," Monty Uncle said to David, extending his hand. "Now don't think all our fellows are like that, trying to bribe."

"Such a shame," Manju Aunty said.

"Like he's been in the war, this fellow looks," Jith Uncle said, clapping David's shoulder. There was a bandage across David's nose, and a red bruise brushed one eye. He did not seem anxious at all about the crowd of people hovering, waiting to greet him and me.

Bangles clinked and silks rustled as relatives embraced me and shook David's hand. They were sympathetic, exclaiming at David's injury and the events of the afternoon, and I wondered if everything that had happened that day would connect him to my family. How ironic that would be, I thought, for an accident to come between him and my family, and for another accident to bring them together.

I refused the sherry Jith Uncle brought me.

"Not even at a party?" he said, shaking his head.

"What I need is food." I looked back at David as I set out for the buffet table under the mango tree. He was touching his whiskey glass to Jith Uncle's. "Remember," I said.

David raised his glass to me.

I sat with my cousins and aunties, eating fish patties and prawns on toast. They leaned forward in their seats and asked me about the car accident and the police station, and I saw how relieved they were to have such pressing topics to discuss. No one asked about David's family, or about our registry office wedding, which no one in our families had attended, or about the small Charlottesville apartment where David and I had been living for almost four months. My body got tenser and tenser, watching David drain glass after glass in the background, listening to his laughing get raucous. I wondered if I should take Jith Uncle or Sonia Aunty into my confidence and ask for their help in removing David before he made a scene. But that would turn them against him.

When I saw David and Jith Uncle head toward the fish pond, I followed them.

"Hey, hey, hey!" David said, lurching as he clasped me around the waist. "Jith is showing me his golden carp. See it?"

A wide mesh of thin green wire covered the pond. There was a flash of orange in the murky water as the carp slid away from a group of thinner black fish. It disappeared under a lily pad.

"We put that mesh there after a kingfisher grabbed the golden carp one day," Jith Uncle said. "Pedris heard the splashing and saw it wriggling in the fellow's beak. Pedris threw a stick and the bird dropped the fish. No ill effects, looks like. That fish is hardy. Sonia was worried about how it was going to fare in there. Those black fellows sometimes fight. But see, it can take care of itself." Jith Uncle raised his glass in a toast to the fish.

"Did you see how fat it is?" David said. He crouched unsteadily at the edge of the pond. "If you forget the feed, that one is still going to survive." When he stood up, the reek of his breath made me feel sick.

"Not fat, men," Jith Uncle said. "That fish is getting ready to lay eggs. Soon we will have a lot of golden carp." He took David's arm. "Come, come. Time for another drink. And some food for you. I don't want you to get too tipsy." He laughed.

"Come inside with me for a minute," I said to David, so that I could remind him again to not overdo his drinking.

The night he had got on TV, there had been a party at David's fraternity house. I had told David I would come to the party later; I wanted to go shopping with Fallon to help her buy a dress for her cousin's wedding. When I called David from Bloomingdale's, while Fallon was paying for her dress, he was already drunk. He began belting out a Steve Miller song. I could barely get any words in. The crackling cell phone line disconnected as he was singing about "the pompatus of love."

By the time Fallon and I got to the fraternity house, the damage had been done. People were drifting away from a thinning crowd gathered on the street. A blue Channel 3 TV van was just pulling away from the curb, and firemen were retracting a rubber hose onto a fire truck parked in front of the house. The left side of the house was charred. The porch was a ruin, its walls blackened, its dignified white railings and part of its roof gone. Smoke still rose from the edge of it. The Adirondack chairs had been reduced to piles of wet ash. The whole place stank of smoke and melted vinyl.

David, wearing no shirt, was guffawing with a small group of his frat brothers under the heavily singed branches of the magnolia tree in the trampled front yard. One of his friends was shirtless too, and two others were wearing only patterned boxer shorts. With them were three girls, one fully dressed and two who appeared to be wearing only men's shirts. Knowing them all, I could tell in one glance what had happened: the porch and part of the house had caught on fire, perhaps because of someone's drunken antics, and everyone had rushed out. The two couples who had evidently been in bedrooms had emerged partially or completely undressed, so David and Bobby, who had been fully dressed, had given the girls their shirts.

What I didn't know until later was this: when a TV crew had arrived to investigate the commotion, David, bare-chested and obviously inebriated, had chosen to be the fraternity's spokesperson, with two sheepish girls, wearing only men's shirts, flanking him. After I heard the horrified phone messages my parents left me, I found a video of the news clip that had been posted online. In it, David was barely coherent and apparently unconcerned about the fire damage to the house. He high-fived the young men standing behind him, congratulating them woozily on getting out alive. The TV crew's bright lights beamed mercilessly on David's bare upper body and on the long bare legs and disheveled hair of the two women beside him. I could see how guilty he must have seemed, on all counts, to my parents. My attempts to explain that his morals were no different from the ones to which they were accustomed did nothing to improve the situation. They refused to entertain phone calls or visits from David.

But now we had come to Colombo on our own, and I had a chance to prove that David could behave responsibly. I didn't want him to ruin it.

"Come on, I want to talk to you," I said.

But he picked me up as if we were in the privacy of our apartment and tried to kiss me.

"Are you crazy? Put me down," I said.

He swayed, almost dropping me. The glass he had been holding shattered on the cement rim of the pond. He set me down, laughing and apologizing for the glass.

"Never mind," Jith Uncle said. "I'll send Pedris to clean it up later, no problem. Let's go and get you a new drink. And something for Dilini."

I told them to go ahead. Glass shards lay scattered on the grass and the edge of the pond. I knew some must have fallen through the mesh. I thought about the golden carp sliding around in the water and worried about it getting cut, its eggs spilling out uselessly.

I perched on one of the small boulders decorating the pond's edge. Behind me, David began his raunchy jokes, the ones he produced when he got very drunk. Pretty soon, I knew, he would be singing or saying things he would regret tomorrow. I hoped he would not climb on the buffet table or crawl around on all fours with my cousins' small children. I hoped the crowd would thin out before things got much worse, so there would be fewer witnesses who would write to my parents complaining about their son-in-law.

"Sitting here for what?" Sonia Aunty said, coming up beside me.

"David dropped a glass," I said.

"Never mind," she said. "The glass you can't put back together." She brushed a piece of glass away with her slipper and sat next to me. "But some things can be undone, Dilini. These days, divorce is not unheard of. Especially if there is incompatibility early in a marriage."

I peered into the water and saw a gleam that I thought might be glass.

I would need something to pull it out, perhaps a pair of tongs from the buffet table. "People misunderstand him. They only see the problems," I said. "And I don't want to undo anything." I stretched my dress taut across my middle so that she could see my bulging waistline.

Sonia Aunty stared at me. "Why didn't you tell me?"

"Only David knows still," I said. I had found out a week after the TV broadcast, and there had been no way to tell my parents without confirming their fears about him or about his influence on me. "But the baby will need her grandparents and the rest of the family. What are you going to write to Mummy?"

Sonia Aunty was silent for a moment. Then she reached over and wiped a drop of pond water off my arm with the *pota* of her red sari. She rose to her feet and pulled me up. "Come, let's go and calm David down," she said. "Jith Uncle was also like that when he was young, shouting and talking nonsense. Drinking too much runs in the family." She smiled, taking my arm. "Wait and see. David is going to fit in very nicely."

Here in This America

MR. PERERA EXHALED a long whistle and opened *The Bonfire of the Vanities* to page 1. It was an American classic, the librarian had assured Mr. Perera, when he had been trying to decide between it and *The Name of the Rose*.

This had been a good Friday afternoon, Mr. Perera thought, leaning back against the wall in the niche by the fire exit. Only six thirty, and the five o'clock rounds were already finished. The traffic on the gym floor had been minimal, so moving the cleaning cart around had been no problem. It had not taken long to spray Lysol on the machine handles, wipe them down, and run the mop over the steps and treads. A PowerBar wrapper snagged under an elliptical machine cord, a pair of headphones some dishonest fellow had appropriated from United

Airlines, a soggy towel, and two empty water bottles on the treadmills, that was all the litter.

It was very cold outside, worse than usual. That might explain why there was no crowd. It was warm enough in his reading area. But he could still feel the cold that had rammed him when he had gone out through the back door with the rubbish bags a few minutes ago. He stretched out his legs, feeling his right knee groan a little. Even after two years in the States, he had not got used to the climate. His friend Derek Abeykoon, from his days at the land commissioner's department, now lived in Miami, Florida. Miami, Derek said, was just as warm as Sri Lanka. Mr. Perera did not believe him, or at least, he thought Derek was exaggerating. Derek had that tendency. Back in the days when they had worked together, every time Derek finished dealing with one of the land files, he had acted as if he had finished a year's work.

When Mr. Perera first began working at Century Gym a month ago, the cold had been a blessing. It had distracted him from the shame of carrying the rubbish bags, bloated to eye-catching size with paper towels and empty plastic bottles, to the dumpsters behind the building. Getting back in from the cold, that was what he thought about; that, the way the wind pulled the moisture off his lips and turned his ears ice-cold, and the words he had said to his wife of thirty-four years when he had decided to take the job.

"This is America," he had said, trying to ignore the sunken expression on Mrs. Perera's face and the way her eyes had become watery. Her eyes were what he had to watch. They said everything. They still had the clean whites he remembered from the early days of their marriage. "Only in Sri Lanka, people care about that kind of thing. Here, no one cares what kind of job you have. True, they are racist sometimes. But class, they are not worried about. A doctor's daughter can marry a truck driver. A lawyer's son can be a waiter. No problem."

"There is no need for you to do this," Mrs. Perera had said. "Are you forgetting that your father was a judge?" She had looked away from him, at the four bangles on her wrist.

"This is only for a short time. Until Nalin gets another job or Sherine finishes her degree." That was too pessimistic, he realized, so he added, "Nalin will, for sure, get a job soon. Long before Sherine finishes. Engineers with good qualifications can always find a job."

"How many applications he has done in the past six months," Mrs. Perera said, shaking her head. She was wearing a pair of small ruby earrings that he had not seen her wear in a long time. They must have been in the bank vault with the few other pieces that had escaped being washed away. Or perhaps she had worn them regularly while they lived in Sri Lanka, and he had not noticed. Mr. Perera realized that he might be paying more attention to her clothing and jewelry now that her manner of dress was so much less familiar. In the past month, she had worn a sari only twice: when they had visited the Athukorales in Clifton on the eleventh and when his cousin's wife's brother had come to dinner with his family last week. The rest of the time, she wore trousers and sweaters, all of which she had bought before Nalin lost his job. Mrs. Perera was still a slender woman, so trousers did not look obscene on her as they did on some American women, Mr. Perera thought. He was thankful that she did not look like Carol Davis, their neighbor on the left, who, although respectable and seemingly of excellent character, did not appear at all ashamed of the way her trousers stuck to her substantial backside.

Mrs. Perera sat down across from him in the armchair facing the sofa. Mr. Perera noticed, with some dread, that a tear had dropped down her cheek and was hanging off the side of her elegant chin. Her eyes had the droopy look that suggested there were plenty more on the way. He straightened his back and prepared for the coming battle of endurance.

"A shame to be doing this with money in the bank," Mrs. Perera said. She dabbed her eyes with a tissue.

"You know perfectly well, rupees are not going to help us." Mr. Perera knew what would come next. If Mrs. Perera were to be believed, dozens of respectable people were buying dollars on the black market every day for exorbitant numbers of rupees.

"Sarath's neighbor's brother brought money out of the country only the other day," Mrs. Perera said, pressing her hand against the chair arm.

"Are you forgetting that my father was a judge?" Mr. Perera said, although he did not think it was necessary to justify his desire to remain an honest man.

Mrs. Perera twisted the hem on one side of her sweater, just as she used to twist the *pota* of her sari. She lowered her eyes to her feet. Even in the winter, she wore open-toed leather sandals. She had not given up wearing her thin gold toe rings. "There has to be another solution, no," she said.

"I have considered every possibility," Mr. Perera said, as firmly as he could. He felt irritated by the generality of her statement. She had not written down every possibility as he had, and considered the feasibility of each, crossing them off the list one by one. She was not practical in that way, even though she had always been exemplary at managing the servants and keeping the household in order.

Mr. Perera realized that the loss of household order must have been very difficult for his wife to face. Next to losing Kamala and Siripala, it might have been the hardest part of the tragedy for her. The deaths of the servants, especially of Kamala, had lain heavily on Mrs. Perera. Kamala had been in their service for thirty years, cooking their meals, cleaning house, and when the children were small, taking care of them.

"Ah, yes, Kamala, she was almost like your family, no?" Derek had said, clucking sympathetically, when Mr. Perera phoned him after arriving in the States. Mr. Perera was not offended by his friend's comment because he understood what Derek meant. Mrs. Perera had been very fond of Kamala. She had trusted Kamala completely; she never saw the need to lock up her jewelry or check Kamala's suitcase for stolen flour, rice, and sugar when she went to her village to visit family once a month. Mr. Perera, of course, had not known Kamala very well because most of Kamala's dealings had been with his wife. Often, he had seen them sitting on the verandah in the evening shade, gossiping about this and that, Mrs. Perera reclining in her armchair and Kamala sitting on the floor at her side.

Mr. Perera had known Siripala more, although Siripala had only been with them for twelve years. Mr. Perera had been the one to direct Siripala's activities in the garden, urging him to cut back the mango and rubber trees when they looked overgrown or to correct the terracing of the back garden when erosion smoothed out the steps. True, he had not needed to do much directing. Siripala had been an efficient gardener; the lawn was always nicely cut, the zinnia beds weeded, the bougain-villea bushes trimmed, and the fishpond cleared of the leaves that fell into it from the neem tree.

Lately, Siripala had been appearing in Mr. Perera's dreams. The dreams were not like the ones that had plagued him for almost two years after the tsunami. Even now, images from those nightmares crossed his mind from time to time. They were mostly of the horror Mrs. Perera and he had found upon returning home from the hill country, thirteen days af-ter the tsunami. During his waking hours, Mr. Perera did not remember much of what he had seen or smelt. What he remembered was the frame of their wedding picture lying on the filthy floor, on top of the slimy remains of other people's lives the water had washed into their house. The wedding picture, which showed him in an old-style double-breasted suit, and his wife in a beehive hairdo and her great-grandmother's dia-monds, had been missing. The frame's carved silver had been oxidized and crusted with mud. He had stood there with his mind empty, holding the frame. He could not get used to the new views he had from the back garden. The sky was stark over their house, no mango and rubber tree branches to break up the blinding white. The water had washed away the wrought iron fence separating the house from the beach, and the glassy sweep of the sea seemed threateningly near.

Thankfully, the nightmares had ended. He suspected that his wife still had them. Sometimes she cried out in her sleep, sudden high-pitched calls that woke him up. But she always said, "I don't remember any dreams," looking out through the small windows of the New Jersey house they now shared with their son and his wife. She never spoke of Kamala or Siripala, although until Nalin lost his job, she had sent an airmail envelope with fifty dollars to each of the servants' families every month.

In Mr. Perera's recent dreams, Siripala seemed less a servant than a mentor. In the last one, he had shown Mr. Perera how to sweep leaves and twigs off the lawn, which was green again, as if the tsunami had never happened. "Hold like this," Siripala had said, placing Mr. Perera's hands on the ekel broom. "Hands too close together, you won't be able to sweep nicely." A hole yawned, inexplicably, in the middle of the lawn. But Siripala was not perturbed. "You can fill the hole with the leaves," he said. The handle of the ekel broom, which Mr. Perera had never used in his waking life, was smooth. It was, to his relief, long enough to pack the soft neem leaves down into the hole.

"What about a sales clerk job?" Mrs. Perera said.

Mr. Perera realized that while he had been reminiscing, she had been waiting to hear about the other possibilities he had considered.

"Doreen said her son-in-law's sister had taken a job at Nordstrom, as a sales clerk, when she was finishing her degree. That is better, that job."

Mr. Perera shook his head. This was the problem with his wife—she did not give him enough credit. What, she thought he would not have checked for those kinds of jobs? "I applied for every single one in the paper," he said, trying not to sound annoyed. "Also I went to the mall and looked. Then even Dunkin' Donuts, McDonald's, Burger King."

Mrs. Perera sucked in her breath. She shrank down in her armchair, torturing the edge of her sweater. "Why did you go and try that? Preparing food for other people?"

"Chandrika, you have to give up these ideas," Mr. Perera said. But new tears were dripping down her face, and he felt his breathing get shallower. "This is a different country," he said. "Preparing food, washing clothes, cleaning toilets even for other people, these are honorable occupations here."

Mrs. Perera's shoulders were shaking a little now, and Mr. Perera understood, sadly, that she was grieving the loss of everything she had had in Sri Lanka: her comfortable life, her status in society, her ideas about respectability. He tried not to think about how different his life was, here in Kinnelon, but he could not help noticing how people treated him. When they had shopped at Keells supermarket in Colombo, the blue-uniformed salesgirls had called them sir and madam and handled their weekly grocery bill, which was certainly much bigger than their own monthly paychecks, with awe. The security guard had snapped to attention as he blew his whistle for the Pereras' driver to bring their Subaru to the automatic sliding doors so that the Pereras would not have to get their shoes dirty walking through the dusty parking lot. Here in Kinnelon, the cashiers at the Stop & Shop barely glanced at them. It was the same at the Bank of America. Here, he was not a big shot, so no personal banker came out beaming and bowing to shake his hand and guide him into an inner office with extracold air conditioning; instead, he stood in line with people dressed in ill-fitting jeans and sullied shoes, waiting his turn to speak to an anonymous teller.

Mr. Perera shook off his thoughts and turned his mind to the task at hand. "Don't you remember the dinner party at Mr. Underwood's house?" he said, leaning forward to pat his wife's hand.

Mrs. Perera wiped her cheeks with a tissue and looked at him hesitantly.

Mr. Perera saw, in her eyes, the memory coming back. Mr. Underwood was the CEO of Underwood & Deacon, where Nalin had worked until six months ago. On the Fourth of July, Mr. Underwood had held a dinner party at his home for his employees and their families. His house was a mansion constructed from pale stone. A front window ran from floor to roof, displaying a semicircular staircase, an oddly elongated chandelier, and a very large painting of two thin black women. The house could, no doubt, have held the five hundred–odd guests, but the party was held outdoors on a lawn that rolled out like a golf course. During the party, Mrs. Underwood had taken Mr. and Mrs. Perera,

Nalin and Sherine, and about fifteen other curious guests to see her chickens. She kept them for the fresh organic eggs, she said. Mr. Perera had thought it strange that Mrs. Underwood would keep chickens on her palatial grounds, remembering the squawking, raggedy hens that shuffled around back gardens of village houses in Sri Lanka, and the stench of their droppings. But Mrs. Underwood's chicken yard was like none he had seen before. There were four chickens, two with scalloped brown and white feathers, and two as pure white as the inside of a coconut, in an enclosure about the size of a children's playground. Around it was Mrs. Underwood's organic vegetable garden, where several long raised beds held greens and trellises bore cherry tomatoes and beans. Mrs. Underwood spoke at length about the chickens' pedigrees and how she had had them flown from a special poultry farm in Canada. While she pointed out a threadbare patch in the plumage of one that a hawk had attacked recently, Mrs. Perera sniffed the air, looking as if she could not believe that the chicken pen was so odorless. Mr. Perera had watched the chickens mincing around, selecting invisible tidbits from soil that looked clean enough to sleep on.

But what had struck him most was Mrs. Underwood's attitude toward Luther, the Underwood's driver. He had been wandering among the vegetable beds that evening. Mrs. Underwood, turning away from her chickens, spotted him. She had raised her sunglasses on to her head and called out to him. "Luther! Have you found anything good?"

And Luther had ambled forward, his dark arthritic-looking fingers cupped around two mounds of small red tomatoes heaped on his palms, saying, "Look at them tomatoes, Edith. Have you tried them yet?"

Edith. Mr. Perera had been shocked at the familiarity of it. He tried, and failed, to imagine Siripala or their own driver, Premasiri, addressing him as Michael, as if he were a friend or a family member. Later, Nalin had told his parents that Mr. and Mrs. Underwood sat in the front seats of their cars when Luther drove, and that once he had seen Luther sitting on a bench outside the office building with Mrs. Underwood, drinking Starbucks coffee and talking. Probably they have lunch together, Nalin had said, shrugging, as if this was such a small thing: the Underwoods, parents and children, eating with the driver and the cook.

"Only in America," Mr. Perera had said.

"Remember?" he said again to Mrs. Perera. He tried cautiously for a little humor. "Even Mrs. Underwood's chickens were from a good family. Still, she was treating that Luther like a friend. That is how it is in America. Drivers, janitors, no problem. Everyone is the same. Created equal. That is what the Constitution says. No caste, class nonsense. This is the best way."

Mrs. Perera's face relaxed. He saw that he had finally won the battle. He pushed his point home, stretching out his legs and trying to look relaxed himself. "Don't worry, no, Chandrika. Just remember, this is a different place, with different customs."

When Mr. Perera looked up from his reading some time later, he saw a lot more bodies in the gym. He looked at his watch, an Omega relic inherited from his father. It was seven-twenty. The dinnertime crowd— mostly trim middle-aged chaps in dress shirts and ties, carrying duffle bags, and young men with ballooned arm muscles and anxious eyes— had begun to arrive. But the crowd seemed unusual; in addition to the men, there were middle-aged women who should have been at home feeding their families.

Then he remembered that it was the day of the biannual party. The staff was invited. During Mr. Perera's two o'clock cleaning rounds the previous Friday, Jeb, the manager, had patted him on the back, and said, "Coming to the party next week, man?" He had not waited for Mr. Perera to answer before walking off. He had called back over his shoulder, "See you there, all right?"

Mr. Perera had called after him, "Yes, okay!" Americans were casual people, he knew. And always busy. Even invitations were done on the go.

Mr. Perera rose to his feet and tucked his book under his chair. His last rounds were at eight o'clock, so he had half an hour to spend at the party. As he made his way toward the aerobics room, music started up.

It was choppy and violent-sounding with too many impolite words, not the kind of music he enjoyed, but he was learning not to pay attention to the songs he heard day in and day out.

The aerobics room was already half full. There was a cluster of people around a long table that must have come out of the storage room. He walked over and helped himself to a paper plate. A woman holding a plastic wine glass was looking at the food on the table, which was covered with an immaculate cloth of white linen. Mr. Perera took a roll, a piece of ham, some cubes of pepper jack cheese, and a few vegetables. He nodded at the woman encouragingly. "Will you have something?" he said.

She seemed to have difficulty taking her gaze away from the food. The tendons on her neck were standing out. There was not much flesh on her bare arms. "No, I'll just have a little wine," she said. She poured herself some Chardonnay and offered the bottle to Mr. Perera.

"I see you around here a lot," she said, as he poured a glass for himself.

"Yes. I do the afternoon cleaning." America, he said to himself, raising the glass to his lips.

The woman nodded. She did not seem surprised. Her eyes strayed to the food on Mr. Perera's plate. "I thought I'd stay and have a drink after my spinning class," she said. "My husband's making dinner." She took a sip from her glass. "If the kids are even home. High school, you know how it is."

"Ah." The wine was sweet in Mr. Perera's mouth. "Your children are in high school. How many children?" He realized that he had not introduced himself. He put down his plate and held out his hand. "Michael," he said. "Michael is my name. Michael Perera."

The woman's fingers, with their frosted pink nails, were chilly from the wine. "June Anderson. Two of my kids are in high school. A sophomore and a senior. And one is in college, at NYU. But he's around here someplace." She turned away to look toward the mirrors, where more people were gathering.

Jeb came up with two young men. "Grab a drink," he said, moving past Mr. Perera to the table.

One of the young men tapped June Anderson on the shoulder. "Mom," he said. "I thought you went home."

June Anderson turned to him. "There you are. I was waiting for you. Did you finish your workout?"

The young man had already turned away. He was reaching for the punch ladle. "No, I just got here," he said over his shoulder.

This was a young fellow who spent some time with the weights, Mr. Perera noted.

June Anderson shook her head. "My son," she said to Mr. Perera.

Mr. Perera nodded, downing the last sip of wine in his glass. He was feeling cheerful.

The young man rejoined them. He scanned the room as if he were looking for someone. Mr. Perera poured himself a little more wine and then offered the bottle to June Anderson.

"Thanks," she said. She seemed preoccupied. She nudged her son. "I thought you were going to be here at six thirty," she said. "Dad's waiting to play that movie. But if you haven't even started your workout..."

The young man was still looking around. "Sorry, Mom. I got held up in Franklin Lakes. The Underwoods were having some people over and Spence wanted me to stay."

Mr. Perera remembered that Spencer Underwood was a Century Gym member. It was at the Underwoods, before Nalin lost his job, before he had considered becoming a custodian, that he had first heard about the gym. "You mean Spencer Underwood, Mr. Harold Underwood's son? Of Underwood & Deacon?"

The young man looked at Mr. Perera for the first time, at his black uniform T-shirt, the Century Gym badge clipped to his collar, his white sneakers.

"This is . . . Michael?" June Henderson said. "My son, Andrew."

Jeb had come up with a plate of meat and cheese. He was wearing cologne, or maybe it was one of the strong-smelling deodorants people liked so much, Mr. Perera thought.

"Mike's the man," Jeb said, through a mouthful of food. "Best custodian we ever had." He slapped Mr. Perera on the back.

Man to man, Mr. Perera thought. "Jeb is the best manager I have had," he said. That was another way Americans were so casual. All the names had to be shortened. Jeb must be what? Jebadiah? He slapped Jeb back, landing a gentle thump between Jeb's muscled shoulders.

"Whoa there, man," Jeb said. He moved away a foot or so and poured himself some punch.

June Anderson's son Andrew was still looking at Mr. Perera. "You know Spence?" he said finally.

"Not very well," Mr. Perera said, waving a piece of broccoli. He was feeling quite jaunty. "I went to dinner at his house. But not his invitation. Edith and Harold's." He corrected himself. "Harry's."

Andrew was looking nonplussed. "Harry? You mean Mr. Underwood?"

Mr. Perera paused to nod, and then continued pouring himself a little more wine. It would help to make the last cleaning round go quickly.

"You sound like you know him well. Did you work for him?" How interested this fellow Andrew was in him now. He was looking at his badge again, Mr. Perera saw.

"No, no, no," Mr. Perera said, wiping a drop of ranch dressing off his lip. "I didn't work for him. I don't know him well. But you know everyone is on a first name basis with them. Not only the company workers. The house maids, drivers, cook, all."

"What are you talking about?" Andrew said. He adjusted his feet, in their blue sneakers, to a wider stance. His mother was looking at him now. He did not pay any attention to her. "The Underwoods are the most formal people I know."

"Formal or not, I don't know." Mr. Perera said. "All I know is, they are American like all of you. All first name basis. Their cooks and maids and drivers sit and eat meals with them."

Andrew started to laugh. His teeth were bigger than Mr. Perera would have expected from the size of his rather small mouth. "Hah! This guy's a riot," he said to his mother. "The Underwoods. Remember I was telling you about the paper Spence wrote for that class? About his dad wanting to stop low-income housing in the area?"

Mr. Perera felt disoriented. Maybe he had drunk enough wine. The connection was escaping him. "What does that have to do with Harry and Edith?"

"Harry and Edith," Andrew said. Mr. Perera did not like the tone of his voice. Sarcastic. Young fellows in this country did not know how to show proper respect to their elders. That was the one thing about America that bothered him. "Harry and Edith didn't want to have to go to the same church as the domestics. That was why Harry"—there was the sarcasm again—"had a campaign to stop an affordable housing project near their house."

"You are a cynical young man," Mr. Perera said. He turned to Jeb for support, but Jeb was shaking his head, his lips pulled back in something that could have been a smile. Jeb rolled his eyes toward the ceiling. "Looks like the Lysol fumes have been getting to Mike," he said, as he pulled Andrew away.

June Anderson had drifted off to stare at the chips. Jeb's words were lying on the surface of Mr. Perera's mind, like second-rate milk powder resisting dissolution in a cup of clouded tea. He put his glass down on the table. Had he been too outspoken? He might have had a little too much to drink, he thought, trying to clear the murkiness in his head. But Jeb had not noticed that he had been standing there with a drained wine glass in his hand. It was the Lysol he had been talking about. Mr. Perera closed his eyes for a moment. He could picture the way his wife's eyes would have dimmed if she had been present.

A corner of the pristine tablecloth had got rucked up, exposing the deep cracks, packed with the grime of many years, in the wood underneath. Mr. Perera pulled the cloth down and smoothed it out. That was his job, here in this America, he thought: to keep the place looking good.

Perhaps for the first time since the tsunami, Mr. Perera had the concrete thought that he missed Siripala. He wished he had got to know the chap better. They had never shared a meal or a drink in the twelve years they had lived on the same piece of land. Siripala had taken his meals at the table in the shed with Kamala and Premasiri, or in his small room in the servants' quarters behind the garage. When dusk fell each evening, Kamala had brought Mr. Perera a tray bearing the silver ice bucket and a cut-glass tumbler, and Mr. Perera had poured himself a whiskey from the carved liquor cabinet he kept under lock and key. From his cane recliner, he had watched Siripala labor at sweeping the lawn and lugging the garden hose from the crotons to the bougainvilleas. Now he wondered what Siripala had thought of him sitting there day after day, sipping his drink. If Siripala were here, could they have a drink together and commiserate about the situations into which life could throw people? Would they laugh together, man to man?

Hello, My Dear

PREMA was glad she had not told Emmett about the email the woman had sent. He would have dissuaded her from inviting the woman home.

Prema had shown Emmett two other emails over the past few months. They had not been like the ones she got almost daily, with subject lines that said Dear trusty friend, Greeting and God bless, Your Miss Irina Pubutu, Attentions please, Please I long your urgent respond. One email she had shown Emmett had been about an orphanage in Bangladesh, and the other had been from a Pakistani man with terminal lung cancer. I understand you want to do some charitable work, but don't get duped, Emmett had said, as if he had some special knowledge she did not have. He said the emails were scams, and likely not even from the Indian subcontinent.

Prema stepped out onto the porch, hugging her shoulders against the cold, and scanned the white length of Breakneck Road. The air had the familiar, faintly tinny taste Prema associated with winter in Wyoming. The snow that had started early that morning was still falling. In the distance, Prema could see the light white dust that had blown onto the crimson rose-printed banner that her neighbor, Mrs. Grant, had hung outside her front door. Every holiday was celebrated to its fullest in Cathaway, perhaps because there was not much else to do so far from any other sizeable town. January had not yet ended. The tinsel streamers, stars, and nylon banners printed with the words "Welcome 2012," had only recently been put away, but Valentine's Day preparations had already begun.

Valentine's Day was when the porch renovation was scheduled to begin. Emmett had already contacted a contractor who would install thick glass and heating vents. The porch would become an inside space that could capture the cheerful sunlight Cathaway offered as consolation to the few residents who disliked the cold. Emmett said it would be a place Prema could sit even in deep winter, even though Prema doubted the possibility. She had not discussed the idea of putting off the renovation with him. She had wanted to meet the woman first, to verify her credibility, before broaching the matter with Emmett.

A dirty cream Chevy with ship-like lines crawled up the road and skidded to a stop in the driveway. Prema watched as a woman crunched over the snow to the porch steps. She looked as if she were a decade or so older than Prema, perhaps sixty-five.

"Hello, my dear," the woman said. That had also been the subject line of the first email she had sent Prema.

Prema had decided to risk inviting the woman because she had not sent a mass-email. The email had been from a Sri Lankan to a compatriot. Now Prema felt she had been right. This woman was too prim and matronly to be a con artist.

"Janice Fernando," the woman said. She removed a glove and held out her hand. It was a plain-looking hand; although the nails were trimmed and clean, they did not look manicured. A gray coat was hanging over the woman's slightly lopsided shoulders. "You must be Prema Mendis."

"A long drive from Flanders," Prema said, as she opened the front door. The smell of the pie Emmett had baked that morning still scented the house.

"Five hours," the woman said, slipping her coat off her shoulders.

Prema shut out the cold and led the woman to the kitchen, reminding herself to be cautious; the woman was a stranger, however innocuous she seemed. She started the tea kettle. "So you said Colombo, Mrs. Fernando?"

"Call me Janice," the woman said, taking a seat at the counter. The tip of her nose was bulbous, which gave her face a slightly coarse appearance. The only makeup she had on was lipstick in a sober shade of brown. "Yes. And you?"

The earnestness in her face reminded Prema of a teacher she'd had in school in Colombo a long time ago. The teacher's name had been Miss Geraldine, and she had taught grade seven English. People had thought her eccentric, although maybe that had only been because she had ridden to school on a bicycle, wearing stout covered shoes that could have belonged to a man. In class, Miss Geraldine had been gentle, more likely than the other teachers to excuse girls for talking too loudly. Prema could imagine her saying, "Hello, my dear," in her soft voice. In fact, now that she had thought of it, she was sure she could remember Miss Geraldine saying those words when she had gone up to the teacher's desk one day.

Prema nodded. "Same here. I've been in Wyoming for eleven years, and for much longer in the US. But I'm sure you can still hear my accent, no?" She could hear her Sinhalese accent get heavier as she spoke. After three decades in the US, she had no problem speaking the American way, so she was surprised at the easy way she slipped into her old language patterns. It was good to let go.

"Ah, yes," Janice said.

Friendly eyes, Prema thought, noticing the wrinkles that radiated toward the woman's temples.

"You, of course, can't tell," Prema said, as she put out Emmett's apple pie. "Not even a small accent. You speak Sinhala? Fernando. That name could be Sinhalese or Tamil or Burgher...?" She said this although she was sure Janice was a Burgher. Janice did not look much different from anyone else in Cathaway, with her light brown eyes. There was a faint brownish tint in her skin, but Flanders, like Cathaway, was situated several thousand feet above sea level, so it would be difficult to avoid a tan.

"I used to speak a little Sinhala, but that was a long time ago," Janice said. "I was ten when I came here. That is why I have no accent. I'm Burgher." Then she added, "I am descended from the Dutch, you see."

Prema paused in the act of reaching for the tea tin at the peculiar way Janice said this, as if Prema had never met a Burgher. Could Janice be so accustomed to meeting people who knew nothing about Sri Lanka that describing herself in this fashion had become second nature? It was possible, Prema thought. Flanders was twice the size of Cathaway, which had only 5,300 people, but it was no doubt as insular a place.

"You still have family in Colombo?"

"No," Janice said. "The few I have are mostly in England and Australia."

"Yes, in Australia, I know there are big Sri Lankan communities," Prema said, pouring water into the teapot. "That is where my sisters live now, in Sydney. They have plenty of people around from home." She wondered whether to ask about the kinds of people Janice knew in Flanders. Janice's email had mentioned that she had no children, so she could not have been part of a parent-teacher association. For years, that had been Prema's main social outlet in Cathaway, outside work. But now the children were grown, and she had no reason to be on a PTA. Was this woman the type of person to join book clubs and township boards? Did she hold dinner parties? It would depend on her husband's disposition, Prema thought.

The first time she had met Emmett, in the dimly lit stacks in the Texas State University library, where he had been an assistant librarian, he had struck her as exuberant; later, she thought that had been because of his bushy eyebrows and the resonance of his voice. By the time she married him at the Church of Our Lady of Guadalupe eighteen months later, she had come to understand that he was a reserved man. She had got used to his shyness and did not mind it, although his reluctance to attend social events had already begun, by then, to narrow their circle of friends. Over the years, his reluctance had increased. His books and his skiing were what mattered to him. He was happy in Cathaway.

Janice started to rummage in her handbag, her head bent and her gray hair concealing her face. She extracted a picture from the bag and handed it to Prema. It was a photograph of a large white-walled house that lay partly in the shade of a tree with spreading branches. "The house I grew up in, in Colombo. It's not in my family now, but I had the picture."

Although the colors on the picture were faded, the design on the upstairs balcony railing, the size of the wood-framed windows, the shape of the roof and its terracotta tiles were strikingly familiar. They reminded Prema of houses she had passed every day as a schoolgirl. The scarlet flowers clumped on the tree branches and strewn on the ground marked the tree as a flamboyant like the one that had flourished outside the house in which Prema had grown up.

"I remember houses exactly like this," Prema said. But there might be similar houses anywhere in the world, she thought. Then she wondered if she was being too suspicious. "Funny how I remember houses, when so many other things, I don't remember," she said, placing cream and sugar on the counter. "You remember so much more when you have someone to talk to about things."

Janice nodded at that, stirring her tea. She took a piece of pie and set it on the plate Prema had put on the counter.

"The thing is," Prema said. "I never cared for talking about Sri Lanka with people outside the family unless they were from home. Easier to fit in that way, no? Especially here in Wyoming. But now my children are grown and gone. And Emmett—my husband—is always either working or going up there." She pointed at the mountain slopes spread out to the east.

Emmett said the Wyoming landscapes were sublime. Sometimes Prema could see what he meant when she looked at the land stretching undisturbed to the horizon. But these days, she mostly saw how blank and white it was and how thirsty the scrubby vegetation looked when the snow finally melted. She would have liked more trees, even if they blocked her view of the mountains. What wouldn't she do to have a few bougainvilleas around?

"Skiing, hiking. That's what Emmett cares about nowadays. When he's at home, a book keeps him happy if he's not baking a pie. Not that I'm lonely." She waved her hand at Mrs. Grant's house in the distance, visible through the long living room window. "I've been here so long. I suppose I know a lot of people. But lately, I've been wishing I knew some people from home."

Janice's eyebrows had come together in sympathy. Prema could see that she understood.

How easy it was to talk to her, she thought. "I used to know so many back in Houston, where Emmett and I met," Prema said. "Well, not so many, I suppose. Maybe twenty, thirty. But we got together for dinners and lunches. Birthdays, graduations, public holidays. Any excuse to wear a sari. Can you imagine wearing a sari here? I haven't seen a single resident from the subcontinent in all the time I've lived here. There, someone was always coming by for a chat, with fish buns or patties or milk toffee. I haven't had any of those for a long time. What's the point of making things only for yourself? Emmett is not so keen on them." Her mouth watered, remembering the fish buns. She sighed. "Don't you miss those things?"

"Oh, yes," Janice said, looking at the photograph that lay on the counter between them.

"Maybe it's age," Prema said. "You know they say people get closer to their nature as they get older. These days, I find myself thinking a lot more about my school days back home."

"I know the feeling. You can't wait to go back and settle down," Janice said.

That took Prema aback. "Oh, no, no, no. I can't do that," she said. "My children are in this country, grown and settling down. Emmett would not be happy there even if he found a job. Where would he ski? And I have been here too long myself to give up the conveniences. You know the last time I went back, ten years ago, how hard it was to find a shop nearby that had some printer paper?" She looked hard at Janice, who was stirring her tea again. "You want to go back and settle, even after so many years?"

Janice clutched her handbag to her chest. "No, no. That is not what I meant. Well, in some ways, I want to, even though it is impossible. Certainly I miss Sri Lanka," she said. "There is no one in Flanders who would understand about where I grew up."

It was because no one in Cathaway knew anything about Sri Lanka that Prema had recently asked Emmett, who managed the local public library, to acquire two books on Sri Lanka: a travel book and a history book.

"That's what I am saying," Prema said. "Emmett understands more than anyone else here, but not the same, no? He's not Sri Lankan."

Janice looked up, her fingers twisting the strap of her handbag. "He's from here?" She looked around the room, and her eyes settled on a family picture in which Emmett stood, smiling and freckle-faced, between Prema and their three grown children.

"Yes," Prema said. "Mendis is my maiden name. Of course, Emmett has visited Sri Lanka with me and the children several times. But the thing is, he doesn't have the same connection. It's the little things you miss, no? Tastes of things. Things people say. Smells. You know, no?"

"I am fortunate to have my husband," Janice said. "Of course, there are no other Sri Lankans in Flanders. That is why we Googled common

Sri Lankan names, trying to find people in other towns. The next best thing to family."

"How is he doing, your husband?" Prema said.

"As well as can be expected," Janice said. She wiped the edge of her eye with a tissue she had produced. "He is worried, of course, because of the urgency of the situation. As I said, we have to find the money within the next two days. Otherwise it will be too late."

"How did he get it in both eyes?" Prema said. "Unusual, no?" She knew something about retinal detachment because one of her coworkers had suffered from the condition a couple of years ago.

"Not so unusual for a man of his age, according to the doctor," Janice said. "Even if we can save one eye . . ." She blew her nose softly. "I don't know how we would manage if he goes blind."

"I didn't understand from your emails why he could not get help from his family. They are still in Sri Lanka you said?"

"To find money so quickly . . . they are not so well off, but yes, they are in Kandy. The house he grew up in wasn't far from the Temple of the Tooth, where Lord Buddha's tooth relic is kept."

Prema stared at Janice. It was such a strange thing to say. Did she really think that Prema might not know about the Temple of the Tooth?

Janice's fingers were clenched around the straps of her handbag. Her neck, above her lint-specked blue sweater, was rigid. She was nervous, Prema realized. It struck her that Emmett might have been right. She ran her mind back over the conversation she had just had. But had it really been a conversation? The woman had not said much. Had she been so eager to find someone from home that she had been gullible? Had the woman just shown up here after reading a book or a web page on Sri Lanka?

"Tell me. Where did you live in Colombo exactly?" she said, keeping her eyes on the woman, who was fingering the string of small black beads looped around her throat.

"Colombo 7," the woman said. Then she added, "The area called

Cinnamon Gardens," in a way that sounded again as if she were reciting from a history book or maybe a travelogue.

The woman had not touched her pie, Prema noticed. She put her own fork down. Here she had been rattling on, when the woman was probably not even from Sri Lanka. "What do you remember the most about Colombo?" she said, trying to keep her voice from sounding strident.

The woman stared down at her cup, which was standing in a small pool of tea that had spilled onto the saucer. "As you said, so many little things. These are things that are hard to put into words."

Prema waited for her to say more. Minutes must have passed in silence. The woman only looked into her tea.

"Surely, you remember something," Prema said.

The woman cleared her throat. "There were cannons on Galle Face Green," she said.

Prema remembered the old cannons clearly, left over from the days of the Dutch colonists, pointing out to sea. But those cannons had been pictured in the travel book that Emmett had ordered for the library. Out of all the things the woman could have remembered, why would she only mention something that was probably in every tourist book on Sri Lanka?

"I don't think I can help you," Prema said. She cleared the counter of the pie and the teapot. She took the woman's half-full cup from the counter and placed it in the sink, not caring about her rudeness.

"Suddenly, this . . ." the woman said.

Prema did not look at her face. She gestured toward the door. "It's getting late. I want to get some work done before my husband gets home from skiing."

The woman got to her feet, holding her handbag to her chest. She followed Prema to the door. "You don't believe me," she said. "You are pushing me out because I can't remember all the details of my childhood?"

Prema said nothing. She opened the door, letting in a blast of cold air.

The woman paused on the porch. "I can remember plenty of little things," she said. "I remember the Cargills in Fort. My parents bought two boxes of apples there one Christmas. There were six small apples to a box. It was the first time I ate apples." She pulled her coat tighter around her shoulders. "But is my telling you that going to convince you that I am from Sri Lanka? Sometimes I myself am not sure where I am from. There or here."

How well Prema remembered the Cargills store at Christmastime. How the bustle and noise of the street stopped suddenly when the store's heavy doors closed. How chilly it had been in the air-conditioned interior. How shiny the tins of English butter biscuits and the red cellophane-wrapped hampers of goodies had looked. She remembered apples there too, from when she had been very young, perhaps five or six. The apples had been small and pale pink, and so exotic that she had been afraid to touch them for fear of spoiling them. Now apples sat heaped in the fruit basket on the kitchen counter, a staple of her weekly grocery purchases. Their smell filled her house.

Prema joined the woman on the porch. The wind had risen, and eddies of snow were moving across the porch steps. "Look, I know what you mean," she said.

The woman opened her handbag, sheltering it from the wind, and took out a sheaf of folded papers. "Here, if you want to see," she said. "The report from the clinic. You can call the clinic if you want to verify his condition. I have given them permission."

Prema took the papers, but she did not look at them. She looked at the woman's shoulders hunched against the cold, and at her face, on which she saw the kind of fear and sadness she might see in anyone who needed help, whether they were from Colombo or Cathaway.

"Maybe you should wait until Emmett gets home." She hesitated, unsure whether to wait outside with Janice or to invite her in again. But it would be too cold outside to wait. "Come in and sit," she said. "When Emmett comes home, I will talk to him and see if we can spare some money for a loan. We had been planning a renovation project, but we might be able to postpone that for a while."

She looked around at the porch, and at the familiar white expanse of the mountains ahead. Putting off the renovation would not be difficult. She was not sure she wanted it done anyway. Even glassed in and heated, the porch would always be between the inside and outside, she thought, never fully one or the other.

ACKNOWLEDGMENTS

THE STORIES IN this collection have appeared, sometimes in slightly different form, in literary journals: "Beauty Queen" in the *Fourth River*, "The Water Diviner" in the *Examined Life*, "The Fellowship" in the *Michigan Quarterly Review*, "Today is the Day" in the *Kenyon Review*, "Sunny's Last Game" in the *Hawaii Pacific Review*, "The Lepidopterist" in *Kaleidoscope*, "Hopper Day" in *Stand*, "Therapy" in the *Summerset Review*, "The Rat Tree" in *Epiphany*, "Security" in the *Saranac Review*, "A Burglary on Quarry Lane" in the *Massachusetts Review*, "Leisure" in the *Notre Dame Review*, "Accident" in the *American Literary Review*, "Here in this America" (titled "A Different Place") in *Quiddity*, and "Hello, My Dear" in *Bluestem*.